"I'd like you **my aunt and uncle this evening,"** Jake said. **"If you're available."**

Caroline's heart constricted. "Why?"

He slipped his hands into his pockets. "So we can discuss you coming to Texas with me."

She felt herself sway as the entire world seemed to start spinning around her. A pressure and warmth on her arm settled her for a moment, until she realized it was Jake's hand on her arm, then the spinning was inside her. Her heart. Her thoughts. "I'm going with you?"

"If that is still what you want."

She nodded, then closed her eyes and told herself to breathe. To remain calm. Actually, to breathe so she could *become* calm, because her insides were in absolute chaos. She looked up at him. At his coal black hair and sky blue eyes, still wondering if she'd heard correctly. "I thought you were coming to tell me no. That I couldn't go with you to Texas."

"You haven't changed your mind about going?"

Without hesitation, she replied, "No, not at all."

He nodded, and there was a softness about his face that she couldn't quite read.

"Well, there is one more thing I need to say, to ask you," he said, "and it might change your mind."

Adamant that wouldn't happen, she shook her head.

With another nod, he cleared his throat. "Well, then, Lady Caroline Evans, will you marry me?"

Author Note

The time for me to start brainstorming this story coincided with an overnight trip that my granddaughter and I were taking for her birthday. There was a concert that she wanted to go to in northern Minnesota, and I agreed to take her and for us to spend the night in a historical bed-and-breakfast. During the drive north, our conversation shifted to this story, and we discussed the idea of how it could begin with an interrupted wedding. We had a fun time chatting about how that could happen, since the hero and heroine had never met. And, well, to make a long story short, I ended up getting pulled over for speeding. Luckily, the kind patrol officer only gave me a warning to slow down and wished Hayley a happy birthday. All in all, it added to the memories we made of a wonderful trip the two of us had together.

I hope you will enjoy Jake and Caroline's story, and their journey from being left at the altar to happily-ever-after.

THE COWBOY'S
ENGLISH LADY

LAURI ROBINSON

HISTORICAL

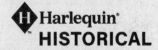

Harlequin®
HISTORICAL

ISBN-13: 978-1-335-54021-8

Recycling programs for this product may not exist in your area.

The Cowboy's English Lady

Harlequin Enterprises ULC
22 Adelaide St. West, 41st Floor
Toronto, Ontario M5H 4E3, Canada
www.Harlequin.com

Printed in U.S.A.

A lover of fairy tales and history, **Lauri Robinson** can't imagine a better profession than penning happily-ever-after stories about men and women in days gone past. Her favorite settings include World War II, the Roaring Twenties and the Old West. Lauri and her husband raised three sons in their rural Minnesota home and are now getting their just rewards by spoiling their grandchildren. Visit her at laurirobinson.blogspot.com, Facebook.com/lauri.robinson1 or X @laurir.

Books by Lauri Robinson

Harlequin Historical

The Captain's Christmas Homecoming
An Unlikely Match for the Governess
A Dance with Her Forbidden Officer
A Courtship to Fool Manhattan

The Redford Dukedom

Captivated by His Convenient Duchess
Winning His Manhattan Heiress

Southern Belles in London

The Return of His Promised Duchess
The Making of His Marchioness
Falling for His Pretend Countess

The Osterlund Saga

Marriage or Ruin for the Heiress
The Heiress and the Baby Boom

Twins of the Twenties

Scandal at the Speakeasy
A Proposal for the Unwed Mother

Visit the Author Profile page
at Harlequin.com for more titles.

Dedicated to my granddaughter Hayley.
Our trip together was a joy from beginning to end!
Love you to the moon and back.

Chapter One

1887

Jake Simpson's jaw was hard set and the thick, stout heels on his boots, made specifically for keeping a man in the saddle while chasing down a maverick cow, echoed off the bricks of the street as he bounded out of the coach that he'd had to hire to take him halfway across London. If ever a man had needed a horse, it had been him. Bullet, his favorite horse back home, would have had him across town in a flash. That's why he'd name the gelding Bullet. The palomino had the speed of a bullet shot from a six-shooter.

Looking at the big, old steepled church in front of him, Jake set a hurried pace, one that was faster than the horses pulling that coach had been. He'd bet two bits to a dollar on that. Every minute he'd spent in that tattered old coach had fueled his ire, and right now, he was mad enough to spit nails straight through a two-by-four board.

After nearly two weeks of traveling—it had taken three days to get from the Texas Panhandle to Galveston, and over a week to cross the Atlantic on a cargo ship packed full of cotton bales, *then* he had to board a train to get him to London—a man should be afforded a decent meal, a bath and shave, and a good night's rest before he had to get down to business.

Jake hadn't been so lucky. Still, it was a good thing he'd picked up a newspaper to pass the time on that train to London. The fact it had been an old one from two weeks ago had irritated him at first, because the fella who'd sold it to him hadn't mentioned that, until he'd come across his cousin's name. The cousin who was the very reason he was here, in London, England. A place Jake hadn't been in fourteen years. Since he was twelve.

A boy of that age was old enough to remember living here, while also being young enough to embrace the adventure of leaving it all behind. Of going to the New World. That's where his father had taken him and his mother. To the center of the United States of America. Texas. Where the population of four-legged creatures far outnumbered the two-legged ones, and a man could be his own man. Not one dictated to him by those who put themselves on pedestals and spouted the rules of society.

In his mind—and Jake had a very good mind, was rarely wrong for the most part—that move to Texas, that adventure, had been the best thing his father had ever done.

Reaching the top of the dozen or so church steps that he'd taken two at a time, Jake shoved open one of the tall, carved wooden doors with one hand, reaching for his curled-brim well-worn hat with the other. It had sheltered him from sweltering sun rays, thunderstorms spitting out rain and hail, and winter blizzards that could freeze a cow's eyes open. But now, out of respect for the Almighty that had been born and bred within him, he removed it and slapped it against his thigh.

With the sound of his heels echoing off both the well-worn floor and tall ceiling, he marched forward, to where another set of double doors stood open, showing rows of pews filled with people on both sides of the aisle and a couple, along with a vicar, standing at the altar.

As he entered the room, the silence made his footsteps even louder. Recognizing the would-be bridegroom as his cousin, Lord Edward Simpson—the reason he'd been traveling for nearly two weeks—shot his anger up another notch. Or two. He was as close to blowing his top as he'd ever been.

Normally, he wouldn't give a midnight hoot about Edward's matrimonial activities, but right now, he was dead set upon stopping things before a single "I do" was spoken. Because his livelihood, the ranch that had been built not only with his blood, sweat, and tears, but those of his mother and father—God rest their souls—depended on this marriage being stopped before it started.

Jake didn't slow his steps as he continued forward, and though there were some hushed mumbles and gaping stares, no one tried to stop him. Perhaps that had something to do with the fact that he wasn't wearing a fancy suit, but instead had on a sturdy pair of work pants, cotton shirt and leather vest, with his saddle bags flung over one shoulder and his Colt revolver stuck in the holster that was always belted around his hips just in case a rattlesnake decided to initiate a challenge. Folks were either too shocked by his attire, or too scared to move.

He didn't care which, but he also wasn't too keen on the idea of a brawl more suited for the Broken Spoke Saloon in Twisted Gulch breaking out in a steepled church in London. Yet, there was no doubt in his mind that if Edward or anyone else *wanted* a brawl, he'd give them one.

Catching a glimpse of his uncle Oscar, Jake gave a

slight nod, then another to Aunt Hilda, who sat beside her husband, before taking the final few steps that brought him to the altar, right between the bride and groom.

"These two hitched yet?" he asked the wide-eyed vicar, who was dressed in a gown as long and white as the woman now standing at his side.

"Hitched?" The vicar seemed to catch the meaning of the word because he quickly followed with, "No, sir, not yet."

Jake nodded, then turned to the woman dressed in white. Her face, actually her entire head, was covered with a long veil of lace, hiding her features and most likely her shock. Regret filled Jake. He didn't like seeing anyone or anything hurt and tried his best to not be the one doing the hurting, but it was better that she knew now that Edward couldn't marry her, rather than regret the marriage later. He gave his head a little shake because this here gal wasn't a whole lot taller than Nellie, his little sister, who was still probably mad at Jake for not bringing her along with him. But this was no place for Nellie. There wasn't anything about this trip that was going to be enjoyable, including stopping this here gal's wedding.

"I beg your pardon, miss," he said.

Since there really wasn't anything else he could think to say to her, he pivoted about, leveled a glare at his yellow-bellied, scum-sucking, scheming cousin. Even as a kid, Edward hadn't been one who could be trusted. Jake remembered that well. He should have remembered that a couple of months ago, too. Well, he *had* remembered, but hadn't realized what it could mean.

Here, too, looking at Edward, Jake couldn't think of anything to say—there was plenty he wanted to say, but none of it suitable for a church—so he grabbed Edward by the back of his collars—shirt and suitcoat, and his ascot—and dragged him from the altar. His hold wasn't so hard it would hurt Edward, but firm enough to let him know that he had no choice but to head down the aisle. Once outside, he'd lay into Edward hide and hair.

"Jake! What's the meaning of this?" Uncle Oscar asked from where he'd stood up from his seat in the front row pew.

"We best talk outside," Jake said, not missing a footstep.

"Father!" Edward shouted.

Jake twisted the material in his fist, tightening the ascot into a noose that prevented Edward from saying anything else, and practically carried his cousin past the gawping onlookers and through both sets of doors, not letting much except Edward's toes touch the ground until they were on the sidewalk in front of the church. Even the steps were too sacred for what Jake had in mind.

Others had followed them outside, and despite the questions being shouted, mainly from Uncle Oscar, Jake spun Edward about so they were face to face. "I have one word for you," he growled, feeling the anger rolling up from his stomach to lace his words. "Faith."

Edward's eyes nearly popped out of his head. That could be because he knew exactly who, not what, Jake was referring to. Or it could be due to the hold Jake still had on his cousin's collars.

Jake uncurled his fingers and gave his cousin a shove hard enough to make Edward stumble as he released him.

"Jacob Simpson!" Aunt Hilda shouted. "I demand to know why you are causing such a scene!"

Turning, Jake eyed the crowd. His aunt and uncle were the only two he recognized—other than Edward, of course—because they were the only family members that he'd seen in the last fourteen years. All three of them, Oscar, Hilda, and Edward, had traveled to Texas for visits since Jake and his parents had moved there. Oscar had been there several times, as had Edward, including the fateful occasion two months ago. "Ask him," Jake said, gesturing with his chin toward Edward.

"Mother, Father," Edward said, rubbing his neck and shaking his head. "I have no idea what he's talking about. Or why he's here!"

Jake planted his hat back on his head. Keeping a cap on his temper, as his mother used to say, was difficult. Jake had to swallow twice before he said, "For one, I haven't *talked* about anything, *yet*. And for two, do you honestly think that I'd travel halfway around the world and barge into a church without a damned good reason?"

The silence that ensued seemed to include the entire city of London. Right then, a rat scurrying about would have sounded like a trampling elephant.

Either the silence or the truth got to Edward, because he was the one to break the quiet. "Whatever he says isn't true," he said. "It's not true."

Jake kept his glare leveled on Edward, while shaking his head. "You either tell them, or I will."

Squirming like the snake he was, Edward straightened his twisted, bright red ascot, and then the lapels of his suit jacket. "There's nothing to tell."

To his way of thinking, Jake had given Edward his one and only chance. It wasn't his way to snitch on anyone, but this wasn't snitching. This was righting a wrong. This was saving his property.

"There's a woman back in Texas," Jake said, eyeing his uncle. "Her name is Faith, Faith Drummond, and she's going to have a baby in a few months." Gesturing with his thumb, he continued, "Edward is that baby's father."

The only saving grace that Caroline Evans could envision as she stood, alone, at the altar, in a church full of people who weren't making a sound, was that the veil covered her face, hiding her expression as they all stared at her. All, including the vicar, who in some ways looked as uncomfortable as she felt.

Could there be a more awkward position to be in? Had it ever happened before? A bride left at the altar moments after the ceremony had begun? Because a man who appeared to be almost bigger than life, surely twice the size of normal men, and wearing a gun on his hip, had literally dragged the bridegroom from the altar, from the church, by the back of his collar like one would a disobedient child. It all seemed inconceivable, but it had happened.

She closed her eyes and swallowed, not sure if the burning in her throat was because she was about to cry, or about to laugh. Most brides would cry—she was sure of that—but she wasn't *most* anything, and the entire scene had been so out of the ordinary, so unexpected, and well, so ridiculous, laughing seemed to be the better option of the two.

All these people were still sitting there in the pews, waiting, as if at any moment Edward would walk back into the church and the ceremony would begin right where it left off. Was she truly the only one who knew that wasn't going to happen? That there wasn't going to be a wedding. No prolonged meal afterward, no sipping of champagne and making small talk. No wedding night.

She let out a tremendous sigh of relief at that thought, because she truly hadn't trusted anything Edward promised.

The next thought made her shiver, because it had to do with the big man, who had had the bluest eyes she'd ever seen and who had clearly needed a shave. She was wishing that he'd dragged *her* away from the altar and down the aisle. Not because she knew him—for she had no idea who he was or why he was so intent upon stopping her wedding—but because then she wouldn't be the one left standing here, wondering what to do.

This truly was an abysmal situation. A hopeless one. Which wasn't new to her. Hope was something she hadn't had for years. She had used to hope, once, but it had always turned into disappointment.

There was only one thing she could do. Luckily, from years of attending services at this very church, she knew the route to the back door, which meant she wouldn't have to walk past anyone.

That's what she did. Turned about, carefully lifted the hem of her dress, and walked past the altar, across a small section of the sanctuary, then exited through a curtained side doorway. She kept right on walking, down the long, somewhat dark hallway to the back door. Grasping the knob, she turned it.

Stepping out into the bright May sunlight felt rewarding. Like an unexpected gift she was being given at this very moment. It was an unexpected feeling, but Caroline wasn't going to contemplate it, nor was she going to stand here longer than it took to close the door behind her. She walked down the steps and across the church yard, then along the street that in a few blocks would deliver her to her aunt and uncle's house.

Unlike in the case of Edward, no one would follow her. The guests filling the pews had not been friends of her family. Most of them had been there for one reason.

They'd been invited by the Duke of Collingsworth. When the son of a duke was getting married to the sister of an earl, and you were invited to the service, you attended, and you gave a gift. A silver platter, candle sticks, an engraved sugar spoon, or creamer. All things that most newlywed couples truly didn't need, but things that society deemed appropriate wedding gifts. The few people Caroline had wanted to invite, her brother, Frederick, had rejected, saying that commoners couldn't attend. She'd had friends who would have been sufficiently aristocratic, once, but that had been years ago, when she'd been young and lived in Bath.

Then again, if she was being completely truthful with herself, she hadn't really wanted *anyone* to come, to witness what she was doing. Marrying Edward. It wasn't something she'd been proud of. Truth was, she was less mortified by having been left at the altar than by having agreed to wed Edward in the first place. She hadn't even invited her best friend, Patsy—Lady Patricia Collins, to most—who wasn't a commoner, and had been the one to tell her about Edward's not-so-stellar reputation.

The only people from her side at the church had been Aunt Myrtle and Uncle James, and of course, her brother. He wouldn't follow her either, because he would have to give their aunt and uncle a ride home. It was too far for them to walk, and they'd long since had to let their coachmen go. Fredrick would be more interested in the gun-toting stranger anyway, and why he'd interrupted the wedding. A wedding Frederick had worked diligently to arrange, despite Caroline's continued objections, protests, and, eventually, open and total opposition.

That likely meant her aunt and uncle would be sitting there until Frederick was ready. Sitting alone in the pews, much like she'd stood alone at the altar. Caroline felt a fluttering of guilt in her stomach. Uncle James and Aunt Myrtle were the only family she and Frederick had, ever since their parents had died over twelve years ago in a train crash between Bath and Bristol. She'd been ten and Frederick fourteen then, and they'd been on the train, too, but had survived. Their father's aunt and uncle had been their only living relatives, and though they were already elderly and without children of their own, they had readily taken the pair of them in.

Letting out a sigh, Caroline glanced up at the sky overhead, as she often did, wondering if her parents were up there, watching over her. She liked to believe they were, and maybe this, the cancellation of her wedding, was the divine intervention she'd sought for years. She'd spent so long wanting her old life back, the one she'd had before they'd died, and later, when she knew that couldn't happen, she had simply wished for a life with more choices.

It wasn't as though she didn't want to get married. She did. Very much. She wanted to be a mother and a wife. Wanted a house full of love and laughter, and the chaos of children chasing after each other, a dog barking and a cat meowing. That was what she used to have, when her parents had been alive. Since they'd moved in with Aunt Myrtle and Uncle James, it had been the exact opposite. Still, they'd been kind and caring over the years, and she was grateful that they had taken her and Frederick in. Her love for them had been the only reason she'd finally given in and agreed to marry Edward, despite knowing all about his reputation for bedding women, which others—especially her brother—had been so keen to ignore.

If only Edward had remained in America. That's what she'd hoped when he had traveled there a couple of months ago. Her heart leaped into her throat, stopping her feet in her tracks, and she flipped back the veil still covering her face, as though that had been the obstacle keeping her from seeing what was suddenly so obvious. That big, blue-eyed man had been an *American*. That was why he had been dressed the way he was and had spoken the way he spoke. Had Edward bedded the man's wife? Had he traveled all the way to England to confront him?

That was exactly why Edward had gone to America in the first place. His excuse had been that he wanted to see to family holdings in the states, a ranch in Texas, but many knew the truth. He had been caught in the bedroom of a married woman, and her husband had threatened Edward's life if he didn't leave London.

But he had returned, more eager than ever to accept Frederick's offer of Caroline's hand. Of course he had been. There was something else everybody was pretending wasn't common knowledge: Caroline knew full well that the duke had finally put his foot down, and told his son to find a woman and marry her, immediately upon his return from America.

Huffing out a sigh, Caroline started walking again. Whether he'd someday inherit the dukedom from his father or not, no woman in their right mind would want to marry Edward, including her. She didn't want a man who had already admitted that he wouldn't be faithful to her. For that matter, she didn't want one who expected nothing more from her than to be a symbol of matrimony, a feeble salve to his battered reputation. A piece of property that he could ignore except for when it suited him.

She hated herself for finally giving in and agreeing to it. Hated the fact that her family was treating her the same way, like she was a piece of property to be bartered and exchanged. Yet, that was indeed exactly what she was to them. Her family needed money. Everything they had had been funneled by her uncle and brother into fruitless research and failed inventions. Caroline was the only thing they had left to sell. Edward had guaranteed that as long as she was his wife, monthly instalments would be deposited in the family's coffers.

Still, she had spent six months refusing him. It hadn't been until the grocer had pulled her aside, asking about a payment, that she'd been forced to accept that marrying Edward was just what she had to do.

There would be no money now, not after that big, tall American had burst into the church and stopped the wedding. Had he assumed he was breaking up a love match? Though every other part of him had emitted fury, there had been a glimmer of sorrow in his sky blue eyes when he'd looked at her, begged her pardon.

If she cared about the man that she'd almost married, she should be concerned that Edward might not survive the encounter with that American man. She still was, just a little; she would never wish harm or worse on anyone. But Edward needed to be responsible, and held accountable for his actions for once in his life. Nothing else seemed to have stopped him from flitting from bedroom to bedroom.

Caroline needed to be accountable for hers, too, and face the fact that her life, and her family's, was now completely ruined. There would be no marriage settlement, and they would go on to lose what was left of the land that their father had left Frederick upon his death. All that would remain of his inheritance would be his title, the Earl of Brittmore. But little good a title did for any of them, other than make Caroline eligible to marry Edward.

Caroline stopped walking, and looked at her aunt and uncle's modest terraced house, and let out yet another sigh. Then, because there was nothing else that she could do, she walked up the driveway, around to the backside of the house, and entered through that door.

"Caroline?" Mrs. Humes, their housekeeper and wife of their butler, Niles, spied her enter the hallway from the kitchen doorway. "What are you doing here?"

"The wedding was canceled," she said, closing the door behind her.

"Canceled? Oh, my." Clutching her ample bosom, Mrs. Humes hurried forward. "Oh, dear, I'm so sorry. What happened?"

Caroline shook her head. "I don't really know. Would you mind coming upstairs and helping me out of this dress?"

"Absolutely, dear." Mrs. Humes laid an arm around Caroline's shoulder as they began walking toward the staircase. "Now, don't you go feeling bad for yourself. You are a lovely woman, one of the prettiest I know, and Lord Edward will come to his senses sooner than later."

Caroline didn't reply, knowing Edward's feelings toward *her*, at least, had nothing to do with the cancellation of their wedding. However, if anybody could finally make Edward "come to his senses," it might just be that big American.

Mrs. Humes, who truly was a dear, and had worked for Aunt Myrtle and Uncle James for years, continued offering consoling words until the beautiful silk wedding dress was lying on the bed and Caroline was wearing one of her well-worn dresses.

"I would like that dress returned to the Duchess of Collingsworth as soon as possible," Caroline said, indicating the wedding gown. "Could you please ask Mr. Humes to deliver it?"

"But you might need it yet," Mrs. Humes said.

"No, I won't." The duke and duchess had always been perfectly pleasant to her, on the couple of occasions that they'd met, and Edward's mother had hired the seamstress and had purchased the material for the dress, so it was only fair to return it to her.

Letting out a sigh, Caroline said, "I will help you prepare a meal. Aunt Myrtle and Uncle James are sure to be hungry when they arrive home."

"No, dear, I can do it," Mrs. Humes said. "You take a rest."

"No, I'd rather be busy." Actually, she'd rather that today had never happened, but that wasn't an option.

Sitting in his uncle's study, a room that had looked a whole lot bigger when he'd been a young boy, Jake ran a hand over his chin. It still needed a good, sharp razor. In the center of the room, his uncle and cousin were arguing back and forth. The two of them were giving Jake a headache, probably because he already knew what the outcome would be. It didn't matter how much they argued or protested; he was hauling Edward back to Texas to marry Faith.

However, the argument had given him insight on why Edward had been in America. The lout had gotten caught in bed with a married woman, by her husband. Uncle Oscar had sent Edward away so he wouldn't end up dead, while Oscar paid off the man and things settled down.

"I can't live in America," Edward said for the umpteenth time. "I have to live here, Father. I'll inherit your title someday."

"Not if you don't change your ways," Jake interjected. "You won't live long enough for that."

Edward paused his pacing in front of the stone fireplace long enough to toss a sneer in Jake's direction.

Dropping the ankle he'd had propped up on his opposite knee to the floor, Jake leaned forward in the high-back leather chair. "Why is it you haven't asked me how Faith is doing? How she ended up at my ranch?"

"How did she end up at your ranch?" Uncle Oscar asked.

"Because Edward didn't use his name," Jake said, still furious over that point, too. "He used *mine* while seducing her, and told her that my ranch was his."

"The ranch is owned by the family," Edward said.

Jake wasn't surprised by Edward's arrogance. Though never willing to do the work, Edward felt he was entitled to everything. "The family owns a herd of cattle," Jake pointed out. "A small portion of the number of head that I run."

"It was grandfather's money that started the ranch," Edward said snidely.

Normally, Jake was good at holding his temper, but that wasn't the case today, and he had to grasp the arms of the chair to keep himself from shooting to his feet. His father had used family money to move them to Texas, but it had been hard work that had built the ranch into what it is today. Hard work was not something Edward understood.

"The Rocking S Ranch was not, nor will ever be part of the dukedom," Uncle Oscar said from where he sat in another high-back leather chair. "It belongs solely to Jake, and it is due to him that our cattle interest in his ranch has been financially successful. Because of his hard work and dedication, our family coffers have expanded substantially."

"Then let him marry her," Edward said. "He already lives in Texas."

Jake's hands, still on the arms of the chair, tightened, but despite how badly he wanted to stand up, he remained seated. "Her name is Faith. Faith Drummond, and she doesn't want to marry me. For some reason, she believes she's in love with you, and she believes you love her. That you promised her marriage." Jake waited a long still moment, before he asked, "Did you?"

"I made a promise to the woman I was supposed to marry today, too," Edward snapped. "The marriage you stopped."

Jake felt a bucketful of remorse for that woman, for ruining her wedding as he'd done. "Is she pregnant, too?" he asked, because that was the bottom line here.

"No," Edward said, then smirked. "Not yet."

Someday, someone would wipe that grin off Edward's face, probably permanently, and probably some woman's husband. Leaning back in his chair, Jake said, "Then your choice should be to do the right thing."

Edward wrinkled his pointed nose, then spun about and sat down in his chair, arms crossed like a defiant wet-behind-the-ears lad. "I won't go to America."

"Yes, you will," Jake said.

"No, I won't."

Jake set his jaw because he wasn't twelve years old, and wasn't going to get caught up in throwing words back and forth like a ball. "Do you know who Faith's father is?"

Edward shrugged. "Doesn't matter."

"Yes, it does." Jake turned to his uncle. "Her father is the lieutenant governor of Texas. A powerful man in a powerful position, and that is my reason for being here. I will not lose my ranch because Edward can't control himself around women."

"You aren't going to lose your ranch," Edward said superciliously.

Jake wished that it wasn't a possibility, because then he wouldn't be here. He ignored his cousin, and continued facing his uncle. "If Leroy Drummond decides to defend his daughter's reputation, which I believe he will once he discovers her condition, I could lose my ranch, and you could lose more than a herd of cattle. He won't let an English man who seduced his daughter, promised her marriage, then abandoned her and returned to England, get away without punishment."

"Do you personally know this Drummond man?" Uncle Oscar asked.

"I know of him," Jake replied. "He was a lieutenant colonel in the war, a district judge after that, and then he served on the Texas Supreme Court before becoming the lieutenant governor. You can believe me when I say he's ordered more than one man to swing from the gallows."

"Does Drummond know it was Edward and not you who defamed his daughter?" Uncle Oscar asked.

"Not yet," Jake answered. "I came here first, so Edward could take responsibility before I speak to Drummond, because I will tell him the truth, so will his daughter." What Jake feared was that Drummond might care more about his daughter's reputation than finding the right man. If Jake didn't comply, which he shouldn't have to, his future, the future of his ranch, could look gravely different than it had looked before Edward's visit to America.

Uncle Oscar let out a long sigh while shaking his head.

Then he nodded. "You will go to Texas, Edward, and you will marry this woman."

"Father! I will be an English duke someday!"

"I wish you could have remembered that before now," Oscar said. "I wish to hell that you would have listened to me when I said this womanizing of yours had to stop!"

The arguing set in again, and Jake, having said his piece and made his point, rose from his chair, and headed toward the door.

"Where are you going?" Edward snapped.

"I'm going to have a bath, and a shave, and a meal," Jake answered, without missing a footstep. "In that order."

Chapter Two

Caroline's heart was beating faster than the wings on a bee as she hurried down the hallway toward the front parlor. From Mr. Humes's description, the man who had just arrived at the front door, requesting to see her, was the American from the church this morning. She couldn't fathom why he would call on her. Frederick still hadn't arrived home. He'd delivered Uncle James and Aunt Myrtle and left again without even coming inside.

Stopping near the doorway to the parlor, Caroline pressed a hand to her stomach in an attempt to quell the nervous jitters, then gave the sides of her pinned-up hair a quick smoothing with both hands. After a deep breath, which she slowly released, she moved, stepped around the doorway.

She was momentarily dazed, because the man standing before her was even taller and broader than she remembered from this morning. Still, she found the ability to keep moving forward into the room that held a selection of mismatched furniture and a rug that had long ago faded from its once-vibrant colors.

Their earlier encounter had been brief, very brief, but it had certainly left an impression. This one was just as startling. The man's black hair was parted on the side, combed back, and it shone with a freshly washed sheen. So did his face, now clean-shaven. Patches of heat tingled Caroline's cheeks as she admitted to herself that he was a very handsome man, and that the utterly charming dimple in one cheek made him not nearly as intimidating as she remembered from the church.

His clothing helped with that aspect, too. Instead of the brown leather vest from earlier, he had on a brown suit coat, and black pants. The ruffles on the white shirt seemed out of place on his broad frame, and the top few buttons were left undone, as if there wasn't enough material for them to be buttoned.

The same hat he'd carried this morning was in one hand, and a bouquet of daisies was in the other.

She came to a stop, and had to blink, wondering if he was real, if he was really standing in her parlor, or if this was some silly dream. Was she sleeping? Had it all been a dream? Had today really happened, or would she wake up and it would be morning, where she would put on the white wedding dress and end up married to Edward? Had the relief that she'd felt the past few hours at the prospect of *not* having to marry Edward also been an illusion?

Perhaps that explained it all. Perhaps this was the answer to all of her prayers not to have to marry Edward? But this man had never been featured in those prayers. She shifted her weight. It felt as if the soles of her shoes were stuck to the polished wood floor. She tried moving a foot, thinking that might let her know if she was dreaming or not.

"Miss Evans," the American stranger said, glancing down at the daisies. "I've come to beg your forgiveness. When I woke up this morning, I had no intention of ruining your wedding, or breaking your heart, and…" He shrugged his massive shoulders. "There's no way I'll be able to sleep tonight with that on my conscience. I understand if you can't forgive me, but I wanted to personally let you know that I'm very sorry for what I did to you."

His tone was so soft, his words so earnest, they didn't seem to match his room-filling presence. More so, this really could be a dream, because no one had ever offered Caroline such a sincere apology in her entire life. However, one thing told her that she wasn't asleep. She could never have conjured up a man like this. He was too unlike anyone she'd ever met. Drawing in a deep breath, she brought her thoughts back to reality and took a step forward. "Thank you, Mr...." She drew a blank, couldn't remember if Mr. Humes had told her his name or not.

"Jake," he said, with a slight shake of his head. "Well, Jacob. Jacob Simpson."

There was a hint of redness on his cheeks. It could be from shaving, but she hadn't noticed it a moment ago.

"These daisies are for you," he said, holding them out toward her. "My mother told me once to never step over daisies trying to get to a rose, and I—" He shook his head and stepped closer. "None of that matters. Here."

A softness filled her insides as she took the bouquet. No one had ever given her flowers. "Thank you, Mr. Simpson." At that moment, it fully occurred to her that this was not a dream. "Simpson?" she repeated. "You are a relative of Edward?"

He'd taken a step back after handing her the flowers, and took another one now, as if he needed to put space between them before answering, "Yes, miss, I am. I'm his cousin, from Texas. I was born here in England, but moved to Texas when I was twelve. That's where I live now. Twisted Gulch, Texas."

Cousin! Embarrassment over her lack of manners made her stutter, "F-forgive me, my lord, I—"

"Please," he said, holding up a hand. "It's just Jake. I own no titles, nor do I wish to."

Instinct was a strange thing, how it could kick in, yet not reveal why. Had she been right about this man's wife and Edward? Or was something else wrong? She was trying to put pieces together, to find the right answer, but needed more information. "Edward visited you recently, in America."

He nodded. "Yes, miss, he did."

What she'd thought earlier today, while walking home from the church, could have been right. That Edward had defiled a woman in Texas that this man loved. Was married to. And that he'd traveled all this way to defend her. Although confirmation of all that wasn't necessary, nor was it her business, Caroline wanted to know. Wanted to be able to tell her brother she'd been right all along. Not that it mattered. Frederick already knew, as did she and half of England, about Edward's penchant for bedding women. Still, she couldn't stop herself from saying "And you are here now, in England, because of his behavior while visiting you."

He bowed his head, gave it a negative shake. "It's not my place to say, miss. I'm sure Edward will pay you a visit shortly, to explain things. Apologize."

No, he wouldn't. Edward never apologized, and certainly wouldn't explain anything. Not to her. There had been no courtship between them. The few times he had visited this house, it had been to see Frederick, where the two of them created the agreement that she ultimately had accepted.

To be fair to Frederick, even though she currently

wasn't of a mind to offer him any fairness in the situation, it was not as though he had lost their wealth through idleness. He and her uncle had always believed they were merely one step away from success. That their latest invention would be the one to bring them fame and fortune. The entire *agreement* with Edward had started out as an investment opportunity. It had been Edward who introduced Caroline's hand into the deal. And it had been Edward who wouldn't go forward with any investment in Frederick and Uncle James's scientific ventures without her inclusion.

She might never know what Edward had done in America, but what she did know was that this man before her, this soft-spoken, gracious man, would also never know that he'd rescued her from making the greatest mistake of her life. Marrying Edward would have been a miserable situation, one that would have continued for the rest of her lifespan.

For that she would be eternally grateful, and remorseful that he, too, had been hurt by Edward. "I'm sorry, Mr. Simpson, for the damage that Edward may have caused you and your wife."

"Oh, no. No. I'm not married, miss."

That confused her. She had been certain that Edward had seduced this man's wife. It must have been his intended then. Either way, it wasn't her place to pry deeper. Even though she sorely wanted to... "Well, Mr. Simpson, I accept your apology, and thank you for the flowers. I've always liked daisies. They are delicate, yet hardy. I remember being a young girl, and seeing them growing wild in the fields."

"They grow wild in Texas, too," he said. "I've come across fields so full of them that it looked like there was snow covering the ground." He took a step toward the doorway. "Thank you for seeing me. I'll be leaving now."

A sense of disappointment washed over Caroline, and she searched for something to say, just so he'd have to stay a bit longer. A foolish thought. There was no reason he would want to stay. Then, suddenly, truly out of the blue, she noticed one more thing about him. "I notice you are not wearing the gun that you were earlier today."

"I didn't have anywhere to put it earlier," he said. "Couldn't leave it on the train or in the coach and my saddle bags were already full." He smiled and winked at her. "But don't worry, I didn't shoot Edward." With a nod, he continued his way to the doorway.

She bit her bottom lip, trying to stop a smile. Not over his comment about shooting Edward, but over that smile of his. How it had brightened his entire face, and deepened the dimple, and the way his eyes had sparkled, and how long his lashes had been for a man.

The sigh she let out was for no other reason than he would most likely forever be the most handsome, most suave, and gallant man that she would ever meet.

It wasn't until late that evening that Caroline learned why Jake Simpson had interrupted her wedding that morning. None of it came as a surprise, but it did disgust her even more than anything she'd heard about Edward in the past. The man had absolutely no scruples.

"Edward is still working on a solution that his father will accept," Frederick said, "so don't despair, a marriage between the two of you is still highly likely."

Caroline stared at her brother without blinking, seriously questioning if this man, who had the same brown hair and brown eyes as she did, and in many ways reminded her of their father, was truly related to her. When her eyes stung from staring so long, she blinked, and shook her head. "Have you completely lost your mind? There is no chance of a marriage. I will not do it. I didn't want to do it before, and I will not, absolutely will not agree to it again." Flustered in so many different ways, she said, "Do you hear me? I will not marry Edward, Frederick, and I mean it."

"Have you forgotten how badly we need the money?" Frederick asked.

"Have you forgotten there is a woman in America who is going to have his child?" she asked in return.

"Edward's going to convince his cousin to marry her."

Caroline's gaze shifted to the other side of the room, where the vase full of daisies sat on the table near the window. Earlier, when the sun had shone in through the window, the rays had reflected off the yellow centers, making them even brighter. No one else had noticed the flowers, except, maybe, for Mr. Humes, but if he had noticed them in Jake's hand when he'd opened the door, the butler hadn't commented on them. Mrs. Humes hadn't said anything either, but she hadn't been in the kitchen when Caroline had found the vase, nor in the parlor when Caroline had placed the flowers on the table.

Caroline hadn't expected anybody to notice. After arriving home and eating the meal she'd helped Mrs. Humes prepare, Uncle James had retreated to the basement as usual, and just as usual, Aunt Myrtle had gone to her sitting room in the back of the house, to sip on her mulled wine and read periodicals or paint. As for Frederick, he'd only arrived home a short time ago, and he wouldn't have noticed if there was a giraffe in the room. He only noticed Caroline was there because he'd requested her presence.

She, meanwhile, had noticed the flowers several times throughout the afternoon and evening, had walked into the room just to see them, and to imagine what a beautiful sight an entire field of them, so many it looked like snow covered the ground, would be. What an amazing thing that would be to paint, too. Her aunt was the painter in the family, but Caroline enjoyed using the watercolor paints when she had spare time on her hands.

Right now, she was thinking that no one, not even Edward, could convince Jake Simpson to do something he didn't want to do. He didn't appear to be the type of man who could be convinced to do anything against his will. However, she could imagine that he would be *very* good at convincing others to do things. He'd grab them by the shirt collar and haul them out the door. That's what he'd done earlier today, and to her way of thinking, it would do Edward good to remember that. And Frederick.

A tiny shiver tickled her spine and she looked at her brother again. "Why would he expect J—his cousin to marry her?"

"Because Jake lives in Texas. It only makes sense."

"That doesn't make any sense." Unless, she surmised, Jake wanted to marry this other woman. He had traveled a very long distance on her behalf. Though Jake had said he wasn't married, he must care for the woman or he wouldn't be in England.

"It makes more sense than Edward marrying her," Frederick said.

Her brother's response was not only unthinkable; it was uncaring and rude, and her only recourse was anger. Rightfully so. She was furious. Had been furious, ever since she'd become nothing more to her brother than something to sell so he could squander away more money on his inventions. Working hard to maintain a small amount of decorum, she slowly pushed herself off the sofa with both hands and rose to her feet. "What would make sense, would be for you to seek employment."

"I work every day," he retorted. "Day and night."

"Burying yourself in the basement with Uncle James is not working," she replied, feeling her temper rising. "It's time that the two of you drop this idea that you're going to make a scientific breakthrough with your weather prediction machine. It's failed every test you've given it."

"Every test has brought us one step closer to success!"

"No, it hasn't," she argued. "It's brought us closer to the poorhouse. You've spent every penny Father left you, and sold off all the holdings in the shipping company and most of the land. You'll soon be an earl with no holdings to speak of."

Frederick's face turned red with anger. "Which is why it's your turn! I've done everything I can."

"I'm not a piece of property you can sell to the highest bidder."

"There is no highest bidder! Edward was the only one interested in marrying you. It's not like you're truly a lady. You certainly don't act like one." Frederick threw his hands in the air. "You have no dowry, nothing to offer. You should be glad he offered to marry you."

"Glad? Glad that you agreed that I would turn my head, let him continue to sneak in and out of women's bedrooms while being married to me? That's not a marriage!"

"Considering you don't want to be married, you should be glad for the compromise."

Too angry to speak, Caroline let out a growl and balled her hands into fists. She did want to get married, but she wanted it to be a real marriage. With kindness and caring and perhaps, love. Furthermore, it was impossible to act like a lady when you lived like a pauper and rarely left the house. When words were finally able to pass her lips, she blurted out, "I'm not marrying him! I'm not! He needs to take responsibility for that woman in Texas, and you need to take responsibility for your own finances."

"And what about you? What responsibility are you going to take?"

"I will take responsibility for myself!" Steaming with rage, she stomped toward the doorway.

"Good luck with that!" Frederick shouted in her wake.

"My answer was no yesterday, it's still no today, and it'll still be no tomorrow," Jake said to his uncle. "I'm not marrying Faith. What I am going to do is haul—" he pointed to Edward while refraining from calling his cousin a few descriptive words, even though they were fitting "—*him* back to Texas to marry her. If he refuses to marry her there, he can voice all his sorry excuses to her father, and face the consequences."

Like last night, they were sitting in Uncle Oscar's study, with its high-backed leather chairs and imposing desk. One wall was lined with bookcases, and another boasted a huge fireplace. Several tall windows faced the street that ran past the three-story town house. Jake could remember being here as a child, and sitting on the floor in front of the fireplace while his grandfather read him the tale about the giant white whale Moby Dick that had bitten off the leg of Captain Ahab. His grandfather had read him other books, too, but that was the one that stuck with Jake all these years later because of how his grandfather could mimic talking like an old sea dog.

He still had that old copy of that book. His grandfather

had given it to him when they'd moved to America. The pages were falling away from the binding now, because he had read it so many times over the years, remembering his grandfather each and every time.

Collingsworth, the family estate, was a fair ride outside of London, and had been where he and his parents had lived, up until moving to America. Back then, he used to be jealous of Edward, who was less than a year older than him, knowing he was here in London, where their grandfather had lived. He'd asked Edward once if their grandfather had ever read him that book, and Edward had laughed and said no, that he didn't need some old man to read to him. He knew how to read himself. Jake had wondered then, and again now, if his cousin would ever realize that he'd been missing the point.

Listening to his grandfather read that story hadn't been just about the story. It had been about their grandfather, about understanding how he'd had an adventurous spirit. Just like Jake's own father had had. That's what his mother had called it. She'd said that's why they'd moved to Texas, because his father was tired of living a life without adventure. Adventure was what they'd found in Texas, building the ranch out of nothing but a piece of land, where Lord Oliver Simpson had become Mr. Oliver Simpson, and had been highly respected. Not because he was a lord, but because he was a determined man fulfilling a quest of creating one of the largest ranches in the state. Jake's father had wanted to build something of his own. Something worthwhile and successful.

Jake had vowed to continue that quest, even before his father had died. It had become his life's ambition and would continue to be.

"I don't disagree that is what should happen," Uncle

Oscar said, pulling Jake's attention back to the present. "But other concerns have been brought to my attention. The question of Lady Caroline Evans."

Jake felt the tug of guilt in his gut. Lady. That was what she was, but he'd called her miss, because that was who he was. He'd never owned a title, nor did he want one. Hadn't even thought about it, until she'd brought it up. Even then, he'd continued to call her miss, out of habit, he suspected. His years of being separated from the family, from the life of lords and ladies, of inherited titles, privileges, and nobility, had made all of those things seem insignificant, but they weren't, not while he was here. She probably considered him little more than a big, gruff buffoon who didn't know or respect the rules of society, which were very different here from what he was used to in Texas.

"Having her wedding interrupted as it was, is sure to affect her reputation," Uncle Oscar said. "Guests who had been at the service are questioning what happened and why."

Jake didn't need to be shown proof to know that. He'd thought about it all night. About her. Caroline. He'd been thinking about her since he'd interrupted her wedding, and had hoped that apologizing to her would help. It hadn't. The regret in his stomach had grown stronger after meeting her. She was a pretty little thing. With eyes as dark brown as a calf's and lashes just as long, and a face that was as close to perfect as he'd ever seen. She'd taken his breath away when she'd gracefully slipped into the parlor of her house. He hadn't so much as heard a footstep before she'd appeared, as if she'd just floated into the room. Even now, just sitting here, he felt an odd stirring in his stomach remembering that moment and how he'd just stood there, staring at her.

A hint of embarrassment struck, too, at how he'd been so tongue-tied, he'd hardly been able speak when it came time for him to apologize. It had put in him in mind of the time he'd been young, real young, and his grandfather had introduced him to the queen. Lady Caroline Evans had that same kind of presence. A regalness and beauty that just left him in awe. That glorious brown hair of hers had been a sight to see, too. It had shimmered like it had a light of its own.

"Besides being jilted, having Edward leave the country to marry another woman may put Lady Caroline in an even more unfavorable light," Uncle Oscar said. "Her brother was here last night, and Edward offered him a substantial amount of money. But rightly so, her brother is very concerned about his family's reputation, and respectfully, our family's reputation. How it would look to society if we merely paid her off."

Jake wanted to point out that the family had done that to others who Edward had wronged, but even as the thought formed, he justified it by recognizing that those women had already been married, and an affair was something that could—perhaps *should*—be paid off and buried. It might be whispered about, but overlooked, whereas paying off Lady Caroline could leave her unmarriageable. He didn't know the society rules for this sort of thing, but fully understood that he held a part in being responsible for what would happen to her. Edward held responsibility, too, but in the end, it had been Jake who'd barged into the church and stopped the wedding.

"Lady Caroline is young, and such an event could cause others to withhold any consideration of marrying her," Uncle Oscar said, confirming Jake's thoughts. "I don't know her well, but the few times I have met her, she was pleasant and personable, despite her sheltered past, and I would like to offer another solution."

Jake twisted his neck at the hair that stood up. Why wouldn't his uncle know Lady Caroline Evans better? Edward hadn't said anything about a wedding when he'd been in Texas. Had he just met her recently? And they'd quickly decided to get married? That could be the case if she had refused to go to bed with Edward until they were married. That was the only reason he could think of for Edward to agree to getting married. To get what he wanted. That was why he did everything, anything. He'd always been selfish. A woman with a sheltered past, who didn't know Edward's true person, could have easily fallen into Edward's ruse of being an upstanding man. Faith certainly had fallen for him.

"I'd like you to consider marrying her, Jake."

Jake's thoughts shattered and his neck twinged as he quickly twisted to look at his uncle. "Beg your pardon?"

"We could suggest that you'd stopped the wedding on her behalf, because you wanted to marry her. It would save her from embarrassment, save her reputation from the zealous gossipmongers," Uncle Oscar said. "And a wife could be an asset for you, Jake."

"He can't marry Caroline," Edward shouted. "I am."

A part of Jake wanted to say that he'd marry her, just to thwart Edward, let him know that he couldn't always have everything he wanted, but deep down, Jake wasn't the vengeful kind. Leastwise, not normally. He rubbed his forehead. This was such a mess. A convoluted heap of trouble that he wished he had no part of. But he had no doubt that Faith's father would leave no stone unturned in avenging her reputation, and he'd be damned if he'd lose his ranch because of Edward. Even though his taxes were paid, no monies were owed to anyone, and there was nothing underhanded happening at his ranch, a man as powerful as Drummond could find something, or create something, out of vengeance if nothing else.

However, he'd be damned if he'd be talked into marrying anyone. That would not work in his life. He had proof of that. Not only was his mother's death a vivid demonstration of how harsh life on a ranch could be, but he also had the still-fresh reminder of Eloise. Eloise Hatcher. The prettiest gal in Twisted Gulch. The gal who had agreed to marry Jake, until he missed the spring social last year. He'd planned on attending, actually had gone, but it had been smack-dab in the middle of spring roundup, and by the time he got off the range, cleaned up, and rode to town, the party was over. Eloise had said that had been the last straw. That she would not marry a man who put his cows before her. The next week, she'd eloped with Calvin Smith.

Jake figured he was better off not having been lassoed by calico and wished her well. Last he'd heard, they were living up in St. Louis, where Calvin was working for a newspaper. He'd tried to start one up in Twisted Gulch, but folks hadn't much taken to the way he'd reported things that weren't exactly newsworthy or completely true.

The folks in Twisted Gulch were friendly enough, and welcomed newcomers, but they were also set in their ways. So was Jake, and he wasn't looking for any more assets than he already had.

"How many other women did you bed while you were in America?" Jake asked, interrupting the back-and-forth that was once again happening between his uncle and cousin. He should have thought to ask it before now, because he needed to know.

The silence that ticked by not only irritated Jake; it got to his uncle as well.

"Damnation, boy!" Uncle Oscar shouted. "Answer him!"

"None!" Edward answered. "Just the one is all."

"If I find out you're lying, I'll have your hide," Jake warned, shooting him a glare hot enough to start a fire without kindling. He couldn't remember ever before being so filled with fury, because damn it, Lady Caroline Evans didn't deserve this sort of treatment. There was only one reason why Edward wanted to marry her so bad, and it wasn't for love. If Jake knew one thing about his cousin, it was that Edward didn't love anyone but himself. At the same time, Jake was vexing over if she was in love with Edward. Faith sure thought she was, which confirmed he would never understand how women thought.

"I'm not lying," Edward insisted. "I was stuck at your ranch most of the time."

"Not enough of the time," Jake said. He let out a long sigh, wishing he could come up with an answer that would untangle everything, but this mess was like barbed wire strung too tight and then let loose, spinning and coiling itself into a balled-up mess that left it good for nothing.

"Jake, I know this is none of your doing," Uncle Oscar said, "and I'm ashamed. Ashamed of my son. Ashamed of what I let happen. But we are all family here, and have to do what is best for the family overall. If you would consider marrying Lady Caroline, consider helping me get this settled here and abroad, I'll be forever in your debt. Whatever you need, I'll be here to help you get it."

Jake had always liked his uncle, had always looked up to him, being his father's older brother and all. It had been Uncle Oscar who had encouraged his father to go to the States, and had supported them financially in making the move, starting the ranch. As had his grandfather before his death. There wouldn't be a Rocking S Ranch if not for the family.

Furthermore, the connections the ranch had to the Duke of Collingsworth had given it a distinction that other ranches didn't have. Town folks and ranch hands back home liked Oscar. Liked the status of nobility. They nettled Jake from time to time about having a visit from the duke, but it was all in fun. They boasted about the connection themselves whenever given the chance.

Uncle Oscar was liked because he was a good man— he just had a rotten son. Things like that happened. Some people were just born selfish. Thought of no one but themselves.

Jake wouldn't have been here if he hadn't thought Uncle Oscar would make Edward do the right thing. He huffed out a breath, and admitted the truth. "I don't need anything, Uncle Oscar. I have everything I need back in Texas."

"I know," Uncle Oscar said, nodding his head. "I'm proud of you. Proud of your father. He did well with you."

What struck Jake then, as Uncle Oscar looked across the room at his own son and shook his head, was how much older his uncle suddenly looked. There were bags under his eyes, and it was as if his black hair was streaked with more gray than yesterday.

If the tables were turned, and he asked his uncle for a favor, Jake knew it would be granted with no questions asked. "I'll consider it," he said, even as a knot formed in his stomach, "but I do ask one thing."

"No!" Edward shouted.

Neither his uncle nor Jake looked at Edward.

"What is it?" Uncle Oscar asked him.

"That Edward doesn't leave this house," Jake answered. "Not until it's time for us to leave for Texas, because I don't trust him."

"Done."

"No!" Edward shouted, jumping to his feet as if he were going to attack his father.

Jake leaped to his feet and planted himself between his uncle and cousin, facing Edward and practically begging him to swing a fist. Edward had always been smaller and weaker, so they had never actually fought physically, but the desire had been there, on both their parts, even as young lads.

"It's all right, Jake," Uncle Oscar said, having stood and now stepped around him. "I've had enough, Edward. Enough! You will not leave this house."

With eyes as wild as those of a cornered mountain cat, Edward let out a growl. "You can't do that to me! I'm not a child!"

"Then stop acting like one," Uncle Oscar said. "But know this. If you so much as attempt to leave, I will disown you."

"Y—you can't do that," Edward said, though not as forceful and snarly as before. "I'm your only son. Your only child. You'll have no one to pass the dukedom to."

Jake didn't move a muscle, not so much as a twitch in his lips, even though he badly wanted to smile. Edward was finally grasping the truth. The truth he should have considered long before now.

"I have a nephew," Uncle Oscar said. "One that I know is capable and would never dishonor our family's name or heritage."

Although Jake wanted to inherit the dukedom about as

much as he wanted to be bit by a diamondback rattler, he didn't let that show. If this threat was what it took to whip some sense into Edward, he'd go along with it.

"He lives in Texas," Edward said, in one last show of bravado.

Jake shrugged. "I could split my time between Texas and England." Then, just to make it sound better: "I've always considered sending Nellie here when she's a bit older, for a secondary education and to get to know her roots." That was true, though at ten, Nellie was still too young to be so far from home. Jake wasn't ready for that, and neither was she, even though he knew she needed more influence than the few women at the ranch. They were good women, but they'd known nothing other than living on the wild plains and rough hill country of Texas. He'd done everything he could to keep Nellie as safe as possible at the ranch, but a time would come when she would want more freedom, and he'd have to grant it to her. There was more to life for a lady than ranch work, and he wanted her to know it.

"We'd welcome that," Uncle Oscar said, laying a hand on Jake's shoulder. "Both your aunt and I. But we don't have to wait until I die for that. Hilda would be beside herself with joy to have a young girl in the house, and I—"

"I won't leave the house," Edward said.

Having Edward secured was a relief, because Jake truly didn't trust his cousin as far as he could throw him. Another thing he appreciated was the new set of clothes he'd finally secured. He'd stood out like a polecat in a litter of kittens wearing the clothes he'd brought with him, and the ones his uncle's butler—a kind-hearted fellow named Winston who ceaselessly addressed Jake as *Master Simp-*

son nonstop—had found for him to wear yesterday had been so tight that he'd been afraid to move his arms, fearing every seam would let loose on the shirt and coat. The pants had made him feel like he was walking around in the wooly drawers he wore under his britches when winter set in back home.

The tailor that Winston had recommended outfitted him *properly* in a set of loose-fitting black britches, a white shirt with *no* ruffles, a blue silk vest and black coat, along with a new pair of boots. Afterward, he stopped at a second store. Not wanting to bring flowers two days in a row, he purchased a small box of chocolates, and then made his way to Lady Caroline Evans's house again. Like yesterday, he'd borrowed one of Uncle Oscar's riding horses, which beat the heck out of renting another coach, but the saddle wasn't nearly as comfortable as his high-back one from home.

That was of little concern, though, considering everything else.

The same elderly man he'd seen yesterday answered the door of the terraced house, and led him into the same parlor. The room was right next to the front door, with windows that faced the street. Sitting there, on a table in front of one of the windows, were the daisies he'd given Caroline yesterday.

"Mr. Simpson," she said, once again entering the room as quiet as a ghost.

"It's me again," he said, managing to untie his tongue quicker today than yesterday. Wanting to correct her address of him, he asked, "Could you just call me Jake, please? That's what I'm used to."

"Very well, Jake." If she found the informality odd, she

was too well-bred to show it. With a slight nod, she said, "I grant you permission to call me Caroline."

"Thank you, Caroline," he replied. "I was hoping we could talk for a moment."

"Certainly." She waved a hand toward the furniture.

There were a couple of chairs, both with legs spindly enough that he was sure they would collapse beneath his frame. The small sofa didn't look a whole lot sturdier, but the legs were shorter and thicker. He walked to it, stood before it and waited until she was seated in one of the chairs. She was wearing a white blouse and gray skirt, and her hair was pulled away from her face and piled atop her head. Once again, he was struck by her beauty. It was so natural. Like a flower, just downright pretty to look at.

It didn't make it any easier to stomach his…assignment. The proposal he'd promised his uncle he'd consider making her. He'd been coerced into this course of action—something that never sat well with him. So much so that it had never truly happened before.

However, her beauty did make all of this seem even more unfair. With her looks, men ought to be clamoring for her attention, but he had to admit to himself that not even beauty could triumph over a soiled reputation.

As he began to sit, he remembered the candy and handed her the box. "These are for you. It's candy." A flash of embarrassment stung his cheeks. He'd never been this nervous. Ever. He was feeling like a fish out of water. No, not quite. More like a fish in the wrong pond. Holding in a sigh, he said, "For not addressing you properly yesterday."

She took the box. "Thank you, very much, but there is no need for you to bring me anything, or to apologize for anything. I accepted your apology yesterday."

He sat on the sofa and held his breath for a moment, making sure the short little legs weren't going to collapse. When they didn't, he said, "I'm aware of that, and thank you for it, but I'd still like for us to talk. If you don't mind."

"Very well." She set the box on the table beside her chair and folded her hands in her lap. "What is it you'd like to talk about?"

"Well, I—I—" He probably should have practiced this. Thought about how to go about asking a woman if she was in love with a man. Edward had *claimed* that he'd already offered her brother money after the wedding that had been canceled yesterday, and claimed that the earl had declined, insisting on the match, which suggested Lady Caroline might be in love with his cousin. But Edward could have been lying about all of that.

Jake wiped at the sweat he could feel popping out on his hairline. He hadn't been this nervous when talking with Faith about Edward. Then again, she'd blasted into his house like buckshot fired out of double barrels, demanding to see him. Caroline was far more prim and proper—calm, and…well, a lady.

It showed right now, as she sat there patiently, with a serene look on her face.

"I am very sorry about yesterday, and I—" He was now questioning if he should have altered his request that Edward be locked up in the house. His cousin should be the one apologizing to her. "The truth is, Edward isn't able to come tell you why I interrupted your wedding."

The corners of her lips curled up slightly, not really a smile, more like a grimace. She lifted her chin slightly as she said, "My brother has informed me why you prevented Edward from marrying me, and I don't expect to ever see Edward again."

"Do you want to see him?" Jake flinched at his own words. He could talk circles around cowboys and other men, and normally didn't mind talking to a woman or two, but this gal was playing havoc on his mind and tongue. Besides being pretty, she was so mild-mannered and, again, prim and proper. "I mean—"

She shook her head. "It doesn't matter what you mean. I have no desire to see Edward. None whatsoever."

"With all due respect, you might be upset with him right now, but in the future—"

"No," she interrupted. "Forgive me for being so rude in interrupting, but I will never wish to see Edward again. Not you, or anyone else will make me change my mind." She picked up the box of candy and stood, holding the box out toward him. "If that is your reason for being here, you can take your candy and leave. Now."

Chapter Three

Caroline wished her hands and knees weren't shaking, but they were, along with most every other part of her. She was also wishing she'd never laid eyes on this American. The very one she'd thought was so charming and suave, and thought that he'd saved her from a life of misery, was now here to throw her back in the water like an unwanted fish.

She'd never been the fanciful type, but since the argument with Frederick last night she had allowed herself to become embedded in whimsical thoughts, dreams that her life could become something that it had never been before. She'd told Frederick that she'd take responsibility for herself and so she'd begun to contemplate options. Ways she could make enough money to live independently. That idea, at least, wasn't new. She'd been trying it for years, with little to no luck. When she had found someone who would hire her, Frederick had stopped it, saying the sister of an earl could not work like a commoner.

She had convinced herself things would be different this time. That she would find a way to earn money and that no one would stop her.

At this moment, that proved inconceivable. Her life would never change, and this man was the reason. He was proving that she'd simply been lying to herself once again. About herself and him.

Why had she convinced herself that she could ever be free of Edward? Jake must want to marry the woman carrying Edward's child after all. She should have remembered that he had traveled all this way on behalf of that woman, so he must care for her. And naturally—though she hadn't seen it until a moment ago—it would be in Jake's best interest for Caroline to agree to marry Edward again, now that he'd exposed his cousin's shameful behavior. That would leave the other woman free for Jake to marry, with his pride intact.

For one reason or another, everyone wanted her to marry Edward.

Including Jake.

This time she would not give in. No matter what, she was not going to marry Edward. She'd rather be an old maid with no hope of ever having a family of her own than be married to a man she loathed. That was a terrible thing, to loathe someone, but Edward's disrespect toward her and other women made him a detestable person, and she had no reason to believe it would ever get better.

Jake didn't reach out to take the candy as he said, "My reason for being here is—"

His words were unexpectedly interrupted by a loud and rumbling eruption that shook the floor and made the windows rattle.

"Oh, for heaven's sake!" she muttered. Her words were louder than intended, but she was beyond frustrated that yet another experiment had gone awry. It was a common enough occurrence, but for it to happen now, of all times, with Jake present, was infuriating!

He'd shot to his feet. "What the—"

Out of habit, she interrupted him by shushing him and raising a hand so she could listen for the bell. Whenever there was a disruption from the basement, there was a string that ran up to a bell hanging in the hallway that either her brother or uncle would pull, letting the rest of the house know that all was fine, just a little mishap.

As the seconds ticked by, her irritation turned into concern. "There's no bell," she said. "There's no bell!" Dropping the box of candy on the sofa, she pivoted and ran from the room, down the hallway. White smoke was rolling out from beneath the door, but as she grasped the knob to open it, she was picked up by the waist and pulled away from the door. "My brother and uncle are down there!" she shouted.

Jake set her on the floor. "Get outside! Get everyone outside!"

"But—"

"Outside now!" He pulled open basement door. "I'll get them!" he said, before disappearing into a billowing cloud of white smoke.

Caroline started to follow him into the basement, but Aunt Myrtle and Mr. and Mrs. Humes were hurrying down the hallway, toward her, shouting, "There's no bell!"

"Get outside!" Jake bellowed up the steps.

"Oh, dear!" Aunt Myrtle exclaimed. "Oh, dear!"

"Come," Caroline said, encouraged to take Jake's advice by the tremor in her aunt's voice and seeing her paper-white face. She steered her aunt and the others toward the back door, which was closest. "Outside. Everyone. Quickly now." Her heart was pounding hard, fearful that one of her greatest fears could be coming true. That the house would burst into flames. Her uncle and brother had never started a fire in the basement before. They had never not rung the bell before, either. "Hurry! Hurry!" She had to get them outside and then get herself downstairs to help Jake.

"To the carriage house," she said, once her aunt and Mr. and Mrs. Humes were outside. The small building might provide them cover if a second explosion happened. "Hurry!"

They went scurrying across the yard. Caroline turned, about to reenter the house, but just then Jake came thundering through the open door. He had one arm wrapped around her uncle and the other pulling Frederick along behind him. Both men were covered in a fine white powder from head to toe.

"There now, my good man," Uncle James was saying. "All is well. All is well."

"Are you all right?" Caroline asked, reaching for her uncle's arm. "Are you hurt?"

"You didn't ring the bell!" Aunt Myrtle shouted, hurrying back toward the steps with her skirt hitched up almost to her knees.

"I couldn't see the string." Uncle James touched his temples with both hands. "I lost my spectacles in the mishap."

"Is there a fire?" Caroline asked, helping her uncle down the steps, and glancing at Jake. He wasn't covered in white, nor did he look ruffled. Instead, he grinned at her as he shook his head.

"There's no fire," Frederick confirmed, walking down the steps. "Just a chemical reaction."

"What were you doing down there?" Jake asked, frowning, and looking as if utterly confused. Rightfully so.

As she often did when it came to her uncle and brother and their experiments, Caroline felt a rush of impatience.

The two of them thought of little else but tinkering in that basement—until it came time to buy more supplies; then they'd travel from one end of London to the other, gathering what they were looking for and not caring what anything cost.

Uncle James squinted. "Who are you?" he asked. "I feel as if I've seen you somewhere before, but I can't say for sure. I lost my spectacles in the commotion. Did I mention that?"

"Jake Simpson, sir," he replied, shaking hands with Uncle James.

"Glad to make your acquaintance, Jake," Uncle James greeted affably. "I never expected to be carried up my own stairs, but thank you. Had that been a real fire, you would have saved my life. I'm James Evans, and this is my wife, Myrtle. That's our housekeeper and butler, Mr. and Mrs. Humes, and this is my niece, Caroline, and my nephew is the other fellow you hauled out of the basement, Frederick, I mean, the Earl of Brittmore."

Caroline had waited politely while Uncle James had been talking, and introducing everyone in the group who now stood near the back steps, but her nerves and a healthy dose of anger spiked when Frederick didn't take the hand Jake held out toward him.

"Mr. Simpson is Edward's cousin," her brother said spitefully. "The one who interrupted the wedding yesterday."

She glared at her brother. "With good reason."

"Oh, my," Aunt Myrtle muttered with a quivering voice, and looking more whitewashed than before.

Caroline moved quickly toward her, but Jake was faster. He already had ahold of Aunt Myrtle's arm.

"I think you should sit down, ma'am," he said. "Right over here, on the stoop."

"Oh, thank you, thank you," Aunt Myrtle said. "I do believe you are right."

Caroline walked on her aunt's other side as he helped Aunt Myrtle step up onto the concrete stoop, and she shot another glare at her brother for standing by and doing nothing but sneering. He knew nothing about Jake's apology yesterday, because she had chosen not to mention it last night, knowing he wouldn't have approved. He never approved of anything she did, or any of the people she considered friends. Not that she could claim Jake as a friend. More of an enemy now that he wanted her to marry Edward…but he had run to both Uncle James's and Frederick's rescue and should be treated with respect for that action alone.

"I think it's best to stay outside for a time," Jake said, helping Aunt Myrtle sit down on the top step. "Your house smells like rotten eggs right now."

Caroline had no doubt about that. The chemicals they used for their experiments often smelled terrible, and she herself had compared a stench rising up from the basement to something rotting more than once.

"Why are you here?" Uncle James asked, scratching his head, which sent a poof of white powder into the air. It was the same color as his hair, eyebrows, and the whiskers covering his face.

"To speak with your niece," Jake replied, giving Caroline a nod as he stepped away from Aunt Myrtle. "About my actions yesterday and what can be done to rectify the trouble I have caused."

"Oh, I see. Well, then, that's quite gentlemanly of you." Uncle James sat down next to Aunt Myrtle. "Sorry about the smell, my dear. It's just sulfur. I must have my ratio wrong. It wasn't supposed to combust like it did. We need to re-create atmospheric pressure to observe how quickly the leeches rise to the top of their jars."

Jake was now standing next to her and Caroline felt a nervous ripple shudder through her. She probably should step sideways, put some space between them, but it was as if the grass beneath her feet had turned into vines, tying her feet to the ground. His height was something she'd noticed before, but it wasn't until now that she recognized that the top of her head barely passed his shoulder. When he glanced down at her, as if knowing she'd been looking up at him, she found her eyes as unable to move as her feet.

"Did he say leeches?"

His whisper was low and gruff, and confusion was legible in every feature on his face. The first was enough to take her breath away, and the latter made her want to smile. "Yes."

"In your basement?"

"Yes," she repeated, still torn between smiling and being mortified over the truth that there were leeches in her basement.

His sky blue eyes widened. "Why?"

"To predict the weather," she replied, with a shrug. Some might believe it; most would not. When it came to her uncle and her brother's experiments, nothing was unusual to her anymore.

"Predict the weather?"

"Yes," Uncle James said, clearly having heard that question. "That is what we are working on. A weather-predicting device. It will change the world. Ships will be able to know when a storm is coming. It will help farmers know when to plant, and save average people from getting caught in a storm." With excitement rising on his wrinkled face, he waved a hand at Frederick. "Boy, run inside and get your aunt a chair to sit on instead of this step, and collect my spectacles while you're at it."

Without waiting for Frederick to agree, Uncle James continued talking to Jake, "Let me explain further. You see, over thirty years ago, a great inventor and surgeon, George Merryweather, created the tempest prognosticator, a marvelous device that proved how sensitive certain species are to the change of electrical atmospheric conditions. Leeches, in particular, become very agitated when a storm approaches. Merryweather's device consisted of twelve jars, each holding rainwater and a leech, and whenever a storm approaches, the leeches climb up the glass and touch a small whalebone attached to a chain that makes a bell ring. Now, our invention, though similar in using leeches and rainwater..."

As her uncle continued talking about his favorite invention of all time, Caroline noted how agitated her brother was to be sent on an errand. Mr. Humes had quickly gone to retrieve the chair for Aunt Myrtle, but no one bar Frederick and Uncle James was allowed in the basement, by their own rules, so there was no one else who could have gone for the spectacles. When he finally produced them, Caroline braved the smell to take them inside and washed the lenses. By the time she returned, she found that Mr. Humes had continued to carry out other chairs, enough for everyone.

Which is how they ended up. Her aunt, uncle, brother, herself, and Jake, who had requested that they all call him by his first name, sitting outside on kitchen chairs and talking about weather machines and other inventions while sipping on cups of tea and catching whiffs of smelly air wafting out of the opened windows.

Caroline felt a sense of dislocation from the group. Though she heard the discussion, and nodded or shrugged at Jake every now and again, it felt as if a part of her was floating beside her, like a ghost, whispering in her ear not to get caught up in the conversation or the laughter that emitted, usually brought on by Jake. He had a wonderful laugh, a deep, happy baritone sound that was practically contagious. But that little whisper in her ear said not to forget the real reason why Jake was here. To remember that no one sitting in this circle had the decency to let her make her own decisions, and that they all demanded one thing from her: to marry Edward, because then they would get what they wanted.

That part of her, that little ghost or whatever it was, was right, because even Frederick was laughing and acting sociable to Jake. More than sociable. He was being friendly, easygoing, in way that she hadn't witnessed in a long time.

When Uncle James invited Jake to dinner, Caroline's ghost, or common sense, or whatever it was, reentered her body with all the commotion that the earlier explosion had caused. This time she was the only one who felt the shattering, because it was all inside her, and shot her to her feet.

With everyone suddenly staring at her, it took a moment to come up with something to say. "The house still smells," she said.

"Ah, yes, there is that," Uncle James said, looking very disappointed, but only for a moment. A hopeful shine quickly returned to his face. "Tomorrow night? It'll be aired out by then."

The way Jake looked at her as he rose to his feet caused an entirely different kind of commotion inside Caroline. She was as unprepared for it as the last one, and the one that had rattled the entire house before that. For some very irrational reason—and she was usually an eminently rational person, particularly, she thought, compared to those around her—she couldn't pull her gaze from his. For a man she once considered intimidating, mainly because of his size, she now knew he wasn't intimidating at all, but instead very likable. So likable, a very real sense of warmth washed over her, just from sharing that long look.

"I still need to speak to Caroline," Jake said, continuing to gaze at her. "If, after our conversation, she agrees, I would enjoy dining with you tomorrow night."

"Oh, she'll agree," Uncle James said. "Won't you, child?"

She pulled her gaze away and pinched her lips together to stop herself from causing yet another commotion. That was what would happen if she said no, she wouldn't agree, and that she would never marry Edward no matter who asked her to. Jake might have charmed everyone else, but she wouldn't fall for it. She wasn't a child, either, but *that* was a useless argument that she'd given up on long ago.

"Would you care to take a walk with me?" Jake asked her. "I'm a little stiff after sitting so long."

"Of course she will," Uncle James answering for her again.

She bit her lips together a little harder.

"It's up to her," Jake said. "Only her."

A tiny shiver rippled through her, and she really wished she had a few moments to recover from the shock of someone suggesting she could make her own decision. Of all the things Jake could have said, that wasn't what she'd expected. "Yes," she heard herself saying. "A walk would be nice."

Jake made a point of saying goodbye to everyone before he looked at her expectantly.

She started walking along the cobblestone walkway that led to the carriage house. His horse was already inside the small pen beside the house, put there by Mr. Humes while they'd been talking. Upon seeing the butler engaged in the task, Jake had quickly risen to his feet and gone to help. Caroline had found that unusual for a member of the nobility, but not surprising from Jake. There was nothing pompous, arrogant, or privileged about him. The complete opposite of Edward.

Yet, Edward was why he was here, and she wouldn't forget that. "You can retrieve your horse now," she suggested.

Jake flashed her a grin. "I expected the walk to be a bit longer."

Refusing to react to his smile, she explained, "We can still go for a walk, but if you bring him along, then you'll have no need to come back and get him after our conversation."

He took a light hold of her arm and steered her down the driveway. "I will collect him after our conversation, and after I walk you home. I would never consider leaving a woman to walk home alone."

"I walk by myself all the time," she said, questioning if she should pull her arm from his hold, only because the heat of his hand was penetrating her dress and making her arm tingle and feel quite fiery. For some reason, perhaps to get her mind off his touch, she added, "I walked home alone from the church yesterday."

"You did?" he asked as they began walking along the side of the street.

She nodded, while admonishing herself for admitting that aloud. As if she'd needed a reminder of how foolish she'd been to be at that church, dressed in all the finery of a blushing, enamored bride, which had been a total illusion. A lie right from the start.

"Why?"

She'd been the one to start this conversation, so she let out a sigh and answered honestly, "Because the wedding was over and I was quite a spectacle standing at the altar with just the vicar."

"Where was your aunt and uncle? Your brother? Couldn't they have given you a ride home?"

It wasn't like her to complain, but then again, it wasn't as if she'd ever had anyone to complain to. "If I'd wanted to become a bigger spectacle by walking into the congregation to ask them to leave with me, yes. But I didn't want that, so I walked out of the back door instead." Ironically—or at least it seemed ironic to her—they were now headed along the very pathway she'd taken on her route home yesterday.

"I'm sorry for your embarrassment, Caroline," Jake said earnestly. "Very sorry for all of it. I truly didn't mean to cause you shame, to make a spectacle out of you. I just— Well, when I read about Edward's wedding in that newspaper, and then figured out that I only had a few hours to stop it, I set my mind on one goal. Keeping him from getting married. I never thought about you, and I should have. I should have handled things differently, and I'm truly sorry, for your sake, that I didn't."

He sounded so sincere a tremendous bout of guilt stirred in her stomach. "I accepted your apology yesterday, and I meant it." The guilt inside her continued to grow, like water in a pot about to boil over, and there was only one way to keep that from happening. Maybe if Jake knew the whole truth, he wouldn't blame her not wanting to marry Edward. "The truth is, I never wanted to marry Edward. You saved me from that yesterday, and for that I'm grateful." She drew in a deep breath, because she didn't want to disappoint him, but she had to tell him. "I won't ever agree to marrying him again. No matter who asks that of me. I won't do it."

Jake stopped. Stared down at her. Those big brown eyes were gazing back at him, and he was struggling to understand why the words she'd just said had tickled his insides so. His common sense told him that he ought to be more concerned about *what* she'd said, not how it made him feel. There was much in her words to focus on, and to contemplate. Clearing his throat to get rid of the lump that had formed there, and ignoring the uptick of his heartbeat, he asked, "If you didn't want to marry him, why were you? Why were you at the church?"

Her eyes clouded over as her gaze shifted, went in the direction of the house they'd left. "Because of them," she said.

"Them, meaning your family?" he asked.

"Yes."

"They wanted you to marry Edward?"

"Yes."

"Why?"

"Money."

Jake knew that was often a motive behind marriage, had been for centuries in the past and most likely would be for centuries in the future, but he couldn't help but think of the people that he'd just met. He'd sat with them and listened to stories about experiments and inventions that seemed interesting and unusual. From what he'd witnessed, he wouldn't have concluded that her family appeared to be focused on money. But perhaps he'd misjudged them... "They believed that by you marrying into the Simpson family, it would provide them with finances?"

Her cheeks puffed as she let out a long sigh. "Edward guaranteed that as long as I followed the agreement, monthly installments of funds would be sent to my family. I should never have agreed to that, and I won't again, so we can end this conversation now, because I will not marry Edward for any reason. I understand that is a disappointment to you, but there is nothing you can say to make me change my mind."

An icy chill wrapped around his spine, making him shiver. He sensed something underhanded had happened that had ultimately led to her agreeing to wed Edward. "I'm not here to change your mind, nor do I wish to end this conversation. In fact, I would like to know what agreement had been reached between you and Edward."

"It wasn't between me and Edward—it was between my brother and Edward."

"What was the agreement?"

Her gaze shot to her house again. "Why does it matter? I'm not going to agree to it again." She then looked at him, with a frown tugging on her brows. "If you aren't here to change my mind, why are you here?"

Why indeed. Why was he mixed up in any of this? Because of his own sense of duty, of what was right, and his desire to protect his property. His heritage. And he wouldn't stop until that was secure. "Earlier today, before

we were interrupted by the explosion. Or combustion."
That's what her uncle had insisted. That it had been a
combustion of wholly inflammable chemicals—no reason
to have feared a fire at all. "You stated you were aware
of why I stopped the wedding. Her name is Faith Drummond, and she feels she is in love with Edward. I came
here today to ask you if you feel the same way."

She grimaced while asking, "If I love Edward? No.
Not at all."

"You were willing to marry him so your family received financial support?"

With a sigh, she nodded.

Not wanting her to think he was disparaging her, he
touched her arm. "That's a legitimate reason for marriage.
Has been forever and will continue to be. There are many
legitimate reasons for marriage."

"That's easy to say, unless you are the person who is
being sold," she said.

As someone who had never been in her position, would
never be in her situation, he not only felt compassion, but
understood how she could feel that way, and recognized
how wrong it was. "No one should ever feel that way,
and I regret that my family was involved in putting you
in that situation."

"So was my family." She pressed a hand to her forehead. "However, this was different from most such…ar-
rangements. I was the one who went along with it, even
though I knew it was wrong from the beginning."

"How was it different?"

"Edward wanted a wife who wouldn't stop him from
continuing with his affairs. He made it perfectly clear that
if I said anything, did anything to stop him, the payments
to my family would stop." She had dropped the hand from

her forehead, but her expression still held pain in it. "Frederick has sold off most of the holdings he'd inherited to fund those experiments and inventions. There is hardly any money left for us to live on, to pay for food supplies. To pay Mr. and Mrs. Humes. And of course, to continue to fund their experiments. Therefore, Frederick decided to find an investor. Edward was the only one who responded to the request, but he countered with his own request. Me. He wouldn't invest any money unless I agreed to marry him and agreed to his stipulations."

A ball of anger was churning inside Jake's gut. That sounded exactly like something Edward would do, because everything was always about him. Always about what he wanted. Yet, even after all she'd said, Jake couldn't help but wonder why Caroline had gone along with it, knowing Edward would never be faithful to her. She was beautiful. A lady. Surely there was a man out there who would want to marry her and support her family simply because he wanted her to be happy. To be cared for.

"They are quite disappointed in me," she said. "Well, Frederick is, Uncle James and Aunt Myrtle go along with him, because… Well, after two years of his search to find an investor, they were happy he'd finally succeeded." She shrugged. "And found me a husband in the process."

Jake felt the frown tugging on his brows. "Did they, your aunt and uncle, know about the agreement? About Edward's affairs?"

"No. That information was known only to Frederick, Edward, and me."

The more she said, the more questions he had, but he didn't want to browbeat her, either.

"I'm sure you were hoping differently," she said, "so you could marry the woman in Texas, but—"

"I'm not interested in marrying Faith," he interrupted. "Edward is marrying her. I'm hauling him back to Texas and won't let him out of my sight until that happens."

"Oh." She looked a bit perplexed.

He felt the same. He still couldn't seem to move past the fact that she'd said *two years* of searching. "Was there another man that you wanted to marry? Before Edward?"

She took a step away from him, as if scared. "No."

He had the gut feeling he should stop this right now, but he was curious to know if there had been someone else that she'd wanted to marry, and her brother put a stop to it, which was why she'd agreed to Edward's demands. Then she could go on seeing that man, under the cover of an acceptable marriage. He hated himself for having such thoughts, because she didn't seem the type, certainly hadn't done anything for him to be thinking along those lines, but he sure did want to understand this.

"Men of means," she said, "want to marry a lady."

"You are a lady."

She shook her head. "No, I'm not. My father was an earl, and my brother now is an earl, but that doesn't make me a lady. Not a true lady. Not in spirit. I've never been to a ball or the theater, never been to a luncheon or a committee meeting, or even a dress maker, other than the one the duchess had hired to sew the wedding dress. I have no experience or prestige that a man would find of value, and I have no dowry, so therefore, I have never had a suitor. The only reason Edward was interested, was because the duke told him that he had to marry as soon as he returned home from America."

Neither his uncle or cousin had told Jake that, but he could imagine his uncle making the request, and Edward complying in this lowdown manner. But now Jake knew she wasn't in love with Edward… Aw hell, he didn't know if that made things better or worse.

"All right, then," Jake said, buying time because Caroline was gazing up at him with those big brown eyes. They were clear, telling him that she'd believed every word that she'd told him, including that because she didn't have experience as a lady or a dowry, that no man would find her of value. That wasn't true, but from his experience, women tended to be on the romantic side. Idealistic, even. Thought there was only one way that things could be. That's what Eloise had thought. That it was her or his cows. He'd known the choice he'd needed to make that night, when she'd said that to him, and had told her so. It was the cows. Would always be the cows because they were his livelihood.

If only this puzzle were as simple to figure out. "There's just one more question I have to ask."

She frowned. Blinked. "What's that?"

"Would you agree to me joining your family for dinner tomorrow evening?"

Chapter Four

Caroline spent the entire day cleaning, using beeswax and lemon juice on every piece of wood, the floors, banisters, tables, arms and legs of chairs, even the doors and frames, hoping to get rid of any lingering rotten-egg smell and the fine white powder dust that had settled into every crevice. She also washed, dried, and pressed anything that was washable and used talcum powder on the rugs and cushions before beating them clean.

She couldn't remember the last time they'd had a guest for dinner, and throughout the day, she asked herself why she'd said yes. Why she kept saying yes when she knew her answer should be no.

Sharing a meal at her home wasn't in the same category as a marriage, though, and Jake was nothing like Edward. They were as opposite as cats and dogs.

All the cleaning truly needed to be done whether they were having a guest for dinner or not, but staying busy was also supposed to keep her from thinking about Jake, but it wasn't working. While her hands worked, her mind had plenty of time to wonder back to thoughts of him and wonder why he was so determined to make Edward marry the woman back in Texas.

There had to be a reason, besides that it was the right

and ethical thing to do. Faith was going to have a baby! Edward needed to marry her! It just seemed that Jake was going above and beyond what most people would. There had to be more of a reason for him to be so determined that he'd traveled halfway around the world.

Perhaps she was wrong. Perhaps there were still good people in the world who wanted everyone to be treated fairly. Jake certainly seemed to have the character to be such a person. In her opinion—whatever that was worth, considering her past mistakes.

All of these thoughts were making her think about herself, too, and her character.

Despite all she'd known, she'd caved and agreed to marrying Edward, and the truth was, it wasn't just because of her family. She wanted a different life from the one she'd been living, and had been willing to do whatever it took to get one. That was nothing to be proud of. She loved her aunt and uncle, and was grateful for how they'd taken her and Frederick in all those years ago. She loved her brother, too, despite all. It was just that she had no future here. No hope for a family of her own. No hope for anything other than what she had right now. For the past couple of years, watching others her age marry and start families, she'd felt as if her life was strangling her.

That same strangling sensation had come upon her yesterday, when talking to Jake. It had been so strong that she'd told him things she'd never admitted aloud. How she knew a title didn't make her a lady. How she'd never been to a ball or any other social event, and had never had a suitor. Admitting all of that should have been so embarrassing that she'd never want to see Jake again, yet she'd agreed to have him join her family for dinner.

Flustered, she pushed herself off the floor, and tossed

the rag she'd used to wipe down the hallway floorboards into the bucket. While carrying the bucket to the kitchen, she told herself that she should have said no. Simply cut any connection to the Simpson family. If she wanted a different life, she was going to have to find it on her own.

After taking care of her cleaning supplies in the kitchen, she set the table in the dining room, relieving Mrs. Humes from that task, and then opened the basement door and shouted down to her brother and uncle that their guest would arrive within the hour. After that, she entered the back parlor, where her aunt was engrossed in painting a landscape with oil paints, and delivered the same message. Then she went upstairs to change her dress.

Her choices were limited. Both of her best dresses were simple day dresses, neither fancy nor considered suitable evening wear for a dinner party. One more example of how she truly wasn't a lady of social standing. Had no true social standing whatsoever.

She'd been in this position before, choosing between the blue-and-white-striped dress and the yellow one with beige lace. Had that truly only been three weeks ago? When she'd chosen the blue-and-white dress and had been escorted to Edward's home by Frederick, to meet the Duke and Duchess of Collingsworth. They had been informed of the wedding prior to her arrival, and that visit had been for the sole purpose of planning the wedding. The duchess had been very nice: besides insisting upon hiring the seamstress, she'd asked which parts of the ceremony were most important to Caroline.

There hadn't been anything that Caroline had considered particularly important. She'd stated that whatever the family wanted would be fine with her. Both Frederick and Edward had said that no prewedding events were necessary, and though she'd had no say in the choice, she'd been relieved to hear it, and relieved that their suggestion had been granted. She'd just wanted to get it over with. And then...

Shaking her head, she put all of that behind her, chose the yellow dress, and found a ribbon close to the same shade to use in her hair.

What felt like mere minutes later, Mr. Humes informed her their guest had arrived. Her heart began to race and she fumbled with the hairpins as she tried to get them in place.

Finding the ability to speak, she thanked the butler and asked him to inform the rest of the family, before she stepped back and stared at her reflection in the mirror. A sense of defeat caused her shoulders to droop, along with her stomach and every other part of her. She'd washed her hair that morning, so it was so silky that the pins wouldn't hold, leaving it looking more like someone had tried to tie a ribbon around a poorly wrapped gift instead of the sleek and elegant chignon that she'd been trying to fashion. She should have just twisted it into a bun and pinned it up like she usually did. That's what she'd done for the wedding. Then again, she hadn't really cared that day, knowing it would be covered by the veil.

Why did she care today? Jake was only joining them for dinner because her uncle had invited him, and she truly had no idea why he'd felt inclined to agree. He certainly could have said no. She could have said no, too, when he'd asked for her agreement.

Flustered for so many reasons, including knowing there wasn't time to attempt to fix her hair, she spun away from the mirror and left her room.

Jake was in the parlor, and seeing him in that same

spot for the third time in a row incited the same reaction
as the other two times. Her breath quickened, her heart
thudded, and her stomach was filled with flutters. He
was wearing a black-and-brown jacket, white shirt, with
a gold vest and ascot, and brown pants. In many ways, he
looked as formidable as he had in the church while wearing his American attire. He was that tall and broad, and
filled the parlor with much the same presence as he had
consumed at the altar.

His handsomeness was just as prominent, too. Parted
on the side, his black hair was combed back in a way that
made his bright blue eyes stand out more.

It truly didn't matter how he was dressed, or whether
his hair was falling across his forehead or not; he simply
had an aura about him that was masculine and righteous.
Not in an arrogant way that said he was due respect and
admiration because of his station in life, but because he
was of good character and was proud of that in an honorable way.

At that moment, she understood why he was here. Why
he'd agreed to have dinner with them. Because he was a
man of deep morals, and still felt responsible for stopping
the wedding. He was committed to making things right,
in some way, even though in her mind, stopping the wedding *had* been right.

She understood that because she suddenly understood
the difference between his character and hers. Stopping
the wedding had been right for her, but not her family.
She'd failed them. They would soon be destitute and rather
than worrying about that, worrying what her actions had
done to them, she'd been thinking about herself, about
wanting a different life.

"These are for you," Jake said, holding out the bouquet of tiny blue flowers. "I'm not sure what they are called, but they remind me of some wild ones that grow in Texas. We call them bluebonnets. Like the daisies, there are fields of them growing wild, but rather than looking like snow, those fields look like the blue ocean waters of the Gulf of Mexico."

She reached out to take the flowers, but as her hand touched his, a zing of fiery heat raced up her arm as quick as a flash of lightning, making her momentarily forget where she was and what she was doing. The result left the flowers tumbling to the floor. Unlike the daisies, the stems of the flowers hadn't been tied with a piece of twine, leaving them tumbling and scattering across the floor.

"I'm sorry," he said, bending down to pick up the flowers.

She'd bent down at the same time, and consequently, they bumped heads. They both jolted backward, and Caroline did her best to hide the heat racing into her face, struggling to maintain enough balance while kneeling down that she didn't tumble over.

"I'm sorry," he replied again, while quickly gathering up the flowers. "It seems the harder I try not to, the more I make myself look like a buffoon."

Recovering her own dignity, Caroline collected the last few flowers. "You aren't a buffoon. It was my fault. I thought I had ahold of them." This time, she forced herself not to react when their hands touched, and again when he took of her arm to steady her as they rose to their feet. "Thank you," she offered, once standing again. "And thank you for the flowers. They are very lovely, but there truly is no reason for you to bring me something on each of your visits."

"There doesn't need to be a reason to give a beautiful lady flowers," he said.

Forget his words. His smile was enough to make her swoon. Of course, she wouldn't do that—swoon, at least not visibly. Inside, though, every part of her was feeling unsteady. Even her mind. It couldn't provide her with a response.

Pivoting about, she walked to the table holding the vase of daisies, and began tucking the blue flowers among the white ones. For more than one reason. It was the only vase in the house, and she needed time to get her insides under control and think of something to say.

She was saved from immediately having to say anything by Mr. Humes, who entered the room carrying a tray holding a small glass container of Aunt Myrtle's coveted port wine and two glasses.

"The rest of the family will join you shortly," Mr. Humes said, setting the tray on the table next to the vase of flowers.

"Thank you," Caroline replied, even though she understood by the twist of Mr. Humes's lips and the apology in his eyes that her uncle and brother were still in the basement and her aunt was still in her parlor. She gave him a nod, then whispered for him to tell them again that Jake was there. Mr. Humes gave a slight bow before leaving the room. They both knew, however, what little good a second, or even a third, reminder would do.

Once the flowers were all in the vase, and despite her nerves still jumping under her skin, she poured the wine into the glasses and lifted them, one in each hand.

Jake was still standing in the center of the room when she turned around and, willing her hands to cooperate this time, she crossed the room and handed him one of the glasses. "Would you care to sit down?"

"Thank you," he said taking the glass, then gestured toward the furniture with his other hand. "After you."

She sat in one of the armed chairs, while he walked to the sofa and slowly lowered himself onto the cushion. They each took a sip off their glasses as a stilled silence filled the room. She searched her mind, trying to come up with some sort of clever conversation, but like so many other things, she wasn't apt in that, either. Luckily, the flowers gave her a subject. "It must be amazing, seeing fields full of flowers."

He nodded. "It is. My mother sure enjoyed it."

"Enjoyed?"

Nodding again, he said, "She passed away shortly after my younger sister was born, over ten years ago now."

"I'm sorry for your loss," she said. He'd learned about her family yesterday, how her parents had died and she and Frederick had come to live with Uncle James and Aunt Myrtle, but no one had asked about his family. The conversation had been too focused on the inventions and experiments in the basement.

"As I am for yours," he said.

"Thank you," she replied, before asking, "Your father, is he—"

He shook his head before she could finish asking her question. "No. He died four years ago."

"Do you have other siblings besides your sister?"

"No, it's just the two of us. Nellie is ten, and was spitting mad when I wouldn't let her come along on this trip with me. I reckon she'll be over that by the time I get home. She's a good kid, but a bit hotheaded at times." His grin grew. "Comes by that honestly."

Caroline knew the bristling inside her was due to her soft spot for children, even though she didn't have a lot of opportunities to interact with them, not like when the Wetherbees had lived next door. They'd moved away two years ago and she still missed all three of the children. Two boys and a girl. The only neighbor to come visit her now was Mrs. Alcott's dog, Toby. He was nice for a dog, other than the way he was forever burying things in the garden. Try as she might, she couldn't keep him from tearing apart her plants as he squirreled away a bone, stick, or other treasure.

Relinquishing thoughts of Toby, her mind settled back on Jake. She couldn't believe he would have left a ten-year-old child home alone, but he had said it was just the two of them. "Who is Nellie staying with during your absence?"

He lifted a brow, and his grin grew slightly. "Is that your way of asking if I left her home alone?"

She opened her mouth to say no, but the burning in her cheeks wouldn't let her lie. "I can't believe you would do that."

He leaned back. "Thank you. I didn't. She's at the ranch, but there are a lot of other people there, too. People looking out for her when I'm there and when I'm not."

Not knowing any pertinent information about ranching, she asked, "But they aren't family?"

"No, but they are as close as that can be without being kin."

Curious to learn more, about his ranch, his sister, and him, she asked, "How many people live there?"

Jake finished the wine in his glass in one swallow. Had to. It was so sweet that his first tiny sip had sent a shiver down his spine. He set the glass on the table beside the sofa, and began listing off names, starting with Lolitta and Luis, the couple who had been there when his father had purchased the ranch from the previous owner.

Talking about back home, about the people there, was keeping his mind from wandering off toward other things. Namely Caroline. She looked exceptionally pretty tonight. Her hair wasn't pulled back as tightly as it had been yesterday or the day before, and a yellow ribbon that matched her dress was woven into the thick brown mass and tied in a bow atop her head. There was a softness to it that made her look more relaxed, and he liked that. Telling her about the ranch made him relax a bit, too, and he liked that as well.

He'd risen with the sun this morning and traveled the two and a half hours to Collingsworth, the manor house he'd been born in. Nothing much had changed in fourteen years at the estate, other than like the house in London, some things looked smaller to him now compared to the memories of a twelve-year-old. Things he hadn't recalled in a long time had filtered through his mind.

Some of the same servants from when he and his parents had lived there were still in residence, and after their initial surprise at seeing him, they'd told him about being excited to have family living here again, full-time. Edward had informed them that his wife—he'd been referring to Caroline—would be in permanent residence at Collingsworth after their wedding. Therefore, they'd also been disappointed to hear the wedding had been canceled.

It hadn't been a surprise to know that Edward's plan had been to send Caroline to the country, and leave her there, alone. It had also increased Jake's ire toward his cousin. So had last evening, when it had been confirmed that Uncle Oscar had told Edward that as soon as he returned from America, he was getting married, and that if he didn't find a wife on his own, one would be found for him.

Edward had returned, made the deal with Frederick, and had left all the finer details of the wedding to his family, assuring them that he and Caroline would be at the church at the set day and time.

His cousin had also admitted that he'd lied again, that he hadn't offered Frederick any money after the wedding. Instead, he'd assured Frederick that the wedding would happen. Uncle Oscar had been irate.

So had Jake. He still was.

Everything that he'd learned, everything that had happened, made him mad over the way Caroline had been treated, and would have been treated after the marriage, but could he really agree to marrying her himself? He not only had the ranch; he had Nellie and all the people he'd just named off that worked for him, who depended on him, and like he'd told Eloise, the cows, his ranch, and the people there would always come first.

A marriage between him and Caroline wouldn't be that much different than she would have experienced if she'd married Edward. Unlike his cousin, Jake wouldn't have been interested in other women, but his ranch would be where his attentions were always focused. And that wouldn't be fair to her. Fair to any wife. He'd tried to explain that to his aunt and uncle, and even proposed a different plan to secure Caroline's future: a financial investment by the Collingsworth estate in Frederick and James's experiments. They'd readily agreed. But would that be enough? Caroline's reputation was still in jeopardy. Damn this tangled situation!

"So," Caroline said, "there's Lolitta and Luis, who take care of the house, there are also Slim, Rocky, Walter, Bernie, Denver, and Clem, who are ranch hands and live in the bunkhouse. And Mack Henderson, the ranch foreman, and his wife, Jane, who live in the original house—cabin, as you call it—that was on the property when your family purchased it. There is also a schoolhouse that your father had built, because Twisted Gulch is over ten miles away, which makes it too far for the children to attend school. So Jane Henderson teaches her two children, Melanie and Boyd, there, as well as Nellie and six or more other children who live on ranches and farms nearby."

"That is all correct," he answered, impressed that she'd remembered every name he'd said. "So, now do you believe that Nellie isn't home alone?"

"I never believed that she was," Caroline answered, as she once again glanced toward the doorway. She'd done that several times.

"I'm assuming your uncle and brother are working on their weather invention," he said.

She nodded. "I suspect time has gotten away from them."

"Is your aunt with them?"

"No, she tends to forget time, too. She's an artist, a painter." Standing, she continued, "If you will excuse me for one moment, I will go hurry them along."

"Actually," he said, not sure how proper it was for him to ask, "if you don't mind, I'd like us to discuss something first."

Her eyes widened, and she slowly lowered back to her seat. "All right. What would you like to discuss?"

"I'm going to just get straight to the point," he said, mainly for himself. He'd been quibbling with it long enough. "I need to get back to Texas. Get Edward and Faith married, and back to work."

She nodded.

He sucked in a solid breath of air. "My aunt and uncle, the Duke and Duchess of Collingsworth, are concerned about your reputation. The way I interrupted your wedding has the potential to cause irrevocable damage to your ability to find a suitable match in the future, and we, the duke, duchess, and myself, would like you to know that we are willing to assist you in any way you may see fit to rectify the situation as much as possible."

Jake couldn't say for sure how his statement was settling with her. She was looking at him with a somewhat blank stare.

She blinked and drew in a visible breath. "First, I need to point out that one would need to have a reputation in order for it to be damaged. I am virtually unknown. As far as your assistance, though I thank you, all of you, the duke and duchess, and you, don't owe me anything, no assistance of any kind."

"We feel that we do," he countered. "You may have been unknown prior, but society does know your name now, and that I interrupted your wedding. It'll be known in the future, too, once word of Edward's marriage to Faith reaches London. We want to prevent any suffering that all of these events may cause."

A frown knitted her brows together. "I don't understand what you are trying to prevent. You can't stop people from talking."

"Perhaps *prevent* isn't the right word," he said, seeing her point. "*Compensate* would be more accurate."

Both of her brows rose. "Compensate?"

"Yes, for the damage we've caused."

She pressed a finger to her lips, as if she needed to keep them together, perhaps stop from saying something.

Jake was contemplating what to say, when a thud and footsteps sounded in the hallway. A moment later, her uncle James appeared in the doorway.

"Hello, Jake," James said, shrugging on a suit coat as he walked into the room. "So good of you to join us for dinner. Frederick will be along shortly, and…" He looked at Caroline. "Go find your aunt, child. Tell her our guest is here."

Jake took a second to calm himself over the way James had addressed Caroline. It appeared to him that she wasn't treated with the respect she deserved by anyone, and that bothered him. Deeply. So did the blush on her face. He didn't like her being embarrassed. Not at all. It wasn't his place to say or do anything, but he wasn't one to stay in his place when others were mistreating someone. Rising to his feet, Jake took a step, which blocked her from leaving her chair. "Your butler informed your wife upon my arrival. I imagine that she will join us when she's able." While speaking, he held his hand out to shake James's. Jake doubted that he needed to say more, considering the way James cowered, yet he couldn't stop himself. "It was kind of Caroline to keep me company while I waited for the rest of you."

"Oh, yes, I suspect it was," James said, shaking hands. "Sorry to have kept you waiting."

"No harm done," Jake said. This time he stopped himself from saying more. Such as informing the man Caroline was the sole reason he was here.

"Well, please, sit down," James replied. "I'm sure Myrtle and Frederick will be along soon."

Jake returned to his seat, and purposefully didn't look

at Caroline. Although he wanted to. Wanted her to know that in his presence, she wouldn't be treated like a servant or a child. At the same time, he didn't want her to be *further* embarrassed by his acknowledgment of the slight.

James instantly began talking about the latest invention he was working on—not the weather one, so he didn't mention the leeches again. Thank the Lord. It was enough to give Jake the shivers knowing there were bloodsucking leeches in the basement. It wasn't long before Frederick and Myrtle joined them, and shortly thereafter, the butler informed them it was time for dinner to be served.

Jake escorted Caroline into the dining room, and chose the seat beside hers, across from Frederick and with James at the head of the table on his left. Myrtle was at the foot of the table, on Caroline's right. Jake noted that the older woman had a smear of blue paint on her cheek.

Caroline must have noticed it as well, because she whispered something and Myrtle used her napkin to rub the paint away.

The meal of ham, potatoes, green beans, bread, and pickles was tasty, and the conversation, led mainly by James, was a continuation of his explanation of his electromagnetic device that could detect metal in the ground, or even inside a person's body. James claimed it would help surgeons find the lead balls of bullets inside the shot person's body.

Jake figured the hole made by the bullet would be a good place for the surgeons to look, but kept his opinion to himself.

"Uncle James," Caroline said, while her uncle was taking a bite of food. "Jake was telling me about his ranch in Texas. Perhaps you would care to hear about that."

"Ranch?" James nodded.

"Yes," Jake answered. "It's currently a little over ten thousand acres."

"Ten thousand acres?" James shook his head. "That would be sixteen square miles, what are you doing with all that land?"

"Most of it is grassland, for the cattle," Jake answered.

"I've heard of the Texas longhorns," James said. "Read about them in the periodicals."

"I have plenty of them," Jake replied. "They are a hardy breed, but the markets like a variety, so we have herds of different breeds, too."

James was a detail man, and asked about specific breeds and numbers, which Jake readily answered, and then went on to answer a plethora of other questions pertaining to the ranch, the land, the weather, the towns nearby, cattle drives, railroads, and more. The conversation continued well past the meal, dessert, and coffee, with James still pelting him with questions even as they'd returned to the parlor.

"I would like to see this ranch of yours someday," James said. "It sounds interesting, and vastly different from our part of the world."

"You'd be welcome anytime," Jake offered. "It is very different from London, but I wouldn't want to live anywhere else. I'll be heading back in a couple of days, and am looking forward to it."

"I bet you could use a good weather machine there," James said. "Let you know when those tornados you mention are approaching."

"You'll have to let me know when you've perfected yours." Understanding it was growing late, Jake nodded to the others. "I thank you all for dinner and a nice evening." He wasn't exactly sure how to request a few moments alone with Caroline, so the two of them could finish their conversation.

"You aren't thinking of leaving yet, are you?" James asked.

"It's getting late," Jake said. "But I do have a couple of things to discuss with Caroline." Turning to where she sat on a chair near her aunt, he asked, "Would you care to take a short stroll?"

She nodded. "It'll just take me a moment to get a shawl."

He stood, and after she left the room, he bade the others farewell, which took a long time, due to another set of questions from James about how long it took to travel to America. Caroline was waiting for him in the hallway, which gave him an excuse to finally make an exit.

"I'm sorry," she whispered as they walked to the door. "I didn't know Uncle James was going to question you so thoroughly. Usually, it's only his inventions he talks about."

"I'm the one who should be apologizing," Jake said, opening the door for them to exit the house. "We talked about my ranch the entire evening."

"I enjoyed hearing about it," she said. "It sounds like a very interesting place."

"I like it, but it's not for everyone." He closed the door behind them and walked beside her down the steps off the front stoop. "It can be rough and wild."

"You mentioned a plan to send your sister to England when she gets older, is that correct?"

"Yes." He had mentioned that during one of James's questions, but hadn't elaborated on how his sister would need to expand her education as she got older. Things that he couldn't teach her, nor could the women who lived at the ranch. "When she gets older. She'll live with my aunt and uncle, go to school here."

"How much older?"

"I'm not sure." He didn't like the idea of Nellie being that far away from him, but knew it would be for her own good, and he would never deny her the chance to learn about the wider world. "I'd like for her to see other places in America first. I've wanted to do that for a long while, but it's hard to find the time." Nellie needed more than he could give her, because his first commitment was to his ranch, and that wasn't fair to her any more than it had been fair to Eloise… He gave his head a clearing shake, to chase away those guilty thoughts. "Enough about me and my ranch. I wanted us to finish our conversation from earlier."

"Yes, the compensation," she said. "To that, I will say again that your family doesn't owe me anything."

They had reached the edge of the yard, and he paused there, looked down at her. "We are willing to pay you the money that Edward promised you, plus more."

Her hair, and the ribbon tied atop it, glistened in the moonlight. So did her big, brown eyes. "Why?"

"Well, it would be an investment in your brother and uncle's experiments, and also, a part of it would be payment for the damage my family caused you." He stopped shy of explaining that it could be used as a dowry.

She closed her eyes for a moment, then looked away when she opened them again. "You want to pay me for not marrying Edward?"

He nodded, but she still wasn't looking at him, so didn't know he'd done so. Something about that made him not want to say *yes* aloud.

Chapter Five

Caroline drew in a fortifying breath. At least she was counting on it being fortifying, because she didn't have anything else to draw upon. She didn't know exactly why her stomach was churning, or why her throat felt hot, fiery. She'd been willing to marry Edward for money, but getting paid *not* to marry him, well, that felt… She wasn't sure what that felt like, other than erroneous.

If having her wedding to Edward unconventionally ended was something that would hurt her nonexistent reputation, getting paid not to marry him was sure to do worse. People would believe she was damaged goods. Shame rose up inside her as her thoughts went down that route—shame, but also a fiery ball of anger. "I did not allow Edward to have his way with me."

Jake took a step back. "I never suggested—"

"Didn't you? Well, that is what everyone will believe." That was now a glaring reality. Gossip was gossip, and she would be that gossip. She might have been unknown, but after word got out of her being paid off, she wouldn't be. She'd be scorned.

"No—"

"Yes," she interrupted him again. "People believe what they want to believe, and because I had no reputation prior to agreeing to wed Edward, they will now give me one." Too close to tears to say more, she shook her head. Marrying Edward had been a terrible idea from the beginning, and now it felt as though her ordeal was never going to end, just get worse. She would be a marked woman. There was no doubt about that. No one would believe she was pure, chaste. Marrying for money was accepted; being paid not to marry someone would be seen as a definitive sign that something was wrong with her, and she'd be ridiculed.

"Caroline, we want to protect you," he said. "We owe you our protection."

Tears were burning the backs of her eyes. All she could do was shake her head again. Then turn, and run to the house.

Not wanting to face her family, she ran to the back door, and then down the hall and up the stairs, thankful not to be seen along the way. Once in her bedroom, she closed the door and leaned her back against it, sucking in air and squeezing her eyes shut, refusing to let the tears burst forward. Whether she wanted to believe it or not, her life was over. Even without having a reputation, without being known to society, not marrying Edward had ruined her life as much as marrying him would have.

Why hadn't she considered all this before now? Why had it taken Jake's offer of money to make her see what was crystal clear? She was now a marked woman. No one would ever want to marry her. She'd never have children to care for, a home of her own. Those were the only things she'd hoped to have by marrying Edward: that someone on the estate would have children that she could help care for, or that she could become involved in children's charities, and have flower beds, gardens, a home she could decorate and take pride in. That would have been enough.

Foolish thinking, because she'd always known hope caused disappointment.

She lost her battle against the onslaught of tears, and it was a long, exhausting bout of crying. So long that her eyes felt like sand was embedded in them when she crawled out of bed the following morning. Her body felt heavy, from lack of sleep, and her mind felt numb from hours upon hours of torturous thoughts and truths.

It was not only her reputation being forever marked that had kept her awake. If Frederick heard that the Duke of Collingsworth was willing to invest in his experiments, he'd head straight over to their front door, hand out. He wouldn't care if she'd be mocked, looked down upon, and scathed with ongoing gossip about being paid not to marry Edward.

All of that and more had played out in her mind through long, sleepless hours, as had any options she might have, and not a single one of those was ideal or even attainable. The manor home where she'd been born, as well as the small acreage where it stood, had not been sold off as of yet. It was a distance from London, and might be safe from scrutiny, but having been unoccupied for so long, it might not be habitable. Furthermore, her aunt and uncle would never move there. Uncle James had said long ago that he couldn't move his workshop, nor could Aunt Myrtle paint anywhere other than her parlor.

She could move to the manor home herself, but that would take money, which she didn't have. If she did, she wouldn't be in this position. The other ultimate truth was that there was no way out of the mess she'd created, and that was truly beyond depressing.

Once dressed, and after completing her morning routine, Caroline left her room to make her way downstairs and assist Mrs. Humes with the morning meal. She had only made it as far as the top of the stairs when she encountered Frederick.

There had been a time when they'd been close, laughed and joked with each other. Now, there was nothing but scorn in his eyes when he looked at her.

"Why are you making this so difficult?" he asked, in a low half whisper.

With her nerves still raw from little sleep and no answers, she was in no mood to deal with him. "Why did you start all of this in the first place?"

His scowl grew deeper. "It was our only option. Now just tell Jake that you'll marry Edward so he can quit coming here every day, go back to Texas, and marry that other woman."

"Jake isn't going to marry that other woman. Edward is."

"No, he's not," Frederick insisted. "Edward himself told me so. He's still marrying you."

"Have you talked to him since he said that?" she asked.

"No, I've tried to see him, but his butler says he's not taking callers."

"Because it's not going to happen. Jake is taking Edward back to Texas with him to marry Faith."

Frederick ran a hand through his dark, thick hair while shaking his head, then pointed down the stairs. "Then why does Jake keep coming over here every day? Needing to talk to you?"

She was not going to tell him anything about Jake's reasons for coming over to visit her, and prayed to high heaven that no one else did, either. Something clicked or ticked in her brain; she noticed that his hand was still pointing down the stairs. Her heart crawled up into her throat, almost seeming to block it completely, leaving her just enough air to ask, "Is Jake here again?"

"Yes. He's in the dining room, having coffee with Uncle James and talking about that bloody ranch of his. It wouldn't surprise me if Uncle James went back to Texas with him. Which would also be your fault for not agreeing with him during his first visit!"

Caroline's first instinct was to tell her brother that Jake had *never* come here to ask her to marry Edward, only to apologize, but Frederick wouldn't care about any of that. He was desperate for money and that was all he could think about, all he could care about.

Frederick flattened himself against the wall. "Well, go on, he's here to talk to you again."

If given a choice of facing Jake after the way she'd run off last night, or standing here arguing with Frederick, she'd prefer neither. Since that wasn't a possibility, she'd choose Jake. Arguing with her brother hadn't done any good for months, and despite the mess her life was in, she liked Jake. Liked the way he sounded, the way he looked, and behaved, and well, just about everything about him was likable. She enjoyed hearing about things in Texas and at his ranch, too. If moving halfway around the world would change anything, that would be where she'd go. To Texas. See those fields of flowers, those Texas cows with three-foot-long horns on each side of their heads, and many of the other things Jake had mentioned last night.

Caroline walked past Frederick, but he caught her arm as she began to descend the steps. "Tell him that you will marry Edward and he can marry that other woman," he whispered, but it still echoed off the narrow passageway.

She wrenched her arm out of Frederick's hold and hurried down the steps. She wouldn't tell Jake any such thing, nor that she would accept his offer of compensation for not marrying Edward, but she would apologize to him. It had been rude to leave him standing at the edge of the front yard last night.

He was indeed in the dining room and rose to his feet as she entered. The unease in his eyes increased the regret she already felt over the way she'd behaved last night. Mustering up a smile, she greeted him. "Good morning."

"Good morning," he returned. "I apologize for stopping by so early."

"I'm glad you did," she answered, before glancing at her uncle. "Excuse us." Giving her uncle no opportunity to respond, she immediately said to Jake, "We can speak in the back parlor." That was Aunt Myrtle's domain, but her aunt never rose before ten in the morning without a very good reason, and the room was the only one that had a door that would provide them with a modicum of privacy.

They walked in silence, down the hallway, past the staircase, to Aunt Myrtle's parlor. The room smelled of paint and hosted stacks of canvas paintings, and easels with works in progress. She gestured for him to enter ahead of her. It might not be proper to shut the two of them in a room together, but that was the least of her concerns. "This is the only place we can speak privately."

"We could take a stroll," he said, glancing into the very cluttered room. "I know it's early, but I'd really like to catch the cargo ship heading to Galveston tomorrow, out of Portsmouth, and I can't do that until things are settled between you and my family."

If only she could leave on a ship, heading anywhere. She didn't care. What she did care about was that others had been affected by her actions, including him. She had no idea what to do about that, but she did owe him an apology. Letting out a sigh, she gestured to the room again. "Please."

He stepped into the room. She followed and closed the door behind them, wishing there was a way to make everything go away. Go back to what it used to be. It seemed incredible that she'd be yearning for her old life. All she'd wanted back then was for everything to change.

There were only two chairs, both splattered with paint, but this wouldn't take long enough that either of them would need to sit down. She stepped away from the door and kept her voice low. "I apologize for the way I left you last night. That was a very inappropriate way to treat a guest, and I'm quite ashamed of the way I behaved."

"I'm sorry I upset you," he replied.

"I appreciate your apologies and the offer of money," she said, needing to get this over with so he could leave, and she could… She didn't know what she could do, but would have to think of something. "I simply can't accept any money, not even as an investment for my brother and uncle. There are too many consequences. And I want you to know that you aren't responsible for any of this. You were the only one doing the right thing."

"I disagree. I stopped the wedding."

"For which I'll forever be grateful, because I was about to make the biggest mistake of my life. You can leave, return to America knowing that I appreciated all you did, and never worry about any of it again."

"I can't do that." He crossed his arms, stared at her. "I do, however, understand your concerns about accepting the money. The reason I came over this morning was to ask for your opinion."

"Concerning what?"

"Concerning what I can do. What my family can do. There has to be a way we can make this better for you. You just tell me what it is, and I'll see it happens."

She had no opinion. There were no answers. No fixes. That was frustrating, as was his insistence in trying to make it better for her. There was nothing either of them could do…

Her next thought barely entered her mind before it was out of her mouth.

"Take me to America with you."

His eyes widened with what appeared to be the same shock that was rippling through her. She opened her mouth to say she hadn't meant to say that, but words wouldn't form. Instead, a wave of additional thoughts washed through her mind, all the ways it might work, might solve her problems. And to be honest, those thoughts were matched by a great, rising wave of excitement, something she hadn't felt in years. In the United States, where no one knew her, she could have the life she wanted. And here, gossipers would believe she'd left the country to save face, to save her family from ongoing embarrassment. With her gone, gossipers would soon turn to the next scandal.

Could this be the answer she'd been searching for?

Jake did his best to conceal the way his shoulders shuddered by keeping his stance steady, his hands and arms still. Taking her with him had been the last thing he'd thought she'd suggest, and he took a moment to contemplate his answer. He wanted to help her, deeply wanted that because he was responsible for her predicament. But taking her with him was simply not an option.

"I'm not asking you to marry me," she said, in an excited tone. "Just take me with you."

Jake responded with the only thing he could think of quickly. "Your life is here."

"What life?" she asked. "Look around. This is my life. An aunt who rarely leaves this room, painting pictures that she stacks in piles, because she doesn't want anyone to see them. An uncle who spends days and nights in the basement, living for nothing except his inventions, and a brother who is so engrossed in those same inventions that he's sold everything he had inherited, including me."

Jake had seen for himself that what she said was true, and all of that was part of the reason he wanted to help her, but he couldn't just take her with him. Just drop her off in a completely unknown country to fend for herself. "I will be taking a cargo ship to America. It doesn't have space for passengers. There are no staterooms. Just hammocks in the lower deck."

She was pacing the small open area of the room, which was filled with piles of canvas paintings, easels, and paint. Dozens of containers of paint and brushes, and also stacks of periodicals, newspapers, and other publications. Stopping to meet his gaze, she said, "I don't care. I don't care how I get there." Her eyes were sparkling with excitement. "This idea just came to me, but it is the answer. With me gone, the gossips will quickly move on to another scandal."

That might be true, too, and even though the thought of disappointing her tugged at his heart, he had to point out, "The scandal of how the Duke and Duchess of Collingsworth forced you to leave the country?"

The shine left her eyes and she shook her head. "No."

He nodded. "That would be quite the scandal, how they sent you to America to fend for yourself."

She looked around the room, tapping her chin as if thinking. "There has to be a way that it's not blamed on them. Perhaps I stay at your ranch? Just for a while? A short while. We could say that you interrupted the wedding because I'd already agreed to go work for you, and I could work for you. I could help take care of your house. And your sister, Nellie. I could teach her about England, so when she does come here, it won't be so foreign to her. I could even return with her, so she wouldn't be alone." She snapped her fingers. "That's it! We could say that you'd hired me to teach Nellie about England, so she'd be prepared to move here."

Dang it. Not only was the excitement back in her voice and the shine in her eyes, but now she was using Nellie to hit him where he was vulnerable. He didn't believe she was doing that on purpose. She was desperate, and he was the one who had put her in that position. His uncle's request, for him to marry her, came to mind, and so did all of the reasons he couldn't do that, but they didn't feel nearly as clear right now. "My ranch isn't as rosy as I may have made it sound," he said, a little desperately. "It's isolated. A long way from town, and town, Twisted Gulch, is nothing like London. Only a few hundred people live there, and though they are good people…" His mind suddenly went to all the single men who would be tripping over themselves to get to her side and offer marriage. He'd seen it before, and didn't appreciate the idea of that happening to her. "It's just different."

"I want different," she said. "That's why I finally gave in and was willing to marry Edward. I have no future here, and I want one. I didn't need him to love me, just give me more freedom than I have here. A garden and flower beds, animals, servants with children, charities that I could help with." She threw her arms in the air and dropped them to her side. "I want anything besides paintings and experiments and explosions in the basement."

He couldn't deny that everyone wanted a future and deserved one, but he needed time to think. He always thought things through, up to and including the decision to come to England. The only thing he hadn't thought completely through had been storming into the church and stopping the wedding, and that obviously had not worked out well.

He'd come here this morning to ask her opinion about the future. It was her life and she should have a say in it. Those were the very words he'd told his uncle last night, when asked if she'd agreed to the compensation. But this… Huffing out a breath, he said, "I'll need to think about this. See if there are any passenger ships sailing to Galveston."

The joy on her face was like nothing he'd ever seen. It lit up the room and made his heart pound so hard he might have cracked a rib. Something inside his chest sure felt uncomfortable.

"I can be ready to leave whenever you are," she said. "Tonight, tomorrow, and truly, it doesn't need to be a passenger ship. A hammock would be fine, and I don't eat a lot, just—" She covered her mouth with one hand for a moment. "Just think about it. Please."

Jake took the long route back to his uncle's home, riding through the park, hoping it would give him time to think about what he should do, but instead, his thoughts went to how different his life had become since leaving

England. He loved his ranch, and his life there, but he hadn't hated his life here. Granted, he'd been young, but he still had wonderful memories about living here and his family. That was the reason he wanted Nellie to experience it, too.

All of those thoughts weren't helping him with the issue at hand. Caroline. Was he letting his mind drift on purpose? So he wouldn't have to think about how beautiful she looked with that shine in her eyes and that excitement in her voice? She was truly likable, and he sincerely wanted to help her. Not only because he was responsible for her misfortunes, but also because she deserved the opportunity to experience life. It wasn't hard to understand why she was so desperate to leave. She'd practically been held hostage at her aunt and uncle's house.

Which was what would happen to her at his ranch, too. It was isolated, and it was rough and wild, and dangerous.

Despite all that, by the end of his ride he'd come to one solid conclusion.

He had to marry her.

Yes, he was as uncouth as a Texas cowboy could be—a buffoon, no less—and she was a mild-mannered English lady, which in itself wasn't a good match. He was the one who'd put her into her current position in the first place, and it was his responsibility to make amends for that. He sure as hell couldn't just haul her to America and drop her off. That would make him a bigger scoundrel than Edward. So would leaving without her.

Furthermore, she was right about Nellie. His sister needed to be prepared for English society when she came to London, and Caroline would be the perfect one to teach her.

Mind made up or not, it felt like he was going against

the grain after his determined decision *against* marriage of any kind, let alone with Caroline. He hated to be forced into things, even by circumstance or his own actions. All in all, he was frustrated in a handful of ways when he entered his uncle's house, but managed to pull up a smile for his aunt Hilda when he encountered her in the hallway.

"Jake, dear, were you already out and about this morning?" she asked.

He hadn't seen her much the past few days; most of his time at the house had been spent being sequestered with his uncle and cousin. "Yes, I went for a ride."

Aunt Hilda—the Duchess of Collingsworth to most— was a pretty woman, with rust-colored hair and green eyes that always held a sense of compassion and care. "I'm sure you found that different from what you are used to."

"Different," he admitted, "but good."

Her smile grew as she nodded. "That's nice. Would you care to join me for breakfast? Your uncle has already left for a meeting this morning, and Edward, well, he's sulking in his suite. I don't know what we did wrong with that boy."

"I don't believe it's anything you did wrong," Jake said. "No matter how they were raised, some people make bad choices."

"Always the diplomat," she said. "You get that from your father." Once again, she asked, "Breakfast?"

"Sure."

"Wonderful." She hooked an arm through his and they started walking down the hallway. "We haven't had a chance to talk much, and I'd love to hear more about your thoughts on sending Nellie over to stay with us."

"That won't be for a while yet," he said, as an image of his sister formed. He could convince Nellie to wear a dress when they went to a special event, but other than that, she wore britches and boots, with a shirt and a cowboy hat. A sigh was building in his chest. His reasons for marrying Caroline just kept getting stronger.

He waited until both he and Aunt Hilda were seated at the breakfast table, her with a small plate holding toast and a single boiled egg, and since he'd already eaten, he just had a cup of tea in front of him, before he said, "I went to see Lady Caroline again this morning."

Aunt Hilda laid a hand on his arm. "Oh, Jake, tell me truly, how is she doing? I'm so worried about her. She is such a genuine and kind woman. I was looking forward to her being a good influence on Edward, but I should have known better. Now I feel so bad for her."

His aunt was genuine and kind herself. Always had been. "I feel bad for the trouble I've caused for all of you," he said.

"Jake, darling, you mustn't." She squeezed his arm. "You did the right thing coming home and telling us about Faith. I feel terrible for her, too. What is she like?"

"She's a good person," Jake said, trying to find a way to describe Faith. She'd arrived at his ranch with all the gusto of a tornado and the anger of a badger. Dang near tore the house apart looking for Edward—of course she thought Edward's name was Jake and that Jake was the one lying to her. It had been a chaotic morning, and him leaving for London the next day had sent her into another fit, insisting that she had to go with him. He'd had to be harsh, threatened to contact her father before she'd settled down and agreed to stay put until he returned. He believed she would.

"She's pretty," he continued, "but in my opinion, Edward may have bitten off more than he can chew. She's

Texas born and bred, which means she's, well, rougher than the women here."

Aunt Hilda lifted her brows. "Really?" Her smile turned secretive as she said, "Well, that is interesting, isn't it? I look forward to meeting her."

Faith was also loud and brash, the complete opposite of Caroline, and that was who Jake wanted to talk about. "Lady Caroline had a suggestion as to how we could help her."

"Oh, do tell. The poor dear does need our help, the gossip is already spreading. Lady Amelia Cavish sent a message today, requesting I join her for tea tomorrow afternoon, and I know it's only so she can prick me with questions about the wedding cancellation and such. She is a dear friend, so I must accept." Huffing out a breath, she shook her head. "Enough about me, what did Lady Caroline suggest?"

"That I take her to Texas with me," he said.

Aunt Hilda nodded as she ate a small slice of her egg, before she said, "Your mother loved it there."

He knew that, but he knew something else. "My mother would have followed my father to the moon if he could have figured out a way to get there," he said. His mother had told him that, and he'd laughed, thinking that was funny. It had been to a twelve-year-old. It had also been when they were crossing the ocean, heading for the New World.

"She would have. That's how it is when you love some-one," Aunt Hilda said.

Love wasn't in this equation, but responsibility was, along with several other things, making him fully under-stand everything added up to one thing. "I've decided in order to take her with me, we need to get married." There, he'd said it aloud, confirming that's what would happen.

"Oh, Jake," Aunt Hilda said with a gush of air. "Thank you. Edward has embarrassed us so many times, but this one, it's too much. Involving not one, but two innocent young women. One of them carrying his child. The other left at the altar. I've been fearful that it's more than your uncle can handle. When he lies down in bed at night, I can feel his heart pounding in his chest because he's so frustrated. So worried."

Jake took hold of the hand she had resting on the table, tightened his fingers around hers. He had been fearing the same thing, that it was too much for his uncle, and his aunt's words only confirmed again that he'd made the right decision.

"We've been so worried about Caroline," Aunt Hilda continued. "She is innocent in all this, and so vulnerable. It's just all the epitome of sadness, and that has practically broken my heart. We've also been worried about you."

Just like his uncle, Aunt Hilda had aged recently. She looked tired, despondent. "There's no need to worry about me."

"I've always worried about you. And Nellie. When your mother died, and we came to visit, I wanted to bring Nellie home with us. Your father wasn't having any of that, and I hadn't expected otherwise. She was his daughter, and I cried half the way home, thinking about that tiny babe without her mother. When your father died, I wanted to bring both of you home with us, but knew you wouldn't agree to that, and I couldn't separate the two of you. You and Nellie were all each other had." She removed her hand from beneath his and cupped one side of his face. "You've done well with her, and I'm proud of you. It's time you both have more. Caroline will be a good influence for Nellie. She has the finer instincts of a lady. She puts me in mind of your mother."

He shook his head, for he didn't see a resemblance between Caroline and his mother. He'd been sixteen when his mother died and was sure he'd forgotten some things about her, but he could pull up her image in an instant, and the sound of her laugh.

"Not in looks," Aunt Hilda continued as she removed her hand from his face and touched his hair. "You inherited your black hair and blue eyes from your mother. It's in Caroline's persona. Soft-spoken and gentle. Kind and caring. Thoughtful. I think your mother would have liked Caroline, liked that someone was there to remind you and Nellie that you have English roots, teach Nellie more about your homeland."

That was all true, and his mind had now shifted to Caroline. "Well, my next step is to ask her." A nervous knot formed in his stomach. "She might say no."

Aunt Hilda let out a tiny half laugh. "She's a shrewd woman, Jake. She knows you're a good man. Honest, trustworthy. Someone that people can count on. You always have been."

He hoped Caroline knew she could trust him, yet he still had concerns. "Texas is a rough place, especially for women."

"And you are a tough man, who is able to withstand any storm that comes along."

"I wasn't necessarily referring to the weather," he said, with his thoughts going to another aspect of Caroline's life. The leeches in her basement. He wasn't afraid of much, and most certainly not leeches, but he was a bit gun-shy when it came to marriage. There was a lot that went along with marriage. At one time he'd thought he'd been ready for all that—a wife and children to inherit the ranch his parents had started and he'd continued—but after the whole mess with Eloise, he'd decided to accept that it might not be in his future.

"I wasn't referring to the weather, either," Aunt Hilda said, looking at him over the top of her teacup. "And, I believe that you've made the right choice. Not only for the family, and Caroline, but for you."

He picked up his teacup, and though the contents were cold, he drank it anyway, as he resigned himself to the fact that fate had won this round, whether he was prepared or not.

Chapter Six

This time, Caroline was outside when Jake arrived at her house, and seeing him dismount the big, black horse made her shiver and quake from head to toe, fearful as to what his answer was going to be. In the hours since he'd left, the idea of going to Texas with him had become the ultimate solution.

Memories of the way she'd begged him had also flitted across her mind. She should be mortified by that. At least ashamed. That's what she'd told herself. And she might have been, if she wasn't so convinced this was the right answer.

She quickly slid the last couple of pins onto the clothesline, holding the freshly washed sheet in place, then crossed the backyard to meet him near the stable, where he was tying his horse to the post. "Hello."

"Hello," he replied, walking toward her.

Willing herself to remain standing still due to the sound of his voice, for it hadn't held his usual affable tone, she pressed a hand to the swirling in her stomach. He'd decided against taking her, and had come to tell her. She should have known he wouldn't see it the same way as she did and shouldn't have gotten her hopes up. She knew better than to hope. It had been illogical for her to make such a request.

"I'd like to invite you to dinner this evening, if you're available," he said.

"Excuse me?" she asked, convinced she'd misheard.

"I'd like you to have dinner with me and my aunt and uncle this evening," he said. "If you're available."

Her heart constricted. "Why?" She knew why. To offer her money again.

He slipped his hands into his pockets. "So we can discuss you coming to Texas with me."

She felt herself sway as the entire world seemed to start spinning around her. A pressure and warmth on her arm settled her for a moment, until she realized it was Jake's hand on her arm, then the spinning was inside her. Her heart. Her thoughts. Questioning everything, she asked, "I'm going with you? To Texas?"

"If that is still what you want."

She nodded, then closed her eyes and told herself to breathe. To remain calm—actually, to breathe so she could *become* calm, because her insides were in absolute chaos.

"You're welcome to invite your family to dinner, too, if you would like," he said.

"No!" She clamped her lips together, still trying to gain control of herself. Not completely sure if it was nerves or excitement that was consuming her, she blew out the air in her lungs and sucked in more. "I would prefer that they didn't attend." She would explain it all to her family once the plans were in place.

"I assumed as much," he said.

Starting to feel normal again, she shook her head, looked up at him. At his coal black hair and sky blue eyes, still wondering if she'd heard correctly. "I thought you were coming to tell me no. That I couldn't go with you to Texas."

"You haven't changed your mind about going?"

Without hesitation, she replied, "No, not at all."

He nodded, and there was a softness about his face that she couldn't quite read.

"Well, there is one more thing I need to say, to ask you," he said, "and it might change your mind."

Adamant that wouldn't happen, she shook her head.

With another nod, he cleared his throat. "Well, then, Lady Caroline Evans, will you marry me?"

She took two steps backward so quickly, her feet tangled in her skirt. He caught her with one hand, or maybe his hand had still been on her arm, she wasn't sure. Her head was spinning again; the world was spinning again. "Marry you?"

"Yes."

"Why?"

"Several reasons, including to encourage people to believe that is why I interrupted your wedding to Edward."

She felt her lips forming an O, but they emitted nothing. What he said made sense. At least she thought it did. Or did she just *want* it to make sense so she could say yes? She'd been prepared to be his employee, but his wife?

Ultimately, it would be better than being Edward's wife. Furthermore, just like the last time someone offered to marry her, she didn't have a choice. This time, however, the idea didn't make her sick to her stomach.

"It won't change what you mentioned this morning," he said. "You will be at the ranch to assist Nellie. Teach her about England, about being a society lady, and return here with her when she's ready. In exchange for that, I'll provide you with everything you need to have a comfortable life, both in Texas and once you return to England."

She wasn't dense, and understood that meant it wouldn't be a real marriage. That was less surprising than the split second where she'd thought it might, and did nothing to deter her. But she was fully aware that she wasn't a society lady, and needed to point that out to him again. "A title alone doesn't make one a lady."

"No, it doesn't, and one doesn't need a title to be a lady," he replied. "My aunt believes you'll be a very good influence on Nellie, and I agree."

The Duchess of Collingsworth was a true lady, and though it would be asking a lot, and there wasn't much time, if she was willing to teach a few things, Caroline was more than willing to learn. Yet, guilt was filling her at the enormity of Jake's offer, everything he'd be sacrificing for her. "You don't have to marry me. I'm sure we can—"

"No," he said. "The only way is for us to get married. If you are worried about what that will all entitle, let me further explain. We will be looked upon as a couple, and married before we leave England. The marriage will be in name only, but I will not embarrass you by carrying on with other women and will expect the same from you. When the time comes for you to bring Nellie to England, you can remain here, I will continue to financially provide for you and—"

"All right," she quickly interrupted, having heard enough. His offer was similar to what she'd accepted from Edward, but this time, it was much more beneficial for her. "Yes, I will marry you, and I agree with all that you've said. Including the invitation to dinner." It might be wrong, because he was giving up much more than she was by agreeing to a false marriage, but she would find a way to make it up to him. She could do that by making sure she knew everything that Nellie would need to know.

"All right, then," he said. "I'll return at seven with a coach."

Just like that, he was gone.

Well, it didn't happen immediately. As she stood there, she watched him untie the reins of his horse, mount the animal, and ride away. It felt like she was watching a dream. A vision. Right up to the point when he turned the corner and disappeared.

Maybe it was all a dream. This entire day.

This entire week.

"Caroline!" came a shout from the house. "We need rags to clean up a spill!"

The sound of her brother's voice, and request, proved it wasn't a dream. It was her life.

Not for long, she thought and with a tiny skip in her walk, she headed toward the house to point out that the rags were in the same spot where they'd been for years.

Four hours later, dressed in her blue-and-white dress, Caroline climbed into the Duke of Collingsworth's luxurious coach without having told any member of her family where she was going or why. There was no need. They wouldn't miss her. Uncle James and Frederick would eat the evening meal in the basement and Aunt Myrtle would eat hers in her parlor. Mr. and Mrs. Humes knew where she was going, and with whom, but she knew no one would feel any need to ask the servants if they knew where she had gone.

Jake climbed in and settled himself on the seat across from her. His size made the coach feel small, and she gathered her skirt closer, tucking the material beneath her knees as she twisted her legs sideways, giving his feet more room.

He had greeted her at the door, told her she looked pretty and she had thanked him, but they hadn't said anything more to each other.

"This…" He waved his hands between him and her as the coach began to roll away from her house. "What's happening between us, the marriage and all, seems like it's becoming awkward, and I don't like awkward."

She let out a sigh of relief and nodded. "I don't, either."

"What do you say that we just think of each other as friends? We can help each other when there's something the other one doesn't understand, and…" He shrugged. "Well, things are just all around easier and more fun when you're doing them with friends."

"That's true." It would be very easy to be his friend. He was very likable and very different from everyone she knew in England. Different in a good way. "Do you have a lot of friends in Texas?"

"A fair number. I consider all the people at my ranch friends, and there's more in town, and neighbors." He frowned slightly. "There are others who are acquaintances, and I prefer to keep it that way. What about you? Do you have a lot of friends here?"

She shook her head. "I have one very good friend. I met her through church a few years ago, but she's very busy, so we don't get to see each very often." Patsy was a real society lady, too, and someone else she could ask for assistance.

"Does she live nearby?"

"No, she lives a few streets away from the Duke and Duchess of Collingsworth. Patsy— I'm sorry," she said, remembering she was talking to and about nobility, "Lady Patricia Collins is the Countess Eastey."

"Eastey?" He frowned slightly. "I remember the Earl of Eastey, he had a son, Nathaniel."

"Nathaniel," she said at the exact same time he had.

They both let out a small laugh, before he said, "Nathaniel Collins."

"He is Patsy's husband," Caroline said. "I met her at church a few years ago and have worked with her in collecting and distributing items for the orphanage."

"That's very kind of you," he said.

"Thank you." She greatly enjoyed doing such things and would forever be grateful to Patsy for seeking her out and inviting her to participate in the activities.

"If your friend is the countess, I'm assuming Nathaniel's father passed away."

"Yes, but I do not know when. Patsy held the title of countess when I met her. Did you know the previous earl or Nathaniel when you were young?"

"Yes, I played with Nathaniel whenever I was in town visiting my grandfather."

"If you don't mind my asking," she said, "why did your family move to Texas?" That had been something she'd been curious about since meeting him.

"I don't mind." A smile took over his entire face. "My father wanted something of his own, something big, and a ranch in Texas was it. He had my grandfather's blessing, and I remember like yesterday when my grandfather told me that I was going to love sailing across the ocean and living in the New World. I think if he'd been younger, he would have gone with us."

"Did he ever visit you in America?"

"No, he died less than a year after we left. His name

was Abraham. Abraham Jacob. We named our first bull after him. Abe. Though he's getting old for a bull, I still have Abe."

The happiness on his face made her smile. "Your grandfather also had a grandson named after him," she said.

"He did. I have another bull—his name is Moby, because of the book my grandfather read to me more times than I could count."

"Do you have a Captain Ahab, too?"

He laughed. "You've read the book?"

That was one of the few books Uncle James owned; otherwise both her aunt and uncle chose periodicals for reading. "I have."

The easy flow of conversation continued until they arrived at his family's home, a beautiful, huge house that could fit three of her uncle's house within its walls. She'd been here once before and the same nerves kicked in now. The ones that made her feel woozy.

"Come on, friend," Jake said, taking ahold of her hand to help her out of the coach. "There's nothing for you to worry about. Including Edward. He's locked in his room."

"Locked in his room?"

"Yes, he's either under lock and key or within my eyesight until I get him to Texas and married to Faith." He winked at her. "Then he's on his own."

She wanted to ask what he meant, but didn't have the opportunity because he swiftly led her into the house. The same house she'd been in not so long ago, sitting in the same elegant front drawing room, with its matching furniture covered in gold velvet. Drinking the same sherry, served in a crystal glass, and discussing the same subject—marriage, a wedding. However, shortly upon joining the duke and duchess in the drawing room, Caroline discovered that unlike the last time, she wasn't expected to remain silent. Her opinion was sought and respected. Not that there was really anything for her to dispute— everybody seemed in agreement that the wedding and their departure for America needed to take place as soon as possible.

Jake couldn't say he was caught off guard, because he knew exactly what would be discussed tonight, yet found himself feeling as if he was losing his sense of control. It had been a long time since anyone had told him what he was going to do, or when, or how. He'd had time to prepare himself and had already discussed the matter with his aunt and uncle earlier today, but now, with Caroline here, he was questioning everything. Including his ability to protect her.

Not from his aunt and uncle: they were as kind and understanding as ever. It was other people he was worried about, and how they'd react to the wedding, how they would treat Caroline, what they might suspect. Aunt Hilda was correct when she'd said that Caroline was innocent in all of this. If only others knew her, they'd understand that. Understand that she didn't have a dishonest bone in her body.

Furthermore, she'd already been quickly ushered into one wedding and the same thing was happening again. It was what needed to happen, but he wished there was a way for her to get used to the idea. Or maybe he wished there was a way for *him* to get used to the idea. The prospect of a wedding in three days was making him more nervous than coming across a rattler, coiled and ready to strike. He didn't think of Caroline as a snake, of course.

It was the whole idea of tying the knot that had his stomach roiling as if he'd eaten something that wasn't settling well. A bit more time to get used to it would be helpful. In several ways. He had to figure out how he was going to explain getting married once he arrived back home. Hauling home a bride was going to raise more than a few eyebrows.

Time was of short supply. But, perhaps, in the long run, seven days one way or the other wasn't going to make that much difference. At least he could hope that it wouldn't. "I'd like to suggest something," he said.

"Certainly," Uncle Oscar said. "What is it, Jake?"

"That we hold the wedding next weekend instead of this coming weekend," Jake replied. Uncle Oscar had acquired a listing of the passenger ships sailing to America, and the soonest one was Sunday, but there was another one next Sunday. Settling his gaze on Caroline, Jake asked, "If that would be all right with you?"

She nodded. "Yes, that would be fine."

He couldn't say if she was relieved or not, nor could he say if he was, either. Putting off the inevitable wouldn't change the outcome. It just might make it easier to swallow. Or he hoped it would. Seems there was a whole lot of hoping that came along with this situation.

"Oh, thank you, both of you," Aunt Hilda gushed. "I must admit how I've feared the questions that could come about due to a hasty wedding upon what had already happened could become quite distressing. An extra week will certainly help with all the details that will need to be seen to, but it will also help with our…" She paused while folding her hands in her lap. "Explanation as to how we found ourselves in this situation."

The hair on Jake's neck rose. He knew why and how they were in this situation. "Explanation?" he asked.

"Yes, it's something I've been thinking about, and your uncle and I discussed it a short time ago. Though it is a bit of a white lie, it's quite believable."

"What is it?" Jake asked, not quite sure he truly wanted to know.

"Well," Aunt Hilda said, "we would like to suggest that an arrangement had been put in place by Caroline's father and your father for a wedding between the two of you before your father traveled to America, but that such an agreement was only recently brought to our attention. We could say that we had sent a message to you in America, Jake, but we thought it was lost, and in order to honor a family promise, Edward offered to step up and take your place. However, you had received the message and came to England expecting to marry Caroline, and found Edward marrying her instead, which irritated you, and that's why you interrupted the wedding the way you did."

Jake understood his aunt's need to somehow make her son's actions look honorable, and he couldn't fault her that. Yet, he had to ask, "Wouldn't people wonder why you didn't give me more time to get the message?"

"Yes, well…" Aunt Hilda fiddled with the lace on the collar of her dress. "We could suggest that the arrangement had a set date. That Caroline had to wed before her dowry expired."

"I don't have a dowry," Caroline said, looking at him with a grimace.

"Nor do we expect one," Uncle Oscar said as he rose from his chair. He crossed the room, refilled his glass from the decanter, and took a drink before turning to face them all again. "The truth is that families in our positions rarely need to explain our actions. Nor do we need to have them accepted by the gossip speculators. The duchess is merely hoping to spare anyone from the embarrassment of such speculators. A small white lie will be accepted as long as we all present a united front."

Jake felt a lie, big or little, would merely make the whole thing more complex. However, it was quite clear that Uncle Oscar was as worried about Aunt Hilda getting through this ordeal as she was him. Once again, Jake found himself blaming Edward. His cousin's behavior was affecting so many lives. Including his.

There was one thing still catching now and then at his heart. There had been a time when he'd thought about having a child himself. A son or daughter to carry on the ranch after he was too old. That wouldn't happen now, and Edward could be blamed for that, too.

"Now," Uncle Oscar said as he returned to his seat, "it is my understanding that your brother, the Earl of Brittmore, has sought investors for his and his uncle's research and inventions, with little luck."

Caroline bowed her head as she nodded.

A jolt of ire rose up inside Jake. "Caroline had no part in that, nor can she be faulted for it."

Uncle Oscar held up a hand. "I'm fully aware of that, Jake, and agree." He turned back to Caroline. "Subsequently, it is my understanding that the earl has sold off most of his inheritance in order to self-fund these projects."

Jake's ire was still growing, but before he could voice it, his uncle shook his head.

"We are all aware that she's not responsible for her brother's actions," Uncle Oscar said. "What I'd like to suggest is that in the newly discovered agreement between her father and yours, and I guarantee that if questioned, such an agreement will appear, there was another small detail. One where her father invested in a piece of land in America, where your ranch is, Jake, and that piece of land is her dowry."

Jake was following his uncle's line of thought. "And if a marriage between the families didn't happen, I'd have to forfeit that land to the Earl of Brittmore." That would make the entire situation believable.

Caroline gasped and shook her head.

"Never fear, Lady Caroline," Uncle Oscar said. "I'm fully prepared to invest in your brother and uncle's business adventures, in exchange for them agreeing to the marriage between you and Jake."

Caroline now had a hand over her mouth, and Jake knew exactly what she was thinking. That her family would agree to anything for an investor to support their experiments and inventions.

"We could then also suggest that Edward is traveling to America with the two of you to oversee your ranch while you and Caroline are on your honeymoon," Aunt Hilda said. "The two of you taking a week to get acquainted before the wedding would support everything we've just discussed."

It wasn't lost on Jake how badly his aunt wanted to save her son from embarrassment of any kind. Nor was it lost on him that he didn't want his family to experience more embarrassment, either.

"Ultimately, our objective is to avoid a scandal for everyone involved," Uncle Oscar said. "This is a way we could quash it, and, if you're concerned about Edward, don't be. He was sent to Collingsworth today, where he will remain until you sail for America."

Jake already knew that Edward had been sent to the country, accompanied by a trusted employee who would make sure he remained there. He wasn't sold on the idea that everyone would believe there had been betrothal years ago, but if it would alleviate the chances of Caroline's reputation being soiled, he saw no harm in it, and looked to her for her opinion. "What do you think about it?"

Her smile wobbled slightly before she nodded. "I suspect it does sound like a plausible explanation as to what had happened."

"Oh, it does," Aunt Hilda said to Caroline. "I was thinking about it all afternoon, for rumors are already spreading, and this would nip them in the bud. You, dear, could join me for tea with a few friends tomorrow, and we could all attend Lady Donavon's birthday ball on Friday night, and then there is..."

As Aunt Hilda continued with a list of social activities, Jake wondered if he'd made things worse instead of better by postponing the wedding for a week. Only time would tell.

The opportunity to apologize, and to see exactly how Caroline felt about it, didn't arise until hours later, when they were in the coach, traveling back to her house, then he said, "I don't have any flowers or candy, but I do find myself seeking your forgiveness again."

"Whatever for?" she asked.

His eyes had adjusted to the darkness, allowing him to see her brows knitted together. "For suggesting we wait a week before getting married."

"Considering you are the one saving two families from scandals, I believe you have every right to make requests."

He sure didn't feel like he was saving anyone from

anything. "We are in this together and I should have consulted you first."

"You did ask me, and I agreed."

"Did you feel as if you had any other choice?"

She didn't respond with a nod or a head shake. Instead, she licked her lips and swallowed visibly. "I understand that a marriage, to me, is not something you expected, or that you want, and that I'm being selfish when I say that going to America with you is a choice that I never expected to have, but it is one I want. Therefore, I am willing to do whatever you suggest. I will not expect anything from you. And if, when we do arrive in America, you want the marriage to end, I will agree. However it can happen, I will agree."

She wanted a different life, and he could relate to that. His father had wanted a different life and had found one. No, he had created one. One that Jake would forever be grateful for being a part of. Grateful for the life he now had. "I do want you to meet Nellie," he said. "But I won't force you to do something you don't want to do. If you discover that you don't want to remain at the ranch, we can discuss our next steps then."

She nodded.

He huffed out a breath. "I guess our next step now is to tell your family."

"I suspect it is."

"Will they still be awake?"

"Oh, yes," she replied, sighing nearly as heavily as he had. "Uncle James and Frederick will still be in the basement and Aunt Myrtle will still be in her parlor."

He reached across the space between them and touched the back of her hand. "I'll talk to your uncle and brother first."

* * *

As the warmth spread up her arm from his hand covering hers, Caroline struggled to find her tongue. Why everything suddenly felt overwhelming was beyond her. She was an active participant this time. Her role was almost the reverse of the one she had played in her near marriage to Edward. Jake was the one being coerced into marriage by *her.* Yet, her hands were as tied as they had been last time.

What was different was that there was no nauseating swirl in her stomach, the pounding ache in her head, or the constant anger. Guilt, though, was present and strong as she realized Jake was probably experiencing all the things she had last time around. "I'm sorry for all of this," she said, "and there is one thing that I'd like to address."

"Certainly."

"Whether I stay at your ranch or not, the possible dissolution of our marriage—those choices will be up to you. You are doing all of this for the benefit of others, and our choices here are limited. Once we are in America, you should have the final say, the final choice, in what happens. You have my guarantee that I will abide by whatever decision you make."

He nodded, but said, "Let's worry about all that when the time comes. Right now, we need to maintain a united front. Including with your family."

The heaviness inside her chest grew. "About that. My aunt and uncle did not know about the agreement between Frederick and Edward."

Frowning slightly, he asked, "Did they question if you wanted to marry Edward?"

"No. They were relieved that I was finally getting married." Not wanting to paint either her aunt or uncle in an unfavorable light, she continued, "It's not that they are un-caring. They've been very good to Frederick and me. It's just that they have their own interests, and though Frederick quickly became a part of those interests, I never did. Therefore, I was just sort of there. Someone no one really knew what to do with." She'd never admitted that to any-one, but it was how she'd always felt—that no one noticed her when she was there, nor did they miss her when she wasn't—like a pet that no one wanted yet couldn't just get rid of it.

The fingers of his hand, still lying atop hers, folded beneath her hand and gave it a gentle squeeze. If he'd been going to say something, she would never know what it would have been, because the coach stopped, and the doorman pulled open the door for them to exit.

To her surprise, Frederick wasn't still in the basement. Instead, he was standing in the open front doorway, glar-ing at her.

Cupping her elbow as they walked toward the door, Jake said, "Frederick, just the person we need to talk to. Would you mind fetching your aunt and uncle so the five of us can have a conversation?"

"Pertaining to what?" Frederick asked.

The scathing look her brother cast upon her was enough to raise her ire, but it also raised her courage. Actually, having Jake beside her might have been the cause of it. For whatever reason, she felt able to lift her chin and say, "The quicker you find them and have them meet us in the parlor, the quicker you will know."

"They are already in the parlor," Frederick said. "Wait-ing for you. Imagine our surprise to learn you hadn't men-tioned to anyone where you had gone."

"Surprise?" She shook her head. "My surprise will

come when I see the inside of the house, for clearly something happened and I wasn't there to collect the supplies needed to clean it up. That is the only reason anyone would have realized I was gone."

The narrowing of Frederick's eyes said she'd hit the nail on the head.

Turning to Jake, she said, "My apologies before we enter the house. I have no idea of what we will discover."

"The house is fine." Frederick stepped aside and swept an arm for them to enter. "See for yourself." Under his breath, Frederick said, "Even though you weren't here, where you belong."

Her spine stiffened. She wanted to belong someplace where she was needed for more than domestic duties. Entering the house, with Jake right behind her, she walked to the parlor, where she did find her aunt and uncle, and instantly noticed the large bandage on her uncle's hand. Concerned, she crossed the room quickly, and knelt down before him. "What happened?"

"I cut my hand on a broken jar," he replied. "Not to worry, Mrs. Humes bandaged it."

"Let me see," she said, already untying the bandage. "What was in the jar?"

"Rain water," he said.

Caroline pinched her lips together as she kept herself from glancing at Jake. He clearly had been stunned over the leeches in their basement. "I'm glad it wasn't a compound of some sort," she said. Unwrapping the last bit of bandage, she was glad to see it wasn't a severe cut that lined the palm of her uncle's hand.

"It's not too bad, is it?" her uncle asked.

"No, it should heal just fine." She rewrapped the bandage back around his hand. "You'll need to keep it bandaged for a few days."

Her uncle nodded. "I will. I was surprised when you weren't here to bandage it."

"I'm sorry that I wasn't here, but Mrs. Humes did a fine job."

"Yes, she did," Uncle James replied, then nodded toward Jake. "She said you were with Jake."

"I was," Caroline said. "I had dinner with him, and now we would like to talk with you and Aunt Myrtle, and Frederick."

"Most certainly." Uncle James looked at Jake again. "Please, have a seat, Jake."

"Thank you, sir," Jake replied. "I'm sorry to learn you were injured."

"It was just a little mishap," Uncle James said.

Jake waited until Caroline had risen and taken her own seat before he sat down beside her.

He looked at her and smiled, before he turned to her family. "Caroline and I have decided to marry, and I am here not only to ask for her hand, but to ask for your blessings in our union."

Aunt Myrtle covered her heart with one hand as she whispered, "Oh, how gallant."

Caroline had to agree. Jake sounded so earnest and sincere that her own heart skipped a beat. Edward had never asked for her hand. Had never spoken to Uncle James or Aunt Myrtle. He'd just made the deal with Frederick, who had told her aunt and uncle about the upcoming nuptials. The nuptials that never happened because Jake had interrupted. Frederick must have also told them something about that, because they'd never asked her about it.

"Well, that is quite the news," Uncle James said. "You certainly have our permission and our blessings."

"Just hold on here," Frederick said. "I'm her brother, and it's my blessing that she'd need to have."

Caroline's stomach clenched. She wasn't about to let Frederick ruin this for her. "No, it's not," she said, knowing she shouldn't use the lie, but felt she had no choice. "I already have our father's blessing. The Duke of Collingsworth has discovered an agreement that was made years ago between our father and Jake's, for the two of us to get married."

"No, he hasn't," Frederick said rising to his feet. "I would have heard about such thing."

"No, you wouldn't have," she argued, and would have risen to her feet if Jake hadn't placed a hand on her knee. "You were just a child, too."

"The Duke of Collingsworth can show you the agreement, if you choose to see it," Jake said to Frederick. "I'd also like to discuss an agreement between us. I'm interested in becoming an investor in your business ventures. Especially the weather-predicting machine."

Frederick's glare in her direction didn't lesson, but he did stiffen. "You are?"

"I am," Jake said, "if we can come to a mutual agreement. However, that is something we will discuss at another time. Right now, we are here to discuss a marriage between Caroline and I, and of course, as her brother, we do hope to have your approval, and blessing."

Frederick didn't comment, just stared at her with eyes filled with distrust. It didn't seem to faze Jake, other than he patted her knee.

"We would like the wedding to be the weekend after next. Saturday morning," Jake said.

Uncle James nodded before he turned to Frederick. "A betrothal doesn't surprise me. Your father was worried that something would happen to him. His own parents, my brother and sister-in-law, died when you were a small child, Frederick, and Caroline a mere babe. An illness swept across the countryside, taking the lives of young and old. After his parents died, Thomas asked Myrtle and I if we'd agree to take the two of you in if something ever happened to him and Maria. I fully believe he would have made an arrangement for Caroline's future. Just as he knew you'd inherit the earldom, he'd have wanted to know that her future was set, too."

Frederick shook his head. "Our solicitor has never mentioned such a thing."

"He may not have known," Uncle James said. "Mr. Fraiser didn't become your solicitor until years after your father died. Prior to that it was Harold Warner, and he himself died shortly after the two of you came to live with us."

Caroline's stomach felt queasy at how easily the lie was being believed.

Not by Frederick, though. He was still shaking his head.

"Edward would have told me about such an arrangement," he claimed.

Jake cleared his throat. "I do not believe my cousin should be brought into this conversation, considering he was clearly attempting to undermine my role in the agreement and take advantage of my absence for his own benefit. I've chosen to overlook it once, but will not overlook it twice. Nor will I tolerate any suggestion that Caroline was anything other than innocent in all that happened in the past."

Frederick seemed to grasp the full understanding of the brevity in Jake's tone and words because he slowly lowered himself back onto his chair.

Caroline had the distinct feeling it was going to be a long ten days.

Chapter Seven

Caroline stared at the array of fashionable gowns, day dresses, underclothing, and other garments, as well as the material and dressmakers filling the room that she'd been led to shortly after entering the duke and duchess's home this morning. Her heart hammered in her chest as she twisted to look at the duchess. Lady Hilda had invited her to once again meet with the seamstress concerning her wedding dress—not the one she had returned to the duchess after her nonwedding to Edward.

Lady Hilda smiled. "New groom, new wedding, new dress. The other outfits are ones that I'd commissioned to be sewn for you a few weeks ago, for your trousseau, and just need final fittings. I also suggest ordering a few traveling outfits, as well as a few more day dresses to wear in Texas. I remember it being very warm the few times I've been there, so lighter materials will need to be chosen."

"Your Grace, this is too much," Caroline whispered. She could count at least two dozen dresses in various colors and styles.

"Not at all, dear. Jake agreed with me." Gesturing toward a corner of the room, the duchess continued, "He purchased those two traveling trunks for you this morning. You'll also need a few carrying bags, but we'll worry about that later. Madam Beauchamp has brought along her best seamstresses so everything will be completed prior to your departure. Today we'll focus on your wedding dress and picking out materials for traveling and day dresses."

Last time, she'd gone to the seamstress's shop downtown. This time, they were in a luxurious bedroom on the second floor of the duke's four-story home. The walls were covered with flocked white-and-gold paper, and the bed covering and chair cushions—the little Caroline could see of them beneath all the dresses and material draped on every surface—were all made from white-and-gold velvet. In one corner, near a large window framed with gold-colored drapes, there were two large, curve-topped traveling trunks. There had been so many other things to think about, Caroline hadn't thought about packing for her journey.

There was so much she hadn't thought about, and so much she didn't know. Except for one thing. She didn't deserve all this, nor could she accept it.

"This way, Lady Caroline," the tall and voluptuous Madam Beauchamp said. "Let's start with the final fitting for this blue dress. It will be perfect for the tea that you'll be attending this afternoon."

Caroline shifted her gaze back to the duchess. Lady Hilda was an intimidating woman, but also kind and compassionate, which showed in her eyes as she smiled in an understanding way.

"Excuse us for a moment, Madam," the duchess said.

"Of course, Your Grace." With a slight curtsey, the modiste led the other three seamstresses to the other side of the room and set them into tasks concerning several baskets of material.

"I apologize, Caroline, for I understand how this could

feel overwhelming," the duchess said. "That is not what I want. I want you to know how much we appreciate what you're doing for our family, the considerable embarrassment you're saving us. And more. I've worried so about Jake and Nellie for years, and I simply cannot begin to explain how relieved I am to know that they will now have you. A fellow Englishwoman to influence Nellie as she grows, and to help Jake. He's done so much on his own, and it's past time that he has someone to share his life with, to lighten his load."

Although Caroline believed the duchess was being truthful, a large, aching lump formed in her throat. "I fear I may not be the best person to fulfill either of those roles," she whispered. "I may have the title, but I'm not a lady."

"I believe you are. You have a very generous heart. You wouldn't be here if you didn't, and that, my dear, is the main thing it takes to be a lady." The duchess touched Caroline's cheek with one hand. "I'm here to help you quash any of the fears you are feeling, and to help you embrace your new life. Not just for the next ten days, but from this day forward, you will forever have my support, and that of the duke."

Caroline wasn't sure why she hadn't felt so fearful and inept when she'd expected to marry Edward. Perhaps then, she truly hadn't cared, and now she did. "What if I disappoint you or Jake? What if I fail?"

"What if you succeed? Think of the wonderful life you'll have. The wonderful life that Jake will have. He won't admit it, but he's needed someone for a long time. If you keep that in mind, it will be impossible to fail."

Caroline wasn't convinced it was as easy as that, but this, all of it, was what she'd agreed to. "Thank you. I shall try to succeed."

"I'm convinced you will," Lady Hilda said as she waved at the modiste to join them again.

The stylish design of the pale blue gown showed an ample amount of Caroline's shoulders and neck, and Jake found himself swallowing hard as she walked down the main stairway of his aunt and uncle's house. He was still getting used to the whole marriage idea, but had to admit, it was getting easier, knowing it was her that he was getting hitched to. She was likable, and he liked her. Liked everything about her.

News of him getting married was going to shock a large number of people back home, and undoubtedly cause a good amount of speculation. Until they saw her; then folks—men and women alike—would believe he'd been smitten from the moment they met. Which wouldn't be completely wrong. However, he was still worried how she would react to life on the ranch. A knot twisted inside his stomach. The dress she was wearing now would hang unworn there, and that made him question if he was indeed doing the right thing.

"Are you planning on attending the tea this afternoon?" she asked.

He held out a hand to aid her off the last step. "No." He winked at her. "Luckily, I've been spared that pleasure."

Her smile grew slightly before she asked, "I was told you wanted to see me."

"I wanted to check on you. See how you were doing."

"I'm fine, thank you."

She certainly looked fine. Exceptionally fine, and beautiful. "You look more than fine," he said.

Letting out a soft sigh, she whispered, "Truthfully, I've never been more nervous."

He smiled at how she confided in him, and searched for a way to ease her worries. "You don't look nervous." Stepping back, he eyed her from tip to top. "You look confident, and beautiful."

She shook her head. "Confident, I am not. I'm attempting to put on a brave face, but fear it'll slip away at the most inconvenient time."

"You don't need to pretend to be brave. You are brave." He lowered his voice and did his best to sound serious. "You have leeches in your basement."

She laughed. "That really bothers you, doesn't it?"

He was happy to see the shine in her eyes on her cheeks. "It makes me shudder. I'm not afraid of those things, but I don't want to live with them."

"They rarely escape, and if they do, they dry up quite quickly outside of water. Faster even when sprinkled with a spoon of salt."

"I'll remember that," he said, letting out a chuckle. "There is something that I wanted to tell you. I believe it might keep that smile on your face."

She eyed him coyly. "Oh? What?"

"The Countess Eastey will be attending today's tea."

Following a slight gasp, her face lit up brighter. "She will be?"

"Yes. I told my aunt that the countess was a friend of yours, and I personally delivered an invitation to the countess a short time ago. She said that she'd be honored to attend." He knew his aunt was committed to supporting Caroline in all ways, but also figured that a friend closer to her own age might be helpful.

"I—I don't know what to say, other than thank you!"

Before Jake knew what was happening, she looped her

arms around his neck and flattened herself against him, hugging him hard and tight.

"Thank you so much!" she said.

His next surprise was how effortless it was to hug her in return. He didn't have to think about it; his body simply reacted. Both arms wrapped around her and held her tight. Perhaps a little harder than necessary, considering the way his blood instantly heated up and started throbbing.

She must have felt what was happening inside him at the same time as him, because they separated as quickly as they'd come together. Both of them took a step back. He stuck his hands in his pockets, not sure what to do or say.

His breathing felt off, coming quicker and shallower than normal.

"Thank you for the traveling trunks, too," she said sounding as breathless as he felt.

"You're welcome," he replied, doing his best to sound normal. In a short time, they'd be living together, as a married couple, and at some point, would have to get used to touching each other on occasion. He'd touched her several times over the past few days while escorting her in and out of the coach and such, so what made today so different? That it was a hug, or that she was the one who'd hugged him first? This was clearly one of those situations where he'd have to figure it out as time went on.

Accepting that, he stepped forward and took ahold of her elbow. "I will escort you to the main parlor."

She frowned slightly. "The tea won't begin for another hour."

He nodded. "I know, but the countess arrived early so the two of you could visit in private."

The shine of excitement returned to her face, and later, after he'd delivered her to the room and bidden his departure, Jake wished he could be a mouse in the corner. Normally, he kept his nose to himself, but he was worried about her. About how she'd said she was nervous and putting on a brave face.

That right there was why he'd been against getting married. Once he got home, he wouldn't have time to be worried about someone day and night. He was only worrying right now because he had nothing else to do, and that was a problem. On the ranch, there were always things that had to be done, even on top of seeing to the cattle. There was wood to cut for winter, fences that needed mending, upkeep on the buildings, crops for winter feed, wells and windmills, and a list of numerous other things.

He had hired hands helping with everything, but worked right alongside them. That wasn't the case here. Uncle Oscar paid for others to maintain all of his properties, so there was nothing that needed to be done around here or even at Collingsworth.

The thought that struck next caused him to pause slightly in his stroll along the hallway. He did know of a place here that could use some work, and could keep him busy for the next week.

It might not get his mind off Caroline, but he figured that nothing would do that, considering the circumstances and all. Staying busy would be the next best thing.

An hour later, confronted by the dilapidated state of the Evans's stables, he determined there was more that needed to be done than he'd first surmised, and with permission from James, set to work.

Much later, he was up on the roof when he saw one of his uncle's coaches pull into the driveway. For no particular reason, leastwise not one that made any sense, his heartbeat quickened. He finished pounding in the last nail on the last shingle of the many he'd replaced, tucked the hammer into his back pocket, then scooted across the roof to climb down the ladder.

"What were you doing up there?" she asked as he met her on the ground.

She was still wearing the stylish blue gown that showed off her peach-colored flesh, and just like the first time he'd seen her wearing it, his breath locked somewhere between his chest and throat. He used the time it took to pull out the nails he was still holding between his lips to regain the breath needed to speak. "Repairing a few shingles," he said, while sliding the nails into the pocket with the hammer. "How was the tea?"

"I'll tell you in a minute," she replied, before turning to speak to the driver and another one of Uncle Oscar's servants. Together they were unloading one of the traveling trunks Jake had purchased for her from the coach.

Jake followed her. While Caroline told the men carrying the trunk to follow her, he lifted out the second trunk and carried it to the door.

"Thank you, sir," the driver said, while he and the other servant carried the trunk up the staircase behind Caroline. "Please leave that one by the door and we'll carry it upstairs directly."

Jake could easily carry the trunk up by himself, but considered the impropriety of him entering Caroline's bedroom and set the trunk down.

Mr. Humes, who was holding the door open, glanced at the trunk as if wondering if he should attempt to carry it.

Considering the man's age and small stature, Jake said, "We'll leave it right there for them."

Mr. Humes smiled as he closed the door. "Would you

care for a refreshment? You've been working for a long time."

"I could use a drink of water," Jake replied.

Mr. Humes nodded. "Would you care to wait in the parlor?"

Jake glanced at the staircase. Figuring it would take Caroline some time getting everything in the trunks organized, he shook his head. "I'll head back outside. Get a bit more work done. If you don't mind, I'll just follow you to the kitchen for that drink."

Mr. Humes agreed, and after drinking down two glasses of water, Jake exited the back door and walked to the stable, where he put away the ladder and other materials he'd used to repair the roof. While his mind was on Caroline, hoping the tea had gone well, he collected the items needed to tackle another repair.

He was on tenterhooks, wanting to hear how the tea had gone, hoping it had gone well, that she'd managed to escape any of the blame for what had happened between her and Edward. Worry on that score was like a sliver that had festered inside him. Still, he'd never regret having stopped that wedding. Edward would have made her life miserable.

Now they would be the ones married. It was the right decision, the only decision, but it would be up to Jake to make sure it wasn't one Caroline regretted.

Focused on the job, he didn't hear or notice anything, until a shadow was cast onto the ground beside him. He twisted about and used a hand to shield his eyes from the sun to see who had joined him.

Once again, there was an uptick in the beating of his heart. She'd changed her clothes, was now wearing a white blouse that buttoned up to her neck and a gray-colored skirt, and looked as pretty as she had in the blue gown. She was just naturally beautiful, and he'd simply have to get used to that.

"What are you doing now?" she asked.

He gave the stake he'd pounded into the ground a final blow from the hammer. "Staking out where to put a fence around the garden to keep critters from digging up your plants."

Her smile grew as she gestured toward the house to the east. "You must have met Toby. That's Mrs. Alcott's dog. They live next door, and he tends to bury things in the garden."

"I noticed him digging over there earlier," Jake replied, gesturing toward the row of carrot greens. The dog had given him an idea for another task to keep him busy.

"Oh, goodness," she said, noticing the section of greens that were strewed about. "I tried roping off the area, but it wasn't enough to keep him out."

He'd seen remnants of the rope fence, which had irritated him, because he'd known it had been her who had put it up. No one else would have worried about a fence or noticed a need for repairs. Her uncle and brother would let the house crumble down around them as long as it didn't restrict their work in the basement. The same for her aunt and her painting. Mr. and Mrs. Humes were not only elderly, but they would never have been given the money for repair expenses. James had said as much when Jake told him that he'd like to do some repairs on the property. "Back home the fence around the garden is as tall as you are," he said, instead of voicing his anger, "in order to keep the deer out."

"Who asked you to do this? And the roof?" she asked. "Frederick?"

He picked up another stake and the shovel, then walked toward the end of the area he intended to enclose with wrought-iron fencing. "No, I suggested it to your uncle."

"Why?" she asked, following him.

"Because I can't spend the next ten days sitting around twiddling my thumbs."

"Well, I can't spend the next ten days having you repair my uncle's property."

"Why not?" He stopped walking to eye the distance between the last stake he'd pounded in and where he now stood.

"Because it's not right," she answered.

"I disagree," he countered, while sticking the shovel in the ground. "Not only will the repairs keep me busy, they'll ease your mind when it's time to leave. Knowing that the place is in as good of condition as possible."

It was a moment before she let out a sigh. "That is true, but you may be busier than you thought the next few days."

"Oh? Why do you say that?"

She knelt down, picked up the stake he'd laid on the ground, and shoved it into the hole he'd made with the shovel. "We might as well work as we talk."

He knelt down beside her to pound the stake in with the hammer. They quickly fell into a routine of staking out the four corners of the garden and where the gate should be, while she told him about the tea. Apparently, there had been a large number of women in attendance— friendly women—and there were now several outings, dinner parties, balls, and other such prewedding events that they were expected to attend.

"I'm sorry," she said. "Lady Hilda was quite insistent

that they were a good idea and I didn't feel as if I could suggest otherwise."

"It's rare that anyone suggests otherwise to Aunt Hilda," he said. "But if there is an event that you don't want to attend, we won't go. Aunt Hilda will understand."

"It's not me," she said, picking up the shovel and walking toward the row of carrots. "It's you. Lady Hilda said that you aren't very keen on social events."

He followed her. "I was twelve when we moved to America, so I never had to attend many, but I was still taught manners, and I promise to not embarrass you."

Smiling, she shook her head. "I never imagined that you would. In fact, I'm quite sure it will be the other way around. I've never attended any, either."

"Sounds like we are two peas in the same pod, in the garden of London society."

"Oh, dear," she said, giggling as she stopped near the torn-up carrot greens, some hosting small orange carrots. "That sounds like it could be scary."

"Or fun. We could take them by surprise."

She laughed harder, which sounded downright musical. "You already did that. Six-shooter and all."

He took the shovel from her and prodded the ground, looking for what the dog had buried. "I explained about that, and won't wear my gun to any of the events."

She giggled. "It makes me laugh when I think about it."

He scanned her face, and could only surmise that she was telling the truth. "I believe you are the only one." He considered telling her about the knife in the shank of his boot, but chose not to—even though he was starting to think she would simply agree with him that one never knew when a knife could come in handy.

"I'm certainly not the only one," she said. "Several of

the ladies today commented on how gallant your actions were that day."

It was his turn to laugh. "Gallant? Clearly, they aren't remembering things as they truly were."

"I think they are," she said, then pointed to the ground. "Have you found what he buried?"

"Nope." He prodded at the ground again, careful to not uproot any other carrots.

"Toby has buried everything from forks to shoes." A tiny frown formed between her brows as she grimaced. "I probably should have been more persistent in shooing him away, but other than burying things, he's a nice dog."

It might have been the sun shining on her face that made her cheeks look pink, or it could have been a blush. Either way, she was downright pretty. More than pretty, which he'd already known, but right now, it was doing things to him. He was glad the boots on his feet had heels made for hooking onto the stirrups of a saddle, because they darn well could be the only reason he was able to stay rooted in place. Especially as a thought struck him. They'd agreed to be friends, and he felt he could rightly call her one now. But he had a lot of friends, and he sure as the dickens had never thought about kissing any one of *them*.

She broke their gaze by glancing down at the ground. He churned over another small section of dirt, looking for whatever the dog had buried, with other thoughts running about in his head like wild horses. Not just about kissing her. About time, and how sometimes it could be a friend, and other times an enemy. Like right now. He had too much of it on his hands, and her there every minute. Things could get dangerous if he got to liking her too much. This whole marriage thing was complicated. A man should like his wife, more than like, but Caroline wouldn't truly be his wife. She'd be more of a companion, to Nellie most of all. Teach her what she needed to know and then accompany her to England in a few years.

That was going to be tough, letting Nellie leave, and if he became too attached to Caroline, it could be tough letting her return to England, too.

He just wouldn't let that happen—getting to attached to her. That's all there was to that. He had restraint. Plenty of it.

"There's something I haven't yet told you about tomorrow."

"What happens tomorrow?" he asked, keeping his eyes on the dirt.

"We are invited to dinner at the Earl of Eastey's residence, if you want to go. Nathaniel will be there. Obviously, considering it's his home."

He couldn't help but glance at her. Of all the events coming up, he was sure that one was at the top of her list. She'd expressed how wonderful it had been to have the countess at the tea today. "Obviously," he repeated teasingly, because she was looking just too cute not to tease a little bit. They were friends, and he teased his friends all the time. "Of course, we'll go. It sounds fun."

"And afterward, we are attending the theater."

He nodded. "All right." The shovel hit something: he knelt down, and pulled a large spoon out of the dirt.

She giggled. "He really is a silly dog."

And she really was adorable, with a heart of gold.

Caroline thought she'd been nervous yesterday before tea at the duchess's house, but it didn't compare to how jittery she felt walking through the lobby doors of the theater. Dinner with Patsy and Nathaniel had been wonderful, with lots of laughs due to the stories that Jake and Nathaniel shared, both of their younger years, and of things that had happened to them in the years since they'd last seen each other. The other couple was with them now, walking through the doorway just ahead of them, and she was holding on to Jake's arm, but neither of those things was quelling her nerves.

The largest glass chandeliers she'd ever seen hung from a tall ceiling made up of patterned gilded plasterwork, and the walls were covered in what had to be silk wallpaper. The floors were patterned, too, and made of sparkling tile. Massive gold-framed mirrors and exquisite paintings hung on the walls, and matching staircases with marble steps and smooth, shining wooden railings swept upward, one on each side of the lobby. Between the staircases was a curtained doorway, with heavy red-and-gold drapes tied back with thick braided gold cords.

It was all so beautiful, she would have liked to examine things more closely, but other than glances in each direction, she kept her gaze on the floor, due to the vast number of people. There were more than she'd expected, and it felt as if every one of them had stopped talking and swiveled about to stare at her.

Jake must have sensed her nervousness, or was aware of the attention their arrival had drawn, because he patted her hand that was grasping on to his arm. "Hold your head up, Caroline," he whispered. "You have as much right to be here as every other person in the room."

Lifting her gaze from the floor, she twisted her neck enough to glance up at him.

His smile was as friendly as ever, and the way he winked at her sent her heart into a pitter-patter. He truly was a kind and wonderful man, and she didn't want to be an embarrassment to him. Walking around with her head down could mean she became just that. Therefore, she lifted her chin and squared her shoulders as they continued forward, following Patsy and Nathaniel to the staircase that would take them to the upper gallery and the private box of the Duke and Duchess of Collingsworth. Lady Hilda had insisted they use that box, to show just how much the family approved of their union.

"That's my girl," Jake whispered.

Her heart pounded a bit harder, which didn't calm her, but she was increasingly grateful that he was the one beside her.

"I should have expected we'd be a spectacle," she whispered. The women at the tea had indeed called him gallant, and she had agreed. Not just in his actions that day at the church, but every day since. The idea of marrying him was stirring her insides in a very unique way.

"Yep," he whispered in return. "Their eyes are almost popping out of their heads because they've never seen a better-looking couple."

Swallowing a giggle, she said, "I don't think that's what they are thinking. Albeit, you look very handsome in your finery."

"I know," he said, "but I think they are looking at you. The women are wishing they could be that beautiful and the men are wondering where you've been all of their lives."

She enjoyed his teasing and the way he could make her laugh. Even now, with her nerves jumping beneath her skin, she couldn't help but giggle at his comment. "You *know* you look handsome?" she asked, teasing him in return.

"Yes. Don't you think so?"

He was the most handsome man she'd ever met. "I do."

"It's these fancy English duds," he said. "Whereas you look stunningly beautiful all the time."

They were still whispering, leaning their heads close together as they maneuvered the marble stairs, and she wondered if that was making people stare more, for heads were still swiveling their way from people on the stairs ahead of them. It didn't help that the lavender-and-silver dress she was wearing, with its off-the-shoulder cuffed sleeves, made her cautious of every breath, hoping the neckline didn't slip any lower.

Jake's dark coat, white shirt, blue waistcoat, and ascot did make him look handsome, but so had the American clothing he'd been wearing that first day, as well as everything else he'd worn since then. Edward wasn't a homely man, but his appearance had always been too ostentatious, and his arrogance had always bothered her, whereas Jake was simply genuine. In his appearance and personality.

They mounted the final step and started down a hallway lined with heavy-curtained doorways. Couples milled about, finding their boxes and entering them. Ahead of them, the Earl and Countess of Eastey stopped and Patsy turned about.

"I'd like to introduce you to some dear friends of ours," Patsy said. "This is the Viscount Reinhold and his wife, Lady Elizabeth Williams. Lord Reinhold, this is Lady Caroline Evans and the Honorable Jacob Simpson."

"I heard you were in town," the viscount said to Jake once the greetings were complete. "Do you happen to remember me? Our fathers were well acquainted."

Jake nodded toward the slender blond man. "If your given name is Alan, then yes, I remember you visiting Collingsworth a time or two. How have you been?"

"Very well, thank you," the man replied. "I've heard about your success in America, mostly from your cousin, and would relish the opportunity to discuss your cattle breeds firsthand."

Jake let out a half chuckle. "From the horse's mouth, you mean. Rather than the other end."

The viscount laughed. "Precisely. Anything Edward says is always taken with a grain of salt."

"Men always find a way for their conversations to include four-legged animals," Lady Williams whispered.

Although that had rarely been her experience, Caroline nodded as if she fully understood and agreed.

"So true," Patsy replied. "While us women never tire talking about weddings. So you'll be pleased to hear, if you haven't already, Lady Williams, that there will be one taking place Sunday next between Lady Caroline and Mr. Simpson. I will be hosting a bridal tea on Tuesday. I was hoping to ask you about the little cakes you served at your sister's bridal tea last fall..."

Lady Williams, a tall, dark-haired woman, pressed a hand over the lace at her throat, the same shade of dark green as her gown. "My chef has simply perfected those, hasn't he? He bakes each cake separately in teacups. I'd gladly have him bake some for your event, but only if you allow me to join you in hosting? I'd be so honored."

"Oh, thank you," Patsy said. "I would appreciate that very much. Shall we meet tomorrow to discuss?"

Caroline hadn't heard about a bridal tea, nor could she fathom why Lady Williams would be interested in participating. She held her questions until after they'd separated from the viscount and his wife, before whispering to Patsy, "A bridal tea isn't necessary."

"Oh, yes, it is," Patsy replied. "You've been a dear

friend to me, helping with the charity causes at the church. The least I can do is to make sure that this time around, your wedding is the talk of London for the right reasons, and Lady Williams is the person who will assure that happens."

Caroline couldn't think of a response, but there was no time, either, because Jake was once again at her side and guiding her through a curtained doorway to the private box.

The view from the box was awe-inspiring. Beyond the railed opening were the curtained stage, the orchestra pit, the elaborate domed ceiling, and the massive number of people seated below. "I've never seen anything like this," Caroline whispered.

"I hope you enjoy the performance," Jake replied, assisting her onto a plush velvet chair at the front of the box.

"I know I will." She'd already admitted that she'd never been to the theater, nor seen a production of any sort, but it was being in his company that truly made it so wonderful.

A uniformed attendant provided them each with a glass of champagne, and Caroline nearly choked on her first sip. Not because of the bubbles or the tartness, but because she had just registered the many sets of eyes that were again peering in their direction from the other boxes and even from the floor below. Though the ladies were using fans to cover their faces, it was clear to her that they were whispering about who was in the Duke of Collingsworth's box.

There was a small table next to the other side of Jake's chair, and she handed him the glass, nodding at the table.

He took the glass and set it down. "You didn't care for it?"

"The champagne was fine," she whispered. "I don't want to spill it on myself, especially not while everyone is staring at us." He grinned, and this time she stopped him from saying anything flippant. "We both know the real reason they are staring."

Leaning closer, he asked, "Do you think it's because they heard about our wedding, or the one I stopped?"

"Both," she replied.

He wrapped his hand around hers and gave it a gentle squeeze. "They truly must have boring lives if that's all they have to think about. I'm glad that we have more important things to occupy our minds."

She frowned, wondering exactly what he was referring to, but didn't get a chance to ask because the lights dimmed and a hush took over the entire theater. Within minutes, she forgot all about the others in the room as she became enchanted with the actors on the stage.

Chapter Eight

The theater outing stayed with Jake, not because of the actors, who he figured had put on a splendid performance, nor because of the people dressed in their finery, including the ones who had approached him, knowing who he was and interested in learning more about his ranch. It was the way Caroline had been completely captivated that lingered in his mind. She'd clearly enjoyed herself, and his stomach sank a bit more each time he thought about it.

Attending a theater performance wasn't something she'd be able to do in Texas. Not unless he took her to one of the big cities, which wasn't likely. There wouldn't be any teas with friends, or fancy dinner parties, or balls.

Balls, like the one they were at tonight. This event was hosted by the Duke and Duchess of Mulberry, good friends of his aunt and uncle, and half of London appeared to be in attendance. The upper half, that was. Caroline was dressed in another stylish ball gown. This one was made of a shimmering yellow material that somehow made the skin on her shoulders, neck, and lower look almost golden.

Once again, he was finding it hard to keep his eyes on her face when all that skin was calling to him to examine it. Not with just his eyes. His hand kept wanting to slide up her arm and glide across that satin-like flesh. Feel the heat and silkiness of it.

Like with his thoughts of kissing her, he was having a hard time convincing himself that he mustn't feel that way toward a friend. His thoughts were far closer to what he'd once had toward Eloise than to any kind of friendship. He'd kissed Eloise, and thought about other things, but only when they'd been together. Otherwise, when he'd been at home working, he'd never thought that much about her.

It wasn't that way with Caroline. He couldn't seem to stop thinking about her. Night and day.

It wasn't fair to blame it on not being busy, either. Besides the stable roof, and the fence around the garden, he'd repaired stalls, and doors, and a broken window in the basement of the house.

He also had talked to Frederick and James, come to an agreement on investing in their inventions. In truth, he was interested in some of the things they'd shown him. Still, it bothered him that neither her uncle or brother seemed to worry or care that Caroline would soon be leaving.

She certainly had a lonely life, and he regretted that marrying him wasn't going to change that for her.

He also regretted that his restraint wasn't as strong as he'd thought.

Caroline was with a group of women a short distance away. She didn't appear to be bored or in need of his rescue. They'd been at the ball for an hour or so, and when she wasn't at his side, he made sure to keep an eye on her because the need to protect her kept getting stronger inside him. So was the need to feel her in his arms.

Jake felt an elbow hit his ribs and turned toward Eastey, wondering what the man needed.

"Halsbury's wife is making her way in this direction," the man said.

"Don't remember that name," Jake said, emptying his glass.

"She's the blonde woman staring at you," Eastey said, "and has a list of conquests as long as your cousin Edward's. The two of them have been carrying on an affair ever since the Earl of Halsbury had a stroke that left him bedridden."

As that information struck, Jake let his gaze flit across the crowd, but made sure to not make eye contact with the blonde woman walking toward them. He was curious to see who Edward was so intent upon putting before Caroline. One glance was enough to confirm that his cousin was as big of an idiot as Jake had always known. The woman wasn't unattractive, but she didn't hold a candle to Caroline.

He wondered whether Caroline knew the woman was Edward's paramour. Either way, it gave him an opening to do exactly what he'd been wanting to do since they'd entered the ballroom. He set his glass on the table, and nodded at Eastey, before he crossed to the gaggle of women and laid a hand on Caroline's back. "If you ladies will excuse us?"

"Of course," one of them, or maybe more, he wasn't sure, replied.

"Shall we dance?" he asked, once they'd moved away from the other women.

Trepidation rose in Caroline's eyes. "Before I agree, I need to let you know that other than a short lesson from

Patsy after her lady's maid did my hair this afternoon, I've never danced before."

A lady's maid to do her hair was one more thing Jake could add to the list of things she wouldn't have in Texas, yet he wasn't going to worry about that right now. "Then it's a good thing I'm here, because I'm a very good dancer. It ranks right up there next to roping and shooting."

She grinned. "Does it?"

"It sure does." He steered her in the direction of the dance floor. "I'm darn good at steer wrestling, too, and I've never met a horse that I couldn't break to ride." None of that compared to dancing, but he couldn't think of anything else to say to ease her mind.

"You're good at fixing roofs, windows, doors and building fences, too," she said.

"Well, that's how it is on the ranch. When something needs to be done, you learn how to do it."

"Is that how you learned to dance? Because it needed to be done?"

"I learned to dance because there's not a barn raising that happens without being followed by a barn dance."

"What's a barn raising?"

They'd arrived at the dance floor, and he grasped her waist and her opposite hand, and let the thrill of all that register inside him before answering, "It's when someone needs a barn and everyone for miles around shows up to help build it."

"Even the women?"

"Yep." He winked at her. "They bring the food." Tugging her a bit closer, he asked, "You do know how to count to four, don't you?"

"Of course."

"That's how you learn to dance. Two steps forward, two steps backwards. One, two, three, four."

"I don't believe that was in Patsy's lesson."

"Then it is a good thing that I'm here." With that, he started moving, leading her in a slow four-count box-step. She caught on quickly, and soon they were moving along beside all the other dancers. The thrill of having her in his arms was even more rewarding than he'd expected. "Did you lie to me, my lady?" he asked. "Because it appears as if you've been dancing as long as you've been walking."

"I did not, Mr. Simpson," she replied, teasing him in return for calling her *my lady*. "Perhaps it was you who lied. For you are truly a skilled dance tutor, and I don't believe you learned that at any barn dance. You must have had an excellent tutor yourself."

"I did. Even though we'd left England, my mother was steadfast in teaching me the manners of an English lord." He grimaced. "However, being here again has only impressed on me how much I have failed my mother when it comes to teaching Nellie the same lessons."

"I highly doubt that," she replied. "You may believe yourself as an unrefined American, but you're wrong."

"Aw, so you have heard exactly what the aristocrats think of Americans."

Her eyes glistened as she replied, "No man should ever be judged by his manner of dress."

"I believe it was more than my clothes that they judged me by at the church that day."

"And I believe, despite that day, you have won them over. Everywhere we go, people are eager to speak with you, and it's clear that nearly every one of them hopes to gain an invitation to visit your ranch."

Of their own accord, his eyes flitted lower, for a quick

glimpse at where the lace of her dress ended and the swells of her breasts began. The sight caused him to draw in a quick breath before he admitted, "There's only one person that I'm interested in inviting to my ranch, and she has already agreed to go there."

The music ended just then, and though their feet stopped, neither of them moved, except that Caroline closed her eyes. All he could think was *What the devil has gotten into me?* Saying that to her? It was the truth; he did want her to see his ranch, but like him, she knew this marriage was simply a means to an end. A way for her to get away from a situation that he'd caused.

She hadn't wanted a marriage any more than he did. Maybe he was just anxious to get back home and get his life back to normal. However, normal was soon going to be having a wife. He'd gotten used to the idea, as out of the ordinary as that may be. Or maybe it wasn't out of the ordinary. Once he made a decision, he didn't look back. There was no sense in that. His father taught him that once you make a decision, you go forward with it, because even if it turns out to be a bad one, you'd learn from it and never make that mistake again.

Caroline opened her eyes and met his gaze again with a gentle smile on her lips. "I know none of this is what you wanted, Jake, and I want you to know how much I appreciate how kind you've been about everything. I promise to do everything I can to make sure you don't regret any of it."

Her sincerity caused a flutter inside him, a softening of sorts, along with a warmth that was somewhat unsettling. Whatever he was feeling right then could become far too serious and uncontrollable, so he tugged his gaze away from her, looking about for an excuse to leave the dance floor. To put some distance between them. Because all of sudden the idea of kissing her was once again front and center, and he could no longer trust his restraint.

Espying the countess and Eastey standing near the doorway, he asked, "Shall we join the others? I believe refreshments are being served."

Her smile was gracious as she nodded, and Jake felt his heart careening downward. He might be good at many things, but right now, he was at a loss. For so long, he'd prided himself on his ability to adjust and adapt. To figure out what needed to be done and to do it, but when it came to Caroline, it was like he was hanging off the edge of a cliff without a rope being dropped down to help him climb back up to solid ground.

As they walked to the edge of the floor, he berated himself. Despite what he was feeling on the inside, he still should have responded. Told her that there was nothing she could ever do to make him regret helping her. That was the solid truth.

The next moment, he did find himself regretting something: he hadn't been paying close enough attention, because the very woman that Eastey had pointed out earlier stepped in front of him. He not only recognized her, but was fully aware of the subtle hush that came over the room.

"Mr. Simpson," she said, eyeing him from head to toe with a long, slow look. "I don't believe we've had the pleasure. I'm the Countess Halsbury." She licked her lips slowly. "Your cousin and I are well acquainted and he told me about visiting your ranch." She ran a finger along the side of her face before she held the hand out toward him. "It sounds so adventurous."

Jake might not understand everything about women,

but he knew the kind who were vain enough to believe they had what every man wanted. Ignoring her hand, he also pushed aside disagreeable thoughts that, if said aloud, would prove to everyone watching just how unrefined he truly could be. At the same time, he couldn't muster up a large degree of manners; therefore his tone was more than a little sharp. "I will inform Edward that you were in attendance this evening." With that, he sidestepped around the woman and continued to guide Caroline forward with his hand on the small of her back.

The shine was gone from Caroline's eyes when she looked up at him a few steps later. "My apologies," she whispered softly. "I'm afraid Edward was well acquainted with more than one married woman."

Not giving a midnight hoot who was looking at them or why, he stopped and pivoted so they were standing face-to-face. Then he pressed a hand to her cheek. "Do me one favor?"

Her eyes widened as she nodded. "Of course."

"Don't ever apologize for Edward, or anyone else. The responsibility for their behavior falls on their shoulders, not yours." Though he was completely serious, he also understood how others might look upon the pair of them having a *serious conversation* immediately after the interaction with the Countess of Halsbury. Knowing he needed to lighten the mood between them, he winked at her. "Including explosions in the basement."

She pinched her lips together as if not wanting to smile. "What about leeches in the basement?"

He was proud of her for understanding they needed to leave the seriousness behind and put on a united front. Smiling, he said, "If it's my basement, then you better apologize."

Her smile broke through. "Do you have a basement?"

"Yes, but I guarantee you aren't going to find any leeches in it." Leaning closer, he said, "Ever."

She giggled. "I still can't believe you are afraid of leeches."

"I'm not afraid. I just don't like them."

"I'm not sure I believe you," she whispered.

"Well, I don't like the idea of them attaching themselves to me and sucking out my blood."

"They much prefer turtle and fish to humans."

He laughed. "You would know that, wouldn't you?"

"You'd be amazed at the things I know," she said.

"I already am." Confident that she was no longer concerned over the countess, and that the hush had left the room, he let his hand slip off her cheek and twisted for them to start walking again. "I'm also hungry. I haven't eaten since noon. I hope they won't make us wait until three in the morning to feed us more than sweet cakes and fruit."

It was the truth; he was hungry, but more than that, he wanted this all to be over. Wanted to get Caroline away from anyone determined to shame or harm her, and he held no doubts that number included the countess. To his thinking, the Countess of Halsbury must have a reason to carry on an affair with Edward, and a reason why she didn't want it to end. Money, most likely. But the more he thought about it, the more nefarious the reasons that crossed his mind became.

Hours later, while in bed in her modest bedroom, which was made more modest in her eyes after spending hours in the glittering and glamorous London mansion, try as she might, Caroline couldn't silence her mind.

After encountering the woman, Caroline had tried desperately not to notice where the Countess of Halsbury was at every moment. As soon as the woman had introduced herself to Jake, Caroline had been mortified, knowing that she was the woman Edward was having an affair with. She was positive that Jake knew it, too, and that had made her gaze wander toward the other woman. The countess was beautiful and that reminded Caroline of her own simple looks. There was nothing about her that would ever make her stand out in a crowd, not like the countess.

The other woman reminded her of other things, too. Not just about herself.

Jake hadn't come to England expecting to marry anyone, never mind her, and though he'd said he wasn't interested in marrying Faith, that didn't mean there wasn't someone back in Texas that he *was* interested in marrying. Not necessarily someone like the Countess of Halsbury, but someone who fit into his life in Texas. Perhaps someone he was already courting, wanted to continue courting.

That thought made Caroline's stomach sink. He'd made it clear that he wouldn't have an affair, and expected her not to, either. It wouldn't be such a sacrifice for Caroline, but there could be someone he cared about.

Despite years of absence from London, he'd fit right in with the upper crust. People had sought him out all night. Some he'd known in the past; others had merely heard about him and wanted to make his acquaintance and learn more about his life and home. What she'd told him about people wanting to visit his ranch was true. Just as true as what she'd said about doing anything to make him not regret marrying her. If that meant she had to look the other way if there was a woman back in Texas, she would do it. There was no other option, and she'd have to tell him that.

She had been fully prepared to do that with Edward, and this shouldn't be any different. It certainly shouldn't cause such an odd sting in her chest. That's what she felt, though—a sharp, intense sting near her heart—and she was smart enough to know why.

Numerous times throughout the ball, Jake had winked at her, taken ahold of her hand or elbow, or led her in a dance. Each event, each one of his actions had made her breath catch and her heart beat faster, but it had been when he'd grinned at her that her insides had really taken a tumble. He had a signature grin that he gave to anybody, but when he looked at her, he provided the kind of smile people share when they were sharing a joke, or a secret. That was true of them, she supposed. They were sharing a very big secret, and he was doing all of this, the marriage, social events, and everything else, all because of her.

She had wanted a different life, and was getting a taste of one now. A bitter taste. It proved how foolish her desperation had made her. No matter what she had wanted, or what her family needed, she should have listened to her own instinct and refused to marry Edward. She hadn't needed to see the beautiful ballroom, with overhead chandeliers that had lit up the gilded-framed paintings on the walls, the tile floors, and the massive buffet table filled with delectable and exotic foods, to know she didn't fit in there and never would.

She couldn't help but worry that she was making the same mistake yet again.

With Jake at her side, it had been easy to smile and pretend, but it all felt superficial. The trip to the theater the night before had held a purpose—that of watching the performance—but the ball had felt as if the performers had been everyone in attendance, putting on a show of their wealth and status. Those same people had also been the audience, gossiping behind lacy fans and strategically placed hands.

Now, lying here with all this going through her head, she had to wonder if she'd feel as out of place at Jake's ranch as she did here, and if she should have appreciated the life that she'd had rather than wanting a different one.

Tossing aside the covers, she left the bed. Her room was small, and made smaller by the large traveling trunks that Jake had purchased for her. One had been placed below her window, and she sat upon it, drew her knees up to her chest, and stared out at the night sky. It was filled with stars, each one twinkling its light in the darkness.

She couldn't stop her mind from returning to thoughts of Jake. He was not only handsome and kind, but he was poised and self-confident, while holding none of the haughtiness and arrogance of so many other men. He was so easy to like. Right from the first moment she'd met him, she'd liked him, and fully understood that he was also an honorable man. One who would never go back on his word, nor back out of a promise.

A heavy sigh puffed her cheeks as it left her. There wasn't anything she could do to change what had happened, nor what was about to happen. They would marry and she would go to Texas with him. But there, she could make sure that their marriage didn't change his life. Didn't change him.

It was the least she could do after all he'd done for her.

Actually, it was all she could do.

And should do. She *must* do everything she could so he could take care of his ranch. It wouldn't be the life she'd wanted, one that had included a family of her own, children running through the house followed by pets and filling the air with laughter, but she would have a job to do. Expectations that she would need to fulfill. There was much she needed to learn in order to teach Nellie all about London society. Therefore, the only option was to put aside the past and embrace events such as tonight, and everything else leading up to the wedding.

Pushing down a stomach-churning sense of panic, Caroline set her feet onto the floor with as much conviction as she could muster. This was now her life, and she was going to make the best of it.

Caroline kept that thought in mind in the following days. Rather than worrying about her own insecurities, she watched every move of the ladies around her, Lady Hilda, and Patsy, and attempted to mimic them in every way. She kept her head up, her shoulders straight, and sought to make every one of her responses to questions sound as ladylike as possible.

Concentrating so hard was exhausting, but she stayed focused. By the time the bridal shower happened, she had almost convinced herself she was capable of fitting in. Almost, because Jake had been in attendance at most of those other events, and with him, she felt as if she had a shield. She wouldn't have that today.

The upper hall of the Eastey home had been decorated with white-and-pink ribbons and vases of flowers. It quickly filled up with women, who took seats at tables draped with lacy cloth and set with dessert plates of flowered fine china and matching cup-and-saucer sets.

As the ladies ate cucumber sandwiches, fruit, cheese, and the miniature cakes that Lady Elizabeth's cook had baked in teacups and decoratively covered with icing, they sipped on sweet punch and wrote down their favorite recipes on the small sheets of paper that Patsy had supplied at each table. Several ladies, having heard about the request ahead of time, had come with a recipe already written down.

Patsy gifted her a lovely wooden box to hold all the recipes, with a small golden clasp and hinges and a top covered with painted flowers. Caroline didn't need to copy anyone or pretend when it came to expressing her gratitude for her friend's thoughtfulness.

"Thank you," she said, placing a tiny kiss on Patsy's cheek. "It's lovely. I will cherish it, and the contents, forever."

"With you traveling so far away, I thought it would easily fit in one of your trunks, and be a reminder of home, and of all of us who will miss you," Patsy replied.

"I am going to miss you," Caroline said, feeling the sting of tears. She would never forget Patsy's kindness.

"Now, now," Lady Elizabeth said, touching the corner of one of her eyes. "No crying. Not today."

Caroline had encountered Elizabeth Williams several times since the theater, and had found the woman as endearing and friendly as Patsy and Lady Hilda. In fact, every woman in the room, whether she'd met them before today or not, was delightful. Patsy had assured her that would be the case, that many of them had been a bride-to-be once, and knew the jitters that went along with that.

It made Caroline wonder why she'd never tried harder to make friends in the past, and why she had settled for the life that she'd had. Things could have been very different if she had just tried. She was doing that now, because she had a reason to, and that reason was Jake.

"When you return to London for a visit, you'll be able to tell us what recipes you use," Patsy said.

"Oh, yes!" Elizabeth exclaimed. "And you'll have to tell us all about Texas. I must admit that I'm a bit jealous. It sounds like such an adventure."

"It does," another woman, Lady Barkleigh, a dear friend of Elizabeth's, said. "One that you'll be undertaking alongside an extremely handsome and gallant man."

The conversation quickly became a giggle-filled conversation about Jake, with comments that had Caroline's cheeks blushing and her heart thudding.

"There's nothing to be embarrassed about," Patsy whispered.

Caroline couldn't help but point out what she'd earlier told Patsy and whispered in return, "Jake and I aren't getting married because we are in love."

"Maybe it hadn't started out that way," Patsy whispered. "But things change."

"This won't," Caroline whispered. "It's what we both agreed to."

The way Patsy smiled and nodded before she turned to join in on the conversation with the other ladies left Caroline feeling that Patsy didn't believe her. It also left her wondering if things could change. If Jake could ever think of her as more than just a friend.

At the same time, she knew she couldn't hope for that, because it wasn't what Jake wanted. He didn't want a marriage that included any of the actions the women were giggling about.

Chapter Nine

The remaining social outings—which included more dinner parties, a museum outing, and another ball—were all easier for Caroline. Not only was she more confident, and dedicated to learning all she could, but she was happy for Jake that it was almost over. He never complained about a single event. If she didn't know better, she'd have thought he was enjoying himself, which was quite endearing. Add in the other small repairs he'd completed at her aunt and uncle's home, and Caroline was utterly convinced there was not a better man on this green earth.

She was also convinced that marrying him might not produce the life she'd always wanted, but it could be a wonderful one just the same. Being his friend was certainly wonderful.

Therefore, when Saturday eventually rolled around, she was no longer nervous, or worried. Instead, she was ready for the next chapter of her new life to start, where she would start to return all the favors that Jake had bestowed upon her.

She awoke with a song in her heart, a feeling she hadn't had for years, and determined that this time around nothing was going to ruin her wedding, she locked the basement door—after making sure no one was down there, of course—and did the same to her aunt's parlor.

There was simply too much at stake to take any chances. She gave the keys for both door to Mrs. Humes for her to unlock them later today.

Madam Beauchamp arrived early, as planned, and to Caroline's surprise, besides her own wedding trousseau, the seamstress had brought new clothing for her aunt, uncle, and brother. While she was in her room, with two dressing assistants and a hairdresser, Madam Beauchamp was downstairs, ruling the others in the house like a colonel in the Queen's Regiment.

By the time the two coaches arrived to transport them to the church, Caroline hardly recognized her entire family. Aunt Myrtle rode in the coach with her, while Uncle James and Frederick rode in the second one.

"I must remember to thank Jake for the new dress," Aunt Myrtle said. "I've never had anything so beautiful in my entire life."

Madam Beauchamp had shared that it had been Jake who had ordered the clothes for her aunt, uncle, and brother.

"He's certainly kind and generous," Aunt Myrtle continued. "I'm happy that you found such a good man. You will have a wonderful life with him, and that's exactly what your uncle and I wanted for you."

Caroline touched her chest, where a warmth was spreading, despite the corset that was so tight she could barely breathe. Though several corsets had been included in her new clothing, she'd never worn one because they all laced up in the back, and she had no maid to help her. Today, Madam Beauchamp insisted one was necessary beneath her wedding gown, with its tight-fitting bodice, high lace collar and cuffs that buttoned up to her elbows. The seamstress had also wanted her to wear a hoop skirt beneath the tiered layers of white chiffon, but in that, Caroline had won, claiming she was too afraid of tripping over the wires.

Drawing in a quick, short breath, which was all she could manage, Caroline did wonder why her aunt had never made such comments before her previous wedding, yet determined that it truly didn't matter. "Thank you, Aunt Myrtle, and thank you for all you and Uncle James have done for me over the years. You gave me a good life, too."

Her aunt shook her head. "Living with two old people. I wanted more for you, but didn't know how to give it to you." Myrtle wrapped her fingers around one of Caroline's hands. "I'm going to miss you, but Jake said you can come visit, and that we can come visit you, too. James says that we will, and I believe him. It's scary to think about crossing an ocean, but I think it would be grand. So very grand."

The corset was so stiff, Caroline couldn't twist enough to give her aunt's cheek a kiss, so she kissed her fingers and patted her aunt's face instead. "I will be back to visit, and I do hope you come to visit, because I shall miss you very much."

Aunt Myrtle leaned over and kissed her cheek. "I had Mrs. Humes put some water paints and a sketch book in one of your trunks. I would like you to paint me a picture of your new home, and send it to me."

"Thank you, that was very thoughtful," Caroline said, struggling harder to breathe. "I will do that. I promise."

Talking made breathing more difficult, so Caroline

merely smiled as her aunt talked about artistic matters until the coach rolled to a stop.

Between the multiple layers of chiffon that made up her skirt, and the corset hugging her midsection, Caroline struggled a little to maneuver her way to the door of the coach. She was relieved when Uncle James appeared on the paving outside, holding out a hand to help her. He had walked her down the aisle the first time, and would again today.

"I've never seen you looking more beautiful," he said.

"Thank you," she said, stepping onto the ground. "You look very handsome yourself." She'd hoped that standing would help her breathe, but instead, she felt lightheaded, and had to close her eyes for a brief moment to catch her bearings.

"I look good in black," Uncle James replied. "Always have." He nodded toward the church, where Frederick was escorting Aunt Myrtle through the door. "Everyone's inside, waiting on you."

She nodded.

"I don't need to say that you got the pick of the litter with Jake," Uncle James said, "you already know that, but I do want to say that I'm happy about the way things turned out. Jake will make you happy, and you will make him happy."

"I hope so," she answered softly, due to lack of air and some very sincere hope.

Uncle James kissed her cheek. "Hope is all it takes, my darling."

She wasn't convinced of that, having given up on hope years ago, but the way both her aunt and uncle were acting—versus the way they had acted at her last almost-wedding—was making her emotions rise. Or maybe that was because she couldn't breathe. Was that the corset, or were her nerves getting the best of her? Last time, she'd been numb and just wanted the event over. This time she was happy to be here. Happy to be marrying Jake. Did that mean…? Perhaps she liked him more than she should. What if she was falling in love with him? He'd never love her back. Could she live with that?

As if he were reading her mind, Uncle James said, "Frederick didn't want us to say anything discouraging about your marriage the first time, and we didn't. We supposed you'd be close enough at hand if anything went awry. But this time, I feel quite differently. I know it's the right thing. It's time for you to have your own life, and Jake will give you a wonderful one. Of that, I have no doubts, but we are certainly going to miss you. You've been a ray of sunshine since you moved in with us, and you can mark my words that your aunt and I will be crossing that ocean to see you."

When his arms folded around her, she held on tight, because she was going to miss him, too—and because she was growing even more lightheaded. No matter how hard she tried to suck in air, it stopped before reaching her lungs.

He held her tight for several moments, then patted her back. "It's time for us to go in now."

She nodded and tried her best to breathe.

Just as it had been when Jake had barreled himself in through the doors less than a month ago, the church was full. Every wooden pew was near to overflowing with people. Standing at the altar, he watched as Frederick escorted Myrtle to the front pew and the two of them sat down, before turning his gaze to the back of the church. At any moment his bride would appear. If, when he'd left home, anyone had told him that he'd return to Texas a married man, he would have laughed in their face. Called them a bald-faced liar. Yet, that was exactly what was about to happen. He'd get married today and leave for his journey home tomorrow as a married man with a wife in tow.

The strange thing was that he wasn't overly mad about it. Perhaps because he knew it was all a façade, that the wedding was simply a way to right a wrong. More than one, actually. He'd come to England to make things right for Faith, and was getting married to make things right with Caroline.

She appeared in the doorway at the end of the long aisle, holding on to her uncle's arm. A long, lacy veil covered her face just as it had the first day he'd seen her, but this time, he knew the angelic face beneath it. Knew the person, too. She was the kindest, most caring woman imaginable and that alone was enough to convince him that she was exactly what Nellie needed.

He'd started doing that more and more, telling himself that Caroline was exactly what Nellie needed. He knew why. It was because he didn't want Caroline to be what *he* needed. The idea of having a wife had been growing on him lately. Seeing that so many of the men he'd known when they were children now had their own children, sons and daughters who were their pride and joy, had churned something inside him.

His ranch was his pride and joy, and he was ready to get back to it so he could think straight again. Think about ranching and cattle, and hayfields and stock markets. All the things that would keep him from thinking about how Caroline wasn't marrying him because she wanted to. She was doing it because she had to. Over the past few days it had become clear just how much she enjoyed the high life that the London society provided. He would never resent her for that and, married or not, once they arrived in the States, he wouldn't hold her to any commitments. She'd be free to find the life she did want. It was the least he could do.

Until then, it was his job to act the happy bridegroom. Ironically, that wasn't a tough job whatsoever.

All on its own, a smile appeared on his face when Caroline and her uncle stopped in front of him, and he held out a hand to take hers. Feeling the chill of her fingers, he folded his hand tighter around hers and gave her a wink, hoping one or the other would ease the nervousness she must be feeling.

She swayed as she stepped up beside him, and then so softly he questioned if he heard her, she whispered, "I can't."

The air locked in his lungs momentarily and he was about to ask what she meant, when she wobbled, and then drooped.

Acting quickly, he caught her around the back and behind the knees before she collapsed. Her entire body was limp, and he hoisted her tighter in his arms, so her head was lying against his chest, as he turned to the vicar. "Don't just stand there! She's fainted."

The man stared at him dumbfounded, as if not knowing what to do.

Completely flustered, Jake hurried past the man toward a side door, with an echo of mumbles and whispers behind him. His heart was racing with concern, and his stomach churning with guilt. He'd done this to her. Forced her into a marriage she didn't want.

Aunt Hilda and the Countess of Eastey quickly arrived at his side. He told them the same thing he'd told the vicar. "She fainted."

"I saw that," Aunt Hilda replied.

"This way," the countess said. "There's a room where you can lie her down across the hall."

Her words *I can't* were repeating in his head, but his concern was for her. Once she came to, they could talk about why she'd gone this far before determining that she couldn't marry him.

There was no sofa in the room the countess led them into, but there was a wooden pew along one wall and Jake gently laid Caroline onto it, then lifted her veil. Shocked by her paleness, for he'd seen dead men with more color on their faces, Jake's hand shook as he touched her cheek then leaned his face close to hers, to feel if any air was coming from her nose or mouth.

"She's barely breathing!" He ran a hand over her torso, checking for its rise and fall, but all in all, she felt as hard as stone. Like no air was going in or out, and that set a sense of panic inside him.

"Let me see," a man said.

"Who are you?" Jake asked, not about to let some stranger touch her.

"This is Dr. Albright," Aunt Hilda said. "He's been our physician for years."

Eyeing the gray-haired man closely, Jake took a step back. Just one. That gave the doctor enough room to lean over Caroline and do the same thing Jake had just done: check to see if she was breathing.

"I've seen this before," the doctor said. "Help me sit her up."

Jake slid a hand under Caroline and lifted her back

so she was in a sitting position, while asking, "What's wrong? Why is she barely breathing?"

"Her corset is too tight," the doctor said. "It's smothering her. Those garments are dangerous to the health of women. I've said it before, and will say it again. It's not natural to…"

As the doctor went on talking about the corsets, Jake took action.

He sat down behind Caroline and pushed aside the veil covering the back of her dress.

After taking one look at the long row of buttons running down her back, he pulled his knife out of the sheath he'd had the bootmaker sew into the lining of his new knee-height boots. It would take an hour to undo all those buttons, and they didn't have an hour.

With one upward swipe, he sliced the threads of a good dozen buttons. The buttons went flying, and there were still more covering the back of her neck and down her lower back, but he could pull apart the material enough to see the crisscrossing ties of the corset. It was no wonder that she was being smothered by it: he could barely get the blade of his knife underneath the silk laces. Again, it took only one quick swipe to sever the laces, and instantly he could hear her gasp, then cough.

Her head was drooped forward, and Jake pulled her backward, so she was leaning against him as she continued to gulp in air. The relief inside him was massive. He couldn't remember a time he'd been that scared.

"Thank you," she whispered between gulps, sounding hoarse.

"Here." The countess held a glass of water near Caroline's face. "Take a sip of water. It'll help."

Caroline lifted her head and complied, then she let out

a groan as she glanced about. "What happened? Why are we in here?"

"You fainted," the doctor said, "because your corset was restricting your air flow."

Caroline swung her legs off the pew and dropped them to the floor. "Oh, no! I stopped the wedding, didn't I?"

Jake brushed the veil away from her face. "Don't worry about that. How are you feeling?"

She closed her eyes and shook her head. "Thankful I can breathe again."

"Well, now," Aunt Hilda said. "We are sincerely grateful for that, too. You gave us such a scare."

"I'm sorry," Caroline said.

"Nothing to be sorry about," Jake said. "It's all fine."

She looked up at him with remorse dulling her normally shining brown eyes. "Has everyone left?"

"No." He nodded at the others. "Just those of us in this room."

The countess had gathered up the buttons and held them out for Caroline to see. "It'll only take a minute to sew these back on and everything will be fine."

"We need a needle and thread," Aunt Hilda said.

"I have some in my bag," the doctor said. "For when I must perform stitches. I'll go get it from my carriage."

"Wonderful. Thank you, Dr. Albright," Aunt Hilda said. "I will tell the guests that the service will continue momentarily."

"I'll explain things to the vicar," Countess Eastey said, following Aunt Hilda and the doctor to the door.

That left them alone, and as Jake met Caroline's gaze, his heart filled with compassion at the moisture gathered in her eyes. "There now, it's all fine."

She shook her head. "Maybe I'm just not meant to get married."

That whispered *I can't* he'd heard earlier echoed in his head again, and though he now believed she'd been trying to say that she couldn't *breathe*, he knew he had to do the right thing. "Well, I don't believe it's a matter of what's meant, but perhaps what you want."

She sucked in an audible and shaky-sounding breath. "I want to marry you, Jake. I do."

At that moment, Jake felt something he'd never experienced. He could only fathom that it was a joy beyond all other joys.

"I didn't do this on purpose," she said. "Mrs. Beauchamp said the stays would loosen as I moved around, but they didn't. They just kept getting tighter and tighter. Truly, that's what happened."

He wrapped an arm around her shoulders and tugged her close to his side. "I believe you. I have no idea how you made it as long as you did with that contraption tied around you, and as long as you want to get married, that's what we will do."

"Do you still want to get married?" she asked, without looking at him.

"Yes." Even if he felt any of his past qualms, which he didn't, he could have been on his deathbed and still wouldn't cancel another one of her weddings.

"Aren't you worried that I'll be an embarrassment to you?" she asked. "After what just happened?"

"Are you worried that I'll be an embarrassment to you after what happened the last time?" he asked in return.

"No."

"Then we agree on that, too."

She let out a sigh. "You really are a good a man."

As happened on a regular basis lately, a great desire to kiss her arose inside him. This time, he couldn't defy it, and gave her temple a soft brush with his lips. "You really are a brave woman."

The door opened, and the countess entered, quickly followed by Aunt Hilda and the doctor. Jake stood and assisted Caroline to her feet, before he stepped aside, giving the women room to assess the damage to the dress and the repairs needed. In an awkward moment, when they were working the corset out from the back of the dress, he questioned if he should leave the room for decency's sake. At the same time, he wasn't about to let her return to the altar alone. They were in this together and would maintain a united front.

Therefore, he stayed, and listened as it was determined that it would take too long to sew on each individual button, so the doctor simply stitched Caroline's dress together.

Aunt Hilda assured the long veil would cover the missing buttons, and no one would know the difference. It was but a few minutes until they all reentered the main church.

He and Caroline waited until the others had returned to their seats, then he took her hand, smiled at her, and asked, "Shall we try this again?"

"Yes."

Her whisper was soft, but the sincerity in her eyes shone brightly. He winked at her as they began to walk forward, side by side, hand in hand.

The vicar was still at the altar, and began to speak as soon as the two of them took their spots.

As if the man was afraid something else might happen, and wanted the event over as quickly as possible, the service was short. There was just enough time for both of them to say their vows and for Jake to slide the shimmering gold band that he'd purchased for Caroline on her finger. The jeweler had shown him several rings with large stones, but none of them reminded him of her. She wasn't showy, but she was real, and that's why he'd chosen this ring. Its sparkle was as bright as her, and the gold was as pure and genuine as she was.

As instructed, he then lifted the veil from her face, and though the kiss he bestowed upon her lips was a chaste, simple one, he felt the effects of his lips merging with hers throughout his entire system. It was as akin to getting struck by a bolt of lightning as he could imagine.

The fanfare that erupted next was more voluble than he imagined it would be. Then again, maybe all the clapping was inspired by relief, because the marriage had finally happened, without any further disruption.

Guests and family crowded around him and Caroline as they exited the church, and the well-wishing comments continued as he escorted Caroline into the open carriage to take them back to his aunt and uncle's home for the wedding breakfast—a breakfast that the staff had been preparing for the past two days.

The crowd was still near when the carriage began to roll forward. After both he and Caroline had waved and then turned about to face forward, he winked at her. "That wasn't so hard now, was it?"

She looked at him as if stunned for a moment, then her head tilted backward as she laughed, laughed with her whole body. He'd seen her smile and giggle, but this was a sight he hadn't seen before. He instantly knew he liked it, and laughed along with her.

"Oh, dear," she said as their laughter faded. "I can't believe that I fainted."

"It took everyone by surprise," he said. Now that it was over, he could admit that he'd faced down cattle rustlers, rattlesnakes, and tornadoes with less fear than he'd felt when she'd fainted.

"I'm sorry."

"Don't be. Weddings are usually rather dull." He draped an arm around her and gave her a sideways hug. "We've managed to change that, twice."

She giggled again, but then a tiny frown formed between her brows. "May I ask you something?"

"Absolutely. Shoot," he answered, feeling much more like his old self. Other than the constant need to touch her. And he wouldn't mind kissing her again.

"Is there someone back in Texas that you were hoping to marry?" she asked.

His thoughts shifted to Eloise, and he considered saying no, but was far more inclined to go with the truth, something he always did. Furthermore, at the moment, he couldn't even remember what Eloise looked like. "She's not in Texas any longer. She's in Missouri. At one time, I thought we'd get married, but she married someone else."

"She did?"

"Yes, she married a newspaperman. Shortly after she'd told me that she'd never marry any man who put cattle before her."

Caroline's frown deepened. "I imagine that there are times in every profession when work must come first."

He hadn't thought about it that way, yet, having lived the life she'd lived and made the sacrifices she'd made, it wasn't surprising that she had. However, the ranch was still going to be very different from anything she'd known here in London. "That's most likely true, but a ranch can make a person feel isolated. Town is a distance away, and unexpected things happen every day. It's very different from here."

She nodded. "I'm looking forward to seeing it. To living there. To meeting Nellie and all the others."

He didn't want her hopes to be built up too high, but at the same time, he loved his ranch and wouldn't change anything about it. "It'll take us a good two weeks to get there."

"You've told me that a couple of times," she said. "I'm looking forward to that part, too. It's been a long time since I've left London."

"It's been a long time since I was on a passenger ship," he said. "It's sure to be a hoot better than the cargo ship I arrived on."

"Did you really sleep on a hammock?"

"I did." He was glad for her sake that they would be traveling in more comfort.

"You've certainly gone to great lengths for your family."

"For my ranch," he corrected. "My father, and mother, worked too hard to create what we have today for me to lose it because of Edward."

"You felt that could happen?"

"I did. As the lieutenant governor of Texas, Faith Drummond's father is a powerful man."

"Do you still fear something could happen?"

"Not as long as we deliver Edward to Faith," he admitted, still believing that Faith would change Edward's life, in a way his cousin might not appreciate. The Countess of Halsbury wouldn't appreciate Faith, either. From what he'd discovered, the countess had been dead set on becoming a duchess, and wouldn't stop at anything in her quest to make that happen, including slowly poisoning her current husband. There was no proof of that, merely speculations, but those speculations were enough to make him worry about how the countess might have gotten rid of Caroline when the time was right, if Caroline had been Edward's wife. That was a frightening thought, but after his conversation with Uncle Oscar, Jake was certain that in a few weeks, no one would need to worry about the Countess Halsbury.

"Are you concerned about getting Edward to Texas?" Caroline asked.

Again, she deserved the truth. "I don't trust him, but I'm not concerned. I won't let him out of my sight until we arrive at the ranch."

Chapter Ten

Though Caroline had reasons to be mortified after the way she'd fainted at the altar, she didn't have the time to let that mortification rear up inside her. Not during the carriage ride, nor when she and Jake arrived at the Duke of Collingsworth's home.

The wedding breakfast was an elaborate affair, complete with champagne, a beautifully decorated, large wedding cake, and more well-wishing than she'd ever imagined. The very guests who'd witnessed her collapse into Jake's arms at the altar acted as if nothing unusual had happened. Was it that which was causing the joy inside her, or could it just be the relief of finally being married, which was an accomplishment in itself?

Another reason for her happiness could be her aunt and uncle, who appeared to be enjoying the event endlessly. Uncle James was talking about his inventions—of course he was—but others were listening with interest, and encouraging him to tell them more, and Aunt Myrtle was just as engrossed in conversations with women discussing things she'd read in her many periodicals.

Then again, perhaps she ought to accept that any joy she was feeling could be traced back to one thing. One person. Jake. He had everyone in the room laughing with his jokes and the stories he was telling, all about Texas and how the arrival of his beautiful bride was going to shock cowboys right out of their boots. She knew he was just teasing in order to keep things festive, but still, her heart fluttered every time he looked at her. Her lips were still tingling from the kiss he'd bestowed upon them at the altar, too.

She understood that it had been just for show, but she couldn't deny how amazing it had been, nor the excitement that filled her when she contemplated being kissed by him again.

What if things were to change between them? What if someday Jake would want to be more than friends?

Dare she hope that her marriage to him could become real? That someday, God willing, they would have children? Be happy living together at his ranch? She knew better than to hope, but could she now? Hope?

Then again, perhaps all these thoughts were simply prompted by the gaiety surrounding her. That would cease once everyone left; a new reality would descend upon her and him tomorrow. The idea of having to travel to America with Edward in tow was enough to make her feel quite queasy.

Lost in her thoughts, Caroline was caught unaware of what had been said, and looked to Jake, standing at her side.

He grinned and teasingly whispered, "It won't hurt."

"What won't hurt?" she whispered in return.

"Our wedding photograph. Aunt Hilda wants us in the front parlor to have it taken."

"Oh." She glanced to where Lady Hilda was walking toward the dining room doorway. "I'm afraid I wasn't listening as clearly as I should have been."

"Are you feeling faint?" he asked, with a serious glint in his eyes.

"No," she quickly replied. "I'm fine. Was just caught woolgathering, I suppose."

Leaning so close his breath tickled her ear, he asked, "About what? Your handsome husband?"

She couldn't help but laugh and lie. "I was thinking about traveling to Texas, and all the things you've said about it. You make it sound like the finest place on earth." That part was true. His face lit up when he talked about his ranch.

He placed a hand on her back to guide her to the door while saying, "It is to me, and I'm excited to show it to you, but I'll let you form your own opinion."

She'd seen him commanding and determined to get his way, but also had seen him being just the opposite, letting her make her own decisions, and believed he would do that again. Besides so many other endearing qualities, he was a man of his word.

They arrived in the parlor, where others had also gathered, but were leaving a large area open near the fireplace. A single chair had been placed there, and a camera on a tripod was pointed toward it.

"Mr. Simpson," said a man dressed in a suit as black as his hair and bushy eyebrows, gesturing toward the chair. "Please be seated, and you, my lady, stand on his right, and place your hand on his shoulder."

They walked to the chair and Jake sat down, but as she settled a hand on his shoulder, he shook his head. "Shouldn't I be the one standing? It's only proper for a gentleman to give the only seat to a lady."

The man was lifting a black drape attached to the camera, and held it in his hands as he explained, "I'd have to move my camera back, and you are so tall that if I did that, you wouldn't be able to see both your faces in the photograph. She's short, so this is how it needs to be." The man then ducked beneath the cloth. "Perfect. Hold still."

Caroline felt Jake's shoulder tighten beneath her hand, and softly whispered, "It's fine."

"I believe my wife's height is *perfect*," Jake said, sternly enough that a silence overtook the room. "She is perfect in every way."

The man tugged off the cloth. "She is, sir. I meant no disrespect. My apologies."

"Accepted," Jake said, "but I still say she should be the one sitting."

Before she realized he was moving, Jake reached around, grasped her waist, and pulled her onto his lap.

"There," he said, holding her tight around the waist with both hands. "Take your picture."

Muffled laughter came from others in the room, and Caroline looked at Jake while moving her feet to make sure her skirt was covering her legs all the down to her shoes. There was little else she could do. It would be useless for her to try and break his hold. "He can't take a picture of us like this."

"Yes, he can," Jake insisted.

"Take your picture, Mr. Cameron," the Duke of Collingsworth said. "You'll never win in an argument with my nephew. Not when he has his mind made up. Besides, he has a point. A gentleman does need to give the only seat to a lady."

"Yes, Your Grace." The photographer slipped beneath the black cloth again. "Look at the camera and hold still."

Jake grinned at her, and winked, before he stared straight ahead.

Sitting as she was, on his lap with his arms wrapped around her, was causing such a commotion inside her, she didn't have the ability to do anything more than fold her hands in her lap. Nor could she control the smile that was tugging on her lips, even after she'd turned to face the camera, because the Duke of Collingsworth was right; no one could win an argument with Jake. He was too confident, too self-assured, for that to ever happen.

The flare of light that went off was so bright she saw stars for several moments afterward.

"I think he blinded us on purpose," Jake whispered in her ear.

"No, he didn't, but no one would blame him if he did," she replied, and then felt Jake's chuckle more than heard it. "Let me up, now. Our wedding is already one people won't forget for some time. They don't need more fodder for gossip."

"A wedding is something no one should forget," he said. "Including the bride and groom."

Their faces were but inches apart, and that too was causing more chaos inside her, because her gaze kept drifting to his lips. They had been so soft and warm when they'd touched hers earlier, and she found herself wishing that their marriage was real, so she could feel those lips upon hers again. Many times. Thinking about it was locking her lungs up as tight as the corset had earlier.

"I don't believe I've had the chance to tell you how pretty you look today," he said. "You always look pretty, but today, you put me in mind of that field of daisies I told you about, because you are just as breathtakingly beautiful, and I'm right proud to have you as my wife."

It was as if parts of her were melting, and she simply couldn't look away from the sincerity in his blue eyes.

Another flare of light happened and caused her to blink, then close her eyes until the stars went away. She also sucked in a breath of air against the overwhelming sensations still playing havoc inside her.

"Damn," Jake grumbled.

She couldn't stop a giggle from escaping. The entire thing, her sitting on his lap, the picture taking, all of it was so absurd, so out of the ordinary, it was funny. That was all there was to it. At least, that was what she was trying to tell herself.

"Are you about done there, picture man?" Jake asked.

"Yes, sir, unless you'd like a photograph of her standing beside you?"

"No, I think my sight has been damaged enough for one day, thank you," Jake replied.

His hold around her waist lessened, and Caroline hastily removed herself from his lap, feeling the heat in her cheeks at everyone witnessing such an act. At the same time, she couldn't help but recognize the happiness that was still filling her heart. Life with Jake was going to be anything but predictable, and that excited her.

He rose and rested a hand in the small of her back, then proceeded to offer a sincere thank-you to the guests and family members, ending it with an invitation for any of them to visit the Rocking S when possible.

Caroline stood beside him as once again, people paraded past them, offering well-wishes and goodbyes. Oddly enough, she didn't need to force the smile to remain on her lips. For the first time that she could remember, she had a future to look forward to.

Most of the others had left when Patsy approached and said to Jake, "Excuse us for a moment?"

"Of course," he replied, with one of his signature grins.

Caroline walked beside Patsy a few steps away for a bit of privacy. "Thank you for everything," Caroline said. "I'm going to miss you very much."

"You'll be too busy to think about me," Patsy said. "And I'm very happy about that. But I do expect letters about everything." Lowering her voice even more, Patsy added, "I told you things would change."

Even as her own hopes were growing, Caroline shook her head. "Nothing has changed."

"Oh, yes, it has," Patsy insisted. "A man doesn't look at a woman the way Jake looks at you without being head over heels in love."

Caroline's heart skipped several beats, even as she shook her head. "He was just—"

"I'm talking about when you fainted," Patsy interjected. "That man loves you."

Caroline couldn't stop her gaze from going to Jake. Though he was talking to Nathaniel, he turned, caught her gaze, and winked.

Right then, something struck her heart. Something amazing.

"Don't be afraid to love him in return," Patsy said.

Caroline wasn't afraid of loving him, but she was afraid. Afraid to hope that her dream could be coming true.

Only time would tell, yet as the day went on, and Jake was still his jovial self, she couldn't deny that her hopes were growing, as was anticipation about what would happen tonight. Would he suggest they make their marriage real?

When he suggested that they retire early, her heart was pounding so hard, she was breathless and filled with such exciting jitters that she could barely climb the stairs beside him.

"We have to be at the train station before dawn," he said, as they walked along the hallway toward the room where her belongings had been delivered earlier today. "It's going to be an early morning."

There wasn't a single part of her that wasn't tingling, or filled with a swirling heat, leaving her incapable of doing more than nodding.

They arrived at the bedroom door, and as he used one hand to turn the knob, open the door, his other one slid down from where it had been holding her elbow and wrapped around her fingers.

Feeling even more anticipation, she looked up at him. At his eyes, the way they gleamed, and at the smile on his lips. Her own tingled, itched, and she licked them.

His eyes never left her face, his smile never faltered as they stood there, silent and not moving. Then, he nodded and placed a tiny kiss on her forehead. "Good night, Caroline."

The air left her lungs with a rush, and the rest of her was awash with a deflated, sagging feeling. "Where are you sleeping?" The words were out before she had a chance to stop them, contemplate them.

"I'll be right down the hall," he said. "A maid will be up to help you out of your dress."

She'd forgotten she was literally sewn into her dress.

More than that, she'd forgotten all she knew about him, and she shouldn't have. Mere hours ago, his uncle had told the photographer that no one changes Jake's mind, and she herself had admitted that he was a man of his word. Why had she expected any part of their arrangement to change? Why had she allowed herself to hope? She knew better.

* * *

Jake stared at the trunk in his room, filled to the top with the clothes he'd purchased since arriving in England. It seemed like a waste to haul them back to Texas. The suits and pants were made for ballrooms and fancy dinners, not riding the range or branding cattle, or even going to town. Twisted Gulch was as opposite from London as a town could get.

It was making him think about Caroline.

Actually, she was all he thought about all the time. There wasn't a prettier gal around. He'd acknowledged that long before he'd pulled her onto his lap for their wedding picture. He probably shouldn't have done that. If he hadn't, he wouldn't be so tied up in knots. What he'd told that photographer was right. She was perfect. Perfect in every way.

She was not only pretty and all sweet smelling, but she was the epitome of an English lady. Prim and proper, soft-spoken, and so trusting.

That's what he'd seen in those big brown eyes last night while standing outside her room—trust. She trusted him. He'd almost broken that trust last night. Had almost gone back on his word of their marriage being in name only. The day—her fainting and how it had scared him, along with everything else—had made him want to go back on their agreement, and that couldn't happen. He couldn't, wouldn't ever do anything to hurt her, not on purpose.

He huffed out a sigh.

Texas, the ranch, Twisted Gulch, were all going to disappoint her, and so was he. He was going to be her greatest disappointment. He knew that deep down inside him and he didn't like that. He'd done his best to make sure he hadn't proven it over the past couple of weeks, but that had been his only job. It wouldn't be that way once they got home.

Actually, starting this morning, it would no longer be that way.

That left him feeling as if the weight of the world was crushing down on him.

A knock on the door had him dropping the lid of the trunk and latching the clasp before he set his saddlebags atop the trunk and granted permission to enter.

"Good morning, Master Simpson," the footman greeted.

"Morning," Jake replied, buckling his holster around his waist.

"Breakfast is being served in the dining room," the footman said. "We'll load your luggage in the carriage while you're eating."

"Thank you," Jake said, collecting his hat off the bed. It felt good to be wearing his old clothes, but he had to admit that they were the only things that hadn't changed since he'd left Texas. He might look the same on the outside as when he'd arrived, but he wasn't on the inside, and he wasn't overly confident that even arriving in Texas would change that.

It was early morning, still dark outside, so lights were lit in the hallway, and a line of light shone out from beneath Caroline's bedroom door. He'd made the right choice, sleeping separately last night, even though it had been as hard as hell to walk away from her. He'd never imagined being just friends with someone would be so hard.

The door opened right then, and she appeared, wearing a yellow dress and matching hat. Despite all he had on his mind, there was enough room to make him wonder if the sight of her would ever not make his breath catch. Just as quickly, he determined probably not. Nor would the time come that he didn't think about kissing her—or have thoughts of a few other things that pulling her onto his lap had ignited.

"Good morning," she said.

"Morning," he replied. "I hope you slept well."

Stepping into the hallway, she shook her head. "Yes, thank you. Although, I was afraid that I'd oversleep and kept waking myself up."

Jake cupped her elbow to escort her down the hallway. "There was no reason to worry. I wouldn't have left without you."

Her eyes glistened as she smiled at him. "I trust that you wouldn't have, but I wouldn't have wanted you waiting on me, either."

There was that trust again, striking him where it counted, because he wasn't even sure he could trust himself when it came to the feelings she kept causing to erupt inside him.

Breakfast was a quick affair, as was the trip to the train station. Although Edward had arrived at the London home last night—another one of Jake's reasons behind their early retirement—Jake had yet to see his cousin. He'd been absent at breakfast. Aunt Hilda had said that she and Uncle Oscar would travel with Edward in a separate carriage to the station, and true to her word, the three of them arrived while Jake and Caroline's trunks were being unloaded.

Seeing his cousin dressed in his English finery was suddenly a poignant reminder to Jake of all that he was taking Caroline away from. It wasn't just the social life that wouldn't be present in Texas. If he hadn't stopped her marriage to Edward, she'd have a life of nobility. He'd thought he was righting a wrong, but maybe his own righteousness had gone too far this time. Was it right of him to put Faith Drummond and her unborn child ahead of Caroline? Ultimately, that was what he'd done.

He'd never been one to second-guess his decisions, but found himself doing so in many ways. It didn't help that he was also battling himself over forbidden desires that just kept growing.

Final farewells were quick, and the sun was just beginning to cast the earth with dawn light when the train left the station. Jake sat next to Caroline, while Edward sat two rows ahead of them. Uncle Oscar had insisted that Edward wouldn't be any trouble, that he now fully understood one misstep would lead to disownment.

That might be true, but Jake wasn't going to take any chances. He had been angry with his cousin ever since Faith had shown up at the ranch, but by now he was beyond irritated. He was flat out mad, and tired. Tired of Edward's selfishness. How it had affected so many lives.

Jake's gaze shifted to Caroline, and concern rippled his spine. She'd lost the color from her face and her eyes were tightly closed. He reached over and touched her hand, causing her to jolt in her seat.

"It's all right," he whispered. Assuming she was distraught because of Edward, Jake added, "I won't let him bother you."

She shook her head. "It's not—" Drawing in a shaky breath, she said, "I haven't been on a train in a long time."

A wave of regret washed over him. He knew her past. Knew her parents had died in a train accident, yet, because he had one goal in mind—that of getting Edward to Texas—he hadn't taken any of her past tragedy into consideration. He released her hand and wrapped an arm around her shoulders, tugged her closer to his side. Ought he to tell her that she was fine and that nothing would happen? That wouldn't take her mind off the motion of the train. Deciding a distraction would be more helpful instead he said, "Tell me about your parents."

She looked at him with a frown.

"Please," he encouraged. "I want to know about them. What they were like. What your life was like with them."

A gentle smile formed on her lips as she said, "My mother was very pretty and was always smiling. Happy. She loved children. We were allowed to play with the children of our servants, and my mother would play tag and hide-and-seek with us. My father would, too." Her smile increased. "Like you, he had the ability to make an entire room break out in laughter. I remember riding on his back as he crawled around, pretending to be a horse, and how excited he was when I received a puppy at Christmastime."

Jake asked about the puppy, and anything else he could think of to keep her talking about her childhood and happy memories. He also answered her questions about his childhood, and practically before either of them noticed, the train ride ended.

"You kept me talking on purpose," she said as they exited the train. "So I wouldn't think about the train ride."

"I kept you talking because I was interested in knowing more about you." That was completely true. He had enjoyed learning about the happy times she'd had in her life, and felt a determination to make sure that she had more in store.

She shook her head, but her smile never faltered. "Thank you, either way. It made the trip enjoyable."

He agreed with that, other than the fact that he had been forced to keep, and still was keeping, one eye on Edward the entire time. The three of them shared a coach to the seaside, with barely a word spoken right up until they were shown to their cabin on the passenger ship.

Uncle Oscar had arranged the accommodations, and for the first time, Jake wondered if he should have enquired more about them. The cabin was spacious and far superior to what he'd experienced on the trip to England. There was a private bathing room, sitting room, and two bedrooms. One for Edward, and one for him and Caroline to share.

Edward loudly expressed his disapproval of the rooms, along with once again declaring his anger over not being allowed to bring his valet on the trip.

In no mood to hear more, Jake picked up the traveling bag Edward had dropped near the door and tossed it at his cousin. "It's about time you learned to dress yourself, and put away your own belongings."

Edward caught the bag and sneered. "I'm not some uncouth buffoon who needs nothing more than a single change of clothing in a saddlebag."

Not interested in taking the bait his cousin was throwing out, Jake simply glared at him until Edward entered his bedroom, then he smiled down at Caroline. "Would you care to take a look around the ship before she sets sail?"

Upon her nod, they exited the cabin, and once he'd closed the door behind them, he locked it.

"Will you lock him in the cabin the entire trip?" she asked.

Jake pocketed the key. "No. Once we are seaward, his behavior will determine how much freedom he has until we reach Galveston."

"What will happen then?"

They began walking along the corridor where others were entering doors and workers were delivering luggage. "After the wedding, we will take the train to the ranch," he replied.

"Wedding?"

He nodded. "Edward and Faith's wedding. I sent a cable when I decided to remain in England a bit longer than scheduled, asking Faith to meet us in Galveston." He was glad that he had done so, and that he'd received confirmation. Being done with Edward would be a considerable relief.

There was still the separate issue of the weight he'd felt this morning, however. It had grown all day, and the act of leaving England behind was playing havoc on his mind. There was only one bed. One for them to share. Because they were married. The how and why their marriage had come about was taking second place in mind, eclipsed by thoughts about the acts that were normally performed by husbands and wives. His desires had gone beyond kissing Caroline, and the two of them sharing a bed was sure to make fighting them even harder.

"Edward doesn't know about his wedding, does he?"

"No, he does not," Jake admitted. "But don't let that worry you."

There was a glimmer in her eyes as she looked up at him. "It's not worrying me. I trust you have everything under control. You always do, and that amazes me. I've never met someone as confident as you."

He smiled and nodded, all the while knowing there

were plenty of things he wasn't very confident about right now. Not with the way she was looking up at him. He wanted her to be able to depend on him for anything. Everything, and that right there might be the biggest challenge of his life.

Caroline's mind was only half on the ship. It was more luxurious than she'd expected. Actually, she hadn't known what to expect. The accommodations were utterly lavish compared to what she was used to, but there was one significant thing consuming her thoughts. That being the single bed in their cabin.

After her disappointment last night, the one that had kept her up half the night, she shouldn't be thinking about sharing a bed with Jake again, yet here she was. He'd made things clear right from the beginning—this was not a real marriage—and thinking any of that would change was foolish. One bed didn't mean anything. Not to him, and she had to stop thinking that it did to her.

That was hard, though. Over the past few weeks, she'd grown accustomed to him touching her—holding her hand, or elbow, touching her back, dancing with him, and other such simple actions. *Growing accustomed* was an understatement. She *enjoyed* him touching her. Enjoyed simply standing or walking beside him. He made her feel safe and protected in ways she'd never felt before. That feeling had increased tenfold during the train ride, when he'd wrapped an arm around her and held her close to his side. The security of his arm around her had made her fears subside and allowed her to remember happier times. Remember things that she didn't ever want to forget again.

He was making her feel that way again, as they examined the ship. The upper and lower decks, the dining rooms, sitting areas, library and music rooms. The glistening wooden walls and floors, beautiful furnishings, and spacious rooms seemed more suited to a London mansion than an ocean liner.

He also introduced her to Captain Goldman, a middle-aged man with dark hair and brown eyes, who was happy to have them sailing upon his ship to Galveston. It was clear the man had been informed in advance of their voyage, and he offered his assistance in making sure the trip was enjoyable.

They were still on the upper deck, surrounded by other passengers, when the ship left port, and despite all she was leaving behind, Caroline didn't experience an iota of remorse as the shore of England grew farther away. She questioned that, for she would miss her family and friends, including the ones she'd recently acquired.

As if he was reading her mind, Jake encircled her shoulders with one arm. "You'll be back, I promise."

The reason he'd agreed to marry her returned full force, making her feel guilty for once again letting it slip away into a crevice of her mind. "With Nellie," she replied.

"Yes."

She withheld a sigh. Not because of Nellie—in all honesty, she was looking forward to meeting her new sister-in-law—but because she'd let hope sneak in when she shouldn't have. "Will you ever return?"

"I imagine I will," he replied.

"For Nellie?"

"Yes, and for myself," he said. "It was good to reconnect with so many people." He winked at her. "And to see your uncle's inventions. As an investor, I'll need to keep abreast of those."

Caroline pinched her lips together at the onslaught of

feelings she had for this man. He'd awakened so many things inside her, not least of which was a sense of freedom she'd never known. However, she was also concerned. "I fear your investments may be a waste of funds."

"They've already paid off," he said.

Confused by that answer, she asked, "How so?"

He dipped his head and kissed her temple. "I got you."

She felt a tiny whimper in the back of her throat at the touch of his lips and the meaning of his statement. It was true in a sense, but she had a longing for it to be accurate in a deeper, more profound way.

Nothing more was said between them as they stood where they were, watching England get farther and farther away. Caroline knew something was happening to her, or perhaps it had already happened. She had thought she was longing for a whole different life, for the things she'd had as a child, and now, she was wondering if all that longing had been for one very simple thing.

Love.

Had she fallen in love with Jake? It wouldn't be that much of a surprise. He was extraordinary in so many ways. So honorable and committed and likable, and well, lovable.

That was all true, but the implications were still enough to worry her. If she had fallen in love with him—even if she hadn't yet and did so in the future—that wouldn't mean he'd ever love her in return. Nor was there any reason that he should, either. Patsy must not have seen what she'd thought she'd seen.

"I suspect it's safe to go let our prisoner out of his cell," Jake said.

Taking a final glance at the now-faraway land, she nodded. "I suspect so."

She wasn't worried about Edward. He might make things more difficult than necessary, but she was convinced that Jake could handle any efforts Edward put forth to thwart their arrival in Texas or in marrying Faith. From the moment she'd heard about Faith, pregnant with Edward's child, she'd felt Jake was completely in the right in making Edward return and take responsibility for his actions.

They made their way across the deck and through the mazes of stairs and galley ways to their cabin. It was an odd situation to be in, traveling with a man she'd almost married and the man she *had* married. The differences between the two men were as stark as her feelings toward each one of them. Edward had only ever seen her as a pawn, and she had no reason to believe that had changed. In many ways, she was as much of a pawn in her marriage to Jake as she would have been in the one to Edward; however, to her, things were very different in many ways.

That led her to another thought. If she didn't want to be seen as a pawn, she had to stop acting like one. She had to become more confident, and committed, and... well, more like a lady of standing, just like she'd had to do back in London.

She felt her shoulders squaring as a sense of dignity rose up in her. There were many reasons for her to be confident. Besides what she'd learned from the other ladies in London, she was married to the most handsome, most confident, and righteous man on earth.

Jake glanced down at her, and she not only returned his smile, but she looped her arm around his. Feeling a need to come up with an explanation, she said, "I never imagined ships could be this large and smooth. It doesn't even feel like we're moving."

"You might feel it more at night," he said. "If you're a light sleeper, you might sense a swaying."

"Did you feel it on your way trip to England?"

"Yes, but I was on a smaller cargo ship, and sleeping in a hammock."

Trying not to think about sharing a bed with him, she asked, "What about when you were a child and traveled to America? Was that on a ship like this?"

"Very much like this one, and there were other children on it. We formed friendships and spent nearly all day, every day, exploring the ship from bow to stern and top to bottom."

"That's how you know so much about this one." She had wondered, because he had seemed very knowledgeable during their exploration of the ship.

He nodded, then chuckled. "I could show you some of the places we got kicked out of as kids."

"What places were those?"

"Mainly the baggage areas, but we also got shooed out of the food storage area and the engine room."

"Good heavens, you were everywhere."

"We were young boys and cooped up on a ship for days on end." Arriving at their door, he paused to retrieve the key from his pocket. "We had to find something to keep us busy."

"That's sound like an excuse for mischief."

He smirked as he inserted the key in the lock. "You sound just like the girls did back then."

Giggling, she playfully slapped his arm. "They were right, and so am I."

They were both laughing when they entered the room, and encountered a red-faced Edward.

Chapter Eleven

Edward's tirade didn't last long. Caroline didn't know what he'd said or what Jake had said, as she'd excused herself and shut the bedroom door while they'd still been staring at each other. It might have been a cowardly act, but she wasn't overly concerned about that.

She had escaped any ties to Edward—he was not her husband—so didn't feel the need to witness any of his drama. Furthermore, she had full confidence that Jake didn't need her help. A pit formed in her stomach. In all actuality, he would probably never need her help. He only claimed to need help with Nellie because she'd suggested it first. She realized that because the Jake she now knew would never admit that he needed help, let alone ask for it. He'd simply been being nice to her, which was the other thing she knew for sure—he was simply that nice. And kind. And lovable.

There was that word again. Love. Needing something to get it out of her thoughts, she opened the trunk she'd kept in the cabin for the voyage to unpack a few things. It sat against the paneled wall, along with his saddlebags and her traveling bag. On top of everything else, and wrapped in paper, was a package that she hadn't put inside the trunk. A note atop was from Hilda, and simply stated, "These arrived after breakfast. I asked Winston to put them in your trunk. Love to both of you."

Caroline's fingers shook as she carefully removed the paper and found two pictures, ornately framed in silver, both of her sitting on Jake's lap. In one, they were looking at the camera, and smiling, somewhat. It was the second one, where they were looking at each other, that made her breath catch and her stomach flutter.

Lowering herself onto the bed, she continued to stare at the picture. If she didn't know better, she'd believe the two people in the picture were deeply enchanted with each other.

Would it be wrong of her to secretly hope that the day would come when this picture would be true? Wrong of her to want love?

Yes, she determined, it would be, because that was not what either of them had agreed to. It would be unfair to expect something different now. Furthermore, allowing herself to hope for such a thing would merely cause disappointment and dissatisfaction in a life that already had the potential to be extraordinary. She was on her way to an entirely new country, a part of the world she'd never imagined seeing, and opportunities she'd only dreamed of. Those were the things she needed to concentrate on, and be grateful for, not some silly hopes that Jake would want their marriage to become a real one, complete with love.

The door opened, and as she glanced up to see Jake entering the room with his signature smile, her heart thudded against her breastbone as if it had already filled itself with silly hopes.

"Edward is exploring the ship," Jake said, while unbuckling his gun belt.

"I'm sure he'll enjoy that," she said, trying her best to sound normal instead of as breathless as she felt.

He grinned while setting his belt, with the gun still in its holster, on the only chair in the room. "I suspect he will. What do you have there?"

She held out the picture, and then quickly picked up the other one for him to see both. "They arrived after breakfast, while we were preparing to leave, and Lady Hilda had Winston place them in my trunk."

He took both pictures, and chuckled while looking at them. "Well, now, I'd say that's a fair likeness of us, don't you agree?"

"Yes, I would agree," she replied.

Jake skirted around the bed to reach the small table by its head and set down both pictures there, utilizing the stands on the back of the frames to make them stand up. "How's the bed? Soft? Hard?"

She pressed on the mattress with one hand, testing it, even though she was still sitting on it. "Soft?" It wasn't feather soft, but it wasn't board hard, either.

He pressed a hand on the mattress. "Not bad." As he removed his hand, he said, "I suspect we should talk about that."

"About what?" she asked.

The room wasn't very large, so he merely needed to take a single step back to lean against the wall. "The bed. I'm not able to provide you with one of your own. From the looks of the number of passengers, it would be difficult to find another room, but even if there was one available, there's still the dilemma of Edward. I don't trust him to have his own cabin. Nor would I want you to be alone in one, and I wouldn't feel comfortable leaving you and

Edward sharing this one, so, that leaves us with this one bed to share."

"I could sleep on the sofa in the sitting room," she offered.

"No. Edward would enjoy that too much."

It took her a moment to comprehend what he meant by that. He didn't want Edward to think they weren't sleeping together as man and wife. "We *are* married," she said, then flinched because that didn't sound like the right thing to have said.

"I know, so we really have one option. To share the bed. I don't want that to make you uncomfortable. I can assure you that all that will happen is sleeping."

It was a good thing that she hadn't let herself believe in silly notions, because he'd just made it clear he hadn't changed his mind. Their marriage would never be a real one. "I never thought otherwise," she said, and repeated it silently as a reminder to herself.

He nodded and slapped the wall before he pushed off from it. "All right, then, the midday meal should be served soon. Should we go to the dining room?"

"Yes, that would be nice," she said, again hoping she sounded normal and not as dejected as she felt.

If he had the ability to kick himself in the ass, Jake would be doing so now. He'd always preferred to face challenges head-on, and thought that was what he'd been doing when pointing out the bed they would be sharing. He'd also, just as foolishly, thought that tackling the topic would get the pit out of his stomach. The one that was there because he didn't trust himself when it came to being in that bed next to Caroline.

He had no choice but to make damn sure nothing happened in that bed expect sleeping. What had he expected? That she'd say she wanted more to happen? That hadn't been a part of their pact, and that wouldn't change. He shouldn't want it to change. She hadn't even seen his ranch yet—which was sure to be a disappointment and the reason she'd want to return to England as soon as possible.

That was another place he would have to think about beds. There was an extra bedroom, where guests slept, and another one that was used for storage and such. He'd have to have that cleaned out, and buy another bed, which wouldn't be a big issue, but having others know he was married and not sleeping with his wife might be.

These were problems he'd never have imagined that he would have. How could he have? He'd accepted the idea of not getting married after Eloise. It would have been easier if he'd stuck to that decision. The problem was that he'd never taken such a quick liking to anyone as he had Caroline. Nor had he had the overwhelming desire to protect someone the way he did her. Not even when it came to righting Edward's wrong against Faith. His ranch and livelihood had been a major concern there, but when it came to Caroline, his concern was focused on her, and how he'd compromised her future by stopping her marriage to Edward.

It was a convoluted mess. One that left him with no option but to focus on making the most of Caroline's future, for in the end, she truly deserved happiness. He wanted her to have that, have the happiness that she'd had once, when she'd been a child.

As they entered the dining room, Jake wasn't surprised that they were greeted by Captain Goldman. Upon meeting the man earlier, Jake had determined that the captain took great pride in his ship, and in his abilities to manage what was essentially a city on the sea.

"Mr. Simpson," the captain greeted, along with a welcoming nod to Caroline. "Mrs. Simpson. Allow me to show you to your table."

"Thank you," Jake replied while placing a hand on the small of Caroline's back, to escort her forward through the already-crowded room. The tables, covered with white linen cloths were surrounded by people dressed in much the same finery as they'd worn during the balls and dinner parties that he'd attended while in London. That made him think about his trunk full of clothing, and how he might have been too eager to don his working clothes this morning and send his trunk to the luggage compartment on the ship.

"I had the pleasure of meeting your cousin," Captain Goldman said.

Jake wasn't surprised that the captain was the first person that Edward had sought. Nor did he believe that Edward wouldn't have taken it upon himself to make demands on his behalf.

"I assure you, sir, that every instruction the Duke of Collingsworth requested will be followed during the voyage."

"I have no doubt of that, Captain," Jake replied, having already informed Edward that he would not find an ally upon the ship. "I also trust you'll inform me of any difficulties that arise."

"Immediately, sir." They arrived at a table where six other people, three couples, it appeared, were already seated. "Allow me to make introductions."

Jake listened and responded to the introduction of each of the table's occupants, but was more focused on Caroline, and how perfectly she embodied the role of sophisticated lady that he'd watched her become back in London. She was poised and friendly, and easily entered conversations with the others at the table. The pit in his stomach grew into a solid rock at the reminder of all the social opportunities he was taking away from her.

The meal was most likely delicious, yet what he consumed might as well have been sawdust and though he answered the many questions asked of him about America, Texas, and his ranch, he didn't find the enjoyment in talking about such things as he usually did.

However, there was one thing that he did take a small amount of amusement from. That was the narrowing glare of disdain coming from an adjacent table where Edward was seated among six other men. They were all notably older, and not the sort that Edward would usually associate with, and his cousin had clearly found yet another source of dissatisfaction. It was uncharacteristically petty for Jake to find delight in that, but he couldn't stop himself from smiling at his cousin, while resting a hand on the back of Caroline's chair.

His earlier conversation with her was swirling in his mind. Nothing would happen in their bed, but he wouldn't allow Edward the satisfaction of knowing that their marriage was anything less than the real thing. That could prove to be a self-inflicted punishment because his desires were already creating a fierce battle inside him... But he'd always been a man of his word, and would continue to be.

"Would you mind if I stopped in the library before going back to our cabin?" Caroline asked after the meal had ended and they were taking their leave of the dining room.

"Not at all," he replied. "Perhaps I'll find a book to occupy my time."

She giggled slightly. "Instead of exploring areas that you shouldn't?"

"That wouldn't be as much fun as it once was." Teasingly, he lifted a brow and grinned at her. "Unless you'd want to join me."

A shine flashed in her eyes as she stifled another giggle. "No, thank you."

Leaning close, he whispered, "Afraid we'll get caught?"

"Yes."

The pinkening of her cheeks was as charming as her honesty, and the energy between them was heating his blood, which was already hot enough, yet he asked, "But the idea is exciting, isn't it?"

She covered her smile with a hand while shaking her head. "Of course not."

"Liar."

Looking up at him with shimmering eyes, she asked, "Why is that? Why do things that shouldn't, excite us?"

"Human nature," he replied. It was also human nature for him to be thinking about kissing her again. The desire hit as unexpectedly as stumbling upon a rattlesnake. Except the snake had a rattle that it would shake in warning. Jake's desires didn't have a warning. They just struck, and it was getting harder and harder to ignore them.

A silence fell between them as they made their way to the library. Jake used what seemed to be endless shelves of books to get his mind and desires under control. There were volumes covering every subject and novels full of imaginative tales and worlds. He chose a book on agriculture dedicated to the growing of wheat, particularly the Russian winter wheat that was becoming extremely successful on the plains of Kansas. Focusing on his ranch, on advancing it in all aspects, was sure to get him back into the right state of mind.

Caroline had chosen a book as well, and as they left the library, he asked, "Would you care to find a chair on the upper deck? The light will be better for reading there." Their cabin had portholes in each room, but the next few days were going to be a challenge and he was cautioning himself when it came to spending too much time alone with her in the rooms. Night time was going to be enough of a test.

"Yes," she answered. "I'd like that."

By the second chapter of the book she'd chosen, Caroline found herself drawing the pages closer to her face. Not due to the lack of light or eye strain from reading. It was because she didn't want anyone else to see what she was reading. By the title, *Rules of Being a Lady*, she'd assumed it would be a book to teach her more about being a lady.

Rather than being an instructional book, it was a novel about a lady who was having an affair with her gardener, and by the second chapter, they were, well…acting out their affair.

In that instance, it could also be considered an instructional book due to the explicit descriptions. Caroline glanced around, hoping that besides not seeing the words she was reading, no one was witnessing the heat she felt in her cheeks.

Others were sitting in the cane chairs spread out on a section of the deck complete with attendants offering drinks and refreshments, some in conversation, and others like her and Jake were reading. For a splinter of a moment, she considered closing her book and returning it to the library. Yet what could only be described as an uncontrollable—shameless, even—curiosity was simply too strong for her to do that.

As discreetly as possibly, she allowed her gaze to once again settle on the pages of the book, where Lady Aurora Burchett and the gardener, Daniel Fox, were removing one another's clothing in the garden cottage. Lady Burchett's older brother, who was her guardian and would never approve of her falling in love with a servant, had left for Paris in the first chapter, and wouldn't return for four weeks. Lady Burchett was convinced he would be bringing home a man for her to wed, and therefore felt her time with Daniel would soon come to an end.

Caroline recognized Lady Burchett's plight in Chapter One, so it would have been easy for her to sympathize, even if Daniel didn't remind her quite so strongly of Jake.

Soon, though, she was completely engrossed in the pages for reasons other than sympathy. She knew that her access to books had been quite limited, but even so, she'd never have imagined there were books with such specifics about...*desires*, and intimacy between a man and woman. The descriptions of how and where Daniel and Aurora touched and kissed each other had more than Caroline's face feeling hot.

The passages were shockingly scandalous, yet she read every word, not wanting to miss a single thing about any of it.

"That must be an interesting book."

The sound of Jake's voice startled her enough that she pressed the book to her chest, afraid of dropping it.

He laughed. "Your nose has been stuck between those pages for over two hours."

Her heart was still racing so hard she couldn't speak. Aurora and Daniel were no longer in the cottage; they were now in a field several miles from the house, where Her Ladyship had ridden out to meet him, intent upon taking advantage of every spare moment they could find to be together. Daniel was still reminding her strongly of Jake, and now, having read certain things, she fully understood why—because of the feelings and sensation that he'd evoked in her since they'd met. The fluttering in her stomach, the rapid beating of her heart, the heat that swirled in the deepest, most intimate part of her— that was how Daniel made Aurora feel. That was why she was imagining herself in the heroine's place, with Jake playing her Daniel… Simply imagining it, or hoping it would someday come to pass? There was a difference, and looking at Jake now, she understood that difference.

"What's the name of it?" he asked.

She blinked and swallowed, because she had to answer. Had to push past the hope. "*Ru*—" She cleared her throat. "*Rules of Being a Lady*."

He lifted a brow, then shook his head. "I'm glad you're enjoying it."

"I am." She had to look away because the heat rushed back into her cheeks. Espying others on the deck—some sitting, some standing, others walking about—she felt reality slowly creep back into her mind. The book was simply a story. No matter how realistic it seemed, it had nothing to do with her and her life. Accepting that, she was able to turn back to Jake. "Have you finished your book?"

"Yes."

"What was it about?"

"Growing wheat."

"Do you grow wheat on your ranch?"

"The ranch is a cattle operation, and we grow feed for them, but we do have additional acreage that could be used to grow wheat. That's something I've been considering for a while."

Wanting to know all she could about the ranch, she asked more questions, engaging them in a conversation that took her mind off Aurora and Daniel, and lasted until they left the deck.

After Jake returned his book to the library and she put hers inside her trunk, where no one but she knew where it was, they spent the rest of the afternoon exploring more of the ship—only the accessible areas—and conversing with the people aboard, including those who had been at their table at lunch.

They were seated with the same group for the evening meal. It wasn't until that meal ended and the pair of them had returned to their cabin that Caroline was able to retrieve her book. The need to know more about Aurora and Daniel had been eating at her ever since she'd tucked the book away in her trunk. The rules of being a lady that Aurora pointed out in the book included who she could and couldn't love, could and couldn't marry, and Caroline was hoping that Aurora would find a way around those rules.

Jake had picked up several newspapers and while he settled in a chair in the sitting room to read those, she sat on the sofa, soaking in every word of her book. Even though she was tired from rising so early and the day's travels, she couldn't stop reading.

There were more vivid scenes of intimacies that had her blushing—particularly because Jake was sitting nearby—but she also had a real sense of anxiety over what was going to happen when Aurora's brother returned.

That happened in the last chapter, and had Caroline blinking away tears when Daniel was found beneath a fallen tree, crushed to death, though he'd also been shot. The rules of being a lady didn't allow Aurora to question anything, nor to mourn as she quickly married Lord Debois, the man her brother insisted upon, and moved to Paris.

Edward entered the room just as Caroline finished the last page, and she quickly took her leave of the room. Once again, she hid the book in her trunk while she took out her nightgown, one of the new ones made of light blue cotton with short sleeves and tiny white buttons from the waist to the neckline.

She climbed into bed and pulled the covers up to her chin. The emotions stirred up by the tragic ending of the book collided suddenly with the knowledge that Jake would soon join her in the bed. That also brought forth the more…intimate sections of the book, things that seemed as astonishing as the ending. Could they be true, or were they, like the ending, simply a made-up story?

Still, the story seemed so real that her heart was truly breaking for Aurora and Daniel, and once again she had to blink away tears.

When the latch of the door clicked at the knob being turned, she flipped onto her side and faced the wall. The table was on her side of the bed, and she had to close her eyes at the sight of their wedding pictures sitting there. It felt as if they were mocking her. She began to wish she'd never read Aurora's book.

There was barely a sound before the light on the wall was extinguished and she felt the mattress move. Jake weighed more than her, so as soon as he climbed on the bed, the mattress dipped to such an extent that she had to grab the edge to stay on her side rather than rolling downhill toward him.

"You don't need to worry about Edward," Jake said.

She tightened her grip on the mattress. "I'm not worried about Edward." She wasn't, but a thought formed. Edward could have been her Lord Debois. Or would that be Jake, because he was the one she'd married? That caused more confusing thoughts to circle her mind.

"Well," Jake said. "I'm sorry he makes you feel uncomfortable. It will only be a few more days."

"He doesn't bother me. I didn't leave the room because of him. I'd finished my book." She opened her eyes and the first thing she saw was the way that the moonlight shining in through the porthole was illuminating their wedding pictures with a golden glow. Add in the rush of memories from the book, and her eyes started stinging again. "Daniel died," was the only excuse she could give to explain the tiny sob that escaped.

The bed shifted so hard she almost lost her grip on the mattress, and grabbed it with her other hand as well.

Leaning over her, Jake asked, "Who's Daniel?"

A wave of emotions washed over her, too many to acknowledge, but one was embarrassment. "A character in the book," she answered, without looking at him.

He let out an audible sigh before he asked, "Why are you holding on to the mattress like that?"

"Because you weigh more than me. If I let go, I'll crowd you."

The mattress shifted again as he lay back down, then an arm slid beneath her shoulders. "Let go of the mattress. You won't crowd me."

"Yes, I will. I'll roll into you."

"You can't hold on to the edge of the mattress all night." He lifted up the covers. "Come on. Let go and roll over."

Just as with the photographer, she knew Jake wouldn't give in, so she released her hold on the mattress. Just as she'd known would happen, her body slid into the dip in the mattress caused by him.

"Now roll over," he said, still holding the covers up so she had room to move. "Get comfortable. I know you're tired. You've been yawning since suppertime."

That was true, and he had to be tired, too. She rolled onto her back and looked at him.

He grinned and tucked the covers under her chin. "There, now, that wasn't so hard, was it?"

"No." What was hard was controlling her thoughts while lying next to him under the covers. She could feel the heat of his body from her toes to her head.

"And you aren't crowding me, there's plenty of room." His arm was still beneath her and he cupped her shoulder with his hand. "Now, tell me about this Daniel character."

More sensations flooded her system. "He was a friend of the lady in the book, and a tree fell on him. Crushed him."

"That sounds like a sad ending."

She sighed. "It was."

He glanced at her. "Everyone dies in *Moby Dick*, except for Ish and the fish."

That made her grin. "You're right, but I don't think I want to talk about that book while on a ship."

He gave her shoulder a squeeze. "Good point. I thought the book you were reading was about rules for ladies."

"There was that, too." Needing to change the subject, she asked, "Did you read anything interesting in the newspapers?"

"A wedding announcement for us."

"That was in last week's paper."

"Some were older than a week, pushing a month, but there were others from other districts. Back home the papers have reports from Washington and foreign countries, real estate and cattle sales, grain prices, and what new goods arrived at the stores, but here, it's all about social functions and the royal family."

The warmth that had been disturbing earlier was now like a cocoon and she was having a hard time keeping her eyes open. Giving in to the need, she let her lids flutter closed. "Were they doing anything interesting?"

"Not interesting enough to stay up talking about it." He tugged her a little closer. "Time to go to sleep."

The best she could muster up was a small mumble in response as she rolled onto her side and rested her cheek on his shoulder.

Chapter Twelve

Jake eased his way out of the bed as dawn was breaking, careful to not wake Caroline, just as he'd done for nearly week. He was both grateful and sorrowful that the ship would be arriving in Galveston today. The bed was lumpy and bowed in the middle, yet he'd looked forward to climbing into it each night. There was a sweet satisfaction in having her snuggled up next to his side, with her cheek resting on his shoulder as she slept.

It was torturous, too. So torturous. At times it took all he had to remember why he couldn't act on the desires that lived inside him day in and day out. He'd become as smitten with his young wife as everyone else who met her. She'd made friends on the ship as quickly as she had in London, and every ship employee, from Captain Goldman down to the cabin maids, was quick to ask if there was anything she needed. He understood why. He was just as eager to please her.

That overwhelming desire to please her was also what kept him able to keep his other desires under control. The ache never went away, and there were times when his dreams were so vivid and real, he awoke throbbing and gasping for air. In those moments, he'd console himself by wrapping both arms around her and holding her tight as she slept.

It was a hell of a position to be in. Married to the prettiest gal on earth and unable to touch her. Well, he did touch her. Every chance he got. Whether it was holding her hand or elbow, or laying his hand on the small of her back. He kissed her temple a time or two as well, and her cheek, because sometimes he just couldn't stop himself.

He tried being mad at himself for getting married, for going to England, and other things that had led up to the situation he was in, but it didn't help, because truth was, he liked being married to her. Liked introducing her as his wife, liked spending time with her, talking and laughing, and just sitting next to each other while reading or visiting with others. She'd become a part of his life and he couldn't imagine not having her in it, even while knowing that in time, that would happen.

After seeing the ranch, discovering the isolated life it provided, she'd be ready to take Nellie and head back to London posthaste.

That was weighing heavy on him, too. He hadn't wanted Nellie to leave for a few years yet, and knew why. He was selfish. Nellie had been his only family and he'd wanted to keep her with him as long as possible. For her sake, he'd always thought. Now, he was wondering if it was because he didn't want to be alone.

There were plenty of others at the ranch, but she'd been his only family for a long time. Caroline was now a part of his family, and he didn't want to be parted from her, either.

Glancing at the bed, where Caroline was still sleeping, he let his gaze settle on the perfection of her face. She wasn't just pretty. She was beautiful, and poised. A perfect English lady. He'd never known he was so selfish, but she had proven he was. He also knew that he wasn't the English lord she deserved. He'd considered himself an American cowboy for years, and this trip had confirmed that. He might not have been born that way, but it was who he'd become. He let out an unsettled sigh and turned to the door.

Having put on his pants and shirt, he carried his hat, socks, and boots out of the bedroom, and after quietly closing the bedroom door, he sat down on the sofa to put them on. Caroline would sleep for at least another hour, and as had happened the past few days, Edward would be in bed for several hours beyond that.

Not today.

Jake rose and strode to his cousin's bedroom door and pushed it open. Edward was sprawled across the bed on his stomach. One foot was hanging over the edge of the mattress and Jake slapped it with his hat. "Get up."

"Why?" Edward mumbled.

Other than seeing one another a few times a day throughout the ship, he and Edward had barely spoken during the voyage. "We need to talk."

Edward huffed out a breath, but threw aside the covers. Jake left the room and waited by the cabin door as Edward got dressed. Once that happened, he led his cousin into the gangway, quietly closing the door behind them.

"I don't know if I should pity you or respect you," Edward said.

Jake shrugged offhandedly, not caring what his cousin thought as they walked toward the stairway.

"I know one thing," Edward said. "I'd be spending a lot more time in bed with my wife than you are, and doing things besides sleeping."

Jake shot a glare at his cousin.

"Don't deny it," Edward said. "You're wrung tighter than a watch spring, and I've seen the way you strip her naked with your eyes."

Jake couldn't deny either accusation, nor was he going to argue them. "You'll have your own wife soon enough."

Edward made a huffing sound. "I know we'll be arriving in Galveston today. There was no reason to wake me and tell me that."

"Faith is in Galveston," Jake said.

Pausing midstep, Edward said, "You said she was at your ranch."

Jake kept climbing the stairs. "She was, until I sent her a cable to meet us in Galveston."

Edward made a hissing sound as he caught up at the top of the steps.

"You have no one to blame but yourself for your current position," Jake pointed out.

"So I've been told."

"Faith is a good woman."

"She's beautiful," Edward said, "but she's also…"

"A wildcat," Jake said. "One you won't be able to control like you thought you could Caroline."

"I never wanted to control anyone. Never wanted to marry anyone, either. I had a damn good life."

"One where you didn't have to worry about anyone except yourself."

"There was nothing wrong with that. I'm young. Have years before I need to settle down."

They arrived at the deck, where the sun was a golden globe on the water-filled horizon. Jake walked to the nearest railing and leaned against it. "Did you not inherit a single thing from your parents?" he asked. "Do you really think it wasn't wrong to expect Caroline to marry you and look the other way while you continued your affair with the Countess Halsbury?"

"I was *forced* to find a bride."

"What was your intention for when Halsbury dies?"

"Dies? He's not dying, he just can't perform. Can't give the countess what she wants." Edward let out a low whistle. "Besides wanting it, she knows how to please a man."

Jake shook his head as he stared at his cousin. "You can't be that gullible."

"There's nothing gullible about it."

Shifting to lean a hip against the railing, Jake crossed his arms. "You weren't her first affair, but once she got her claws in you, she slowly began poisoning her husband, with every intention of moving her social status from countess to duchess as soon as he dies."

Edward stiffened, then shook his head. "That's not true."

"You could have learned about it, if you'd cared about anyone besides yourself. It most likely will be old news by the time you return to London, because what I just told you will be confirmed and dealt with accordingly."

"What did you do?"

"Merely let my suspicions be known so that Faith wouldn't be in any danger, as I sincerely believe Caroline would have been," Jake answered. "You having a wife wouldn't have stopped the countess any more than her having a husband did."

Jake couldn't be sure that Edward was shocked, but his cousin certainly appeared to be unsettled.

"I wouldn't have let anything happen to Caroline," Edward said, with a hint of chagrin in his tone. "I— Well, I've come to realize what an innocent she was, and how gentle and kind she is."

It almost sounded as though the information had shaken Edward to his senses, at least a little. Jake could only hope so, yet he still had more points to make. "She is all of that," he said. "And more. She is also mine. Mine to protect, and I will do so at all costs, as you should do for Faith. If you have any hope, any ambition of someday becoming the Duke of Collingsworth, it's time to change your ways. Time to recognize what you have been jeopardizing, and put that all behind you as you move forward, into the future."

Edward's chest puffed, but he said nothing as he turned and stared out to sea.

Jake left Edward standing there, and wished he knew some similarly sage advice to give himself when it came to his life, his future.

As they were leaving the ship, Caroline couldn't help but think about the book she'd returned to the library this morning. She had reread many parts of it the past few days, but couldn't explain why. Was it because she was hoping stronger than ever that someday she and Jake might have a real marriage? Might they share the scandalous acts that Aurora and Daniel had? Or was she hoping to build up enough resilience to accept her life, accept the rules, as Aurora had done after Daniel's death?

Was sleeping next to Jake, with his arms around her and her head resting on his shoulders, all she would ever have? That alone was remarkable. More than remarkable. It was so very wonderful in many ways, but it didn't quell the desires that danced inside her day and night. Nor did it relieve a tension that lived inside her so strongly that there were times she feared she might burst.

The sleeping arrangement had created a connection between them, and a comfort. She felt no inhibitions about plucking a piece of her hair off his chest while they were lying in bed, or in leaning against him when they were walking along one of the decks and he'd whisper something to her. The closeness she felt toward him gave her an increasing level of confidence, too. It was impossible not to feel a sense of security when he was beside her, nor a sense of pride in being his wife.

It was also impossible not to feel a sense of longing. She wanted to feel his lips upon hers, and so many of the other things that Aurora had felt with Daniel.

She couldn't stop herself from glancing up at him as they left the ship to walk along the massive dock to take them to the shore. He caught her gaze and winked at her.

Her heart quickened as he often caused it to do. She was wearing a dress she hadn't worn before. A lovely gown made of lilac-colored silk, with a square neckline and three scalloped layers of skirts over a lacy underlayer. A small-brimmed, silk hat that matched the dress was pinned to her hair. She'd become more adept at fashioning her hair in more than a simple bun. Like how Aurora's hair was described in the book, she often left a few corkscrews of hair to frame her face. After the first time Jake had twirled one of those corkscrews with a finger, she'd felt excited, believing he liked it as much as Daniel had proclaimed to like Aurora's curls.

A loud, quick whistle pulled her out of her thoughts, and she looked toward the end of the dock, where other passengers were already making their way onto the shoreline.

Jake lifted a hand and waved. His actions made her glance between him and the shoreline again, trying to determine who he was waving at.

"That's Faith," he explained, and glanced over his shoulder at Edward, who was following behind them.

Caroline kept her gaze forward, on the dark-haired woman, who was wearing an attractive gown of yellow and white, and had both hands on her hips. Caroline swallowed at the sudden dryness of her mouth. She couldn't say what caused a bout of nervousness, but it was there, right in the pit of her stomach.

Faith's gaze bounced between her and Jake, and settled on Edward for an extended length of time as they walked closer to where she stood.

"Jake," Faith said with a snap in her voice as they stopped before her.

He gave her a nod, before he said, "Allow me to introduce my wife, Caroline."

"Hello," Caroline said, with nerves still churning inside her. Faith was nearly as tall as Jake, and with her hands still on her hips, her stance wasn't a welcoming one.

But the quick smile she gave Caroline was friendly. "Well, aren't you a cute little thing," she said. "It's right nice to meet you. Jake here is a good man." Her smile disappeared as she looked past them. "Unlike some I know."

"Hello, Faith," Edward said.

"Let's wait over there," Jake whispered.

Caroline was more than willing to do just that, especially when she heard Faith tell Edward that she had every right to plug him with her six-shooter.

"Mr. Simpson?"

"Yes," Jake answered a short, balding man who stepped forward to greet them.

The man held out a hand. "Adam Tucker. Mr. Drummond sent me to collect you. If you have your luggage vouchers, I will see that it is collected and delivered to the hotel."

"Thank you," Jake replied. "This is my wife, Caroline."

After saying hello to the man, Caroline forced herself to watch as Jake pulled slips of paper from his vest pocket, instead of glancing behind her toward Edward and Faith.

"I'll give these to Raymond," Mr. Tucker said, "and then show you to the carriage."

Caroline glanced up at Jake as Mr. Tucker turned to hand the tickets to another man who had stepped closer.

Jake wrapped an arm around her shoulders and tugged her close to his side as they began walking, following Mr. Tucker. "Looks like Faith's father is in town for the wedding."

"It does appear that way." Caroline couldn't say she'd formed a great fondness for Edward, but she did feel a bit sorry for him, even though she knew it was past time for him to accept responsibility for his actions.

The wedding was a brief ceremony that took place that evening in a private room at the hotel. Leroy Drummond was a tall, gray-haired man who had been nothing but kind and welcoming to her and Jake. However, he was also formidable in a way that left Caroline with no doubt he'd been the one to teach Faith how to use the six-shooter she'd mentioned to Edward. Edward would need to tread carefully with this family, and, judging from his demeanor, he understood that.

"All's well that ends well," Jake said, clicking on the overhead light as they entered their hotel room after the ceremony and evening meal that had followed. "For us. Edward's on his own from now on."

She smiled at him as she crossed the room toward the

bureau, removing the pin from her hat. "I hope all goes well for them. Faith certainly is a lively person."

"Lively? She moves like she was shot out of a gun and is just as loud." He removed his hat and gun belt, hung them on the wooden post at the foot of the bed.

Sitting her hat on the bureau, Caroline turned about to face him. What he'd said was true, but she was attempting to sound ladylike. "She is nice and pretty."

He plopped down on the bed and stretched out, folding his hands behind his head. "She is nice, but not as nice as you. Or as pretty."

She should be used to his compliments, because he said things like that regularly, but they still made her face feel warm, and left her unsure what to say in return. Especially when he looked at her like he was right now, as if he could see through her dress. That made more than her face fill with heat. "You do know you're lying on the bed with your boots on."

"I do." He removed one hand from behind his head and patted the mattress. "Just checking it for softness. Feel it yourself."

She stepped over and placed a hand on the mattress.

As quickly as he'd pulled her on his lap on their wedding day, he pulled her onto the bed beside him. Both of his arms were wrapped around her, holding her tight. "I think it'll do, don't you?" he asked.

She didn't dare think too deeply. Not with the commotion happening inside her. "I think that now we are both lying on the bed with our boots on."

His lips brushed her forehead with an enticingly soft touch. "Do I look like I care?"

With her insides melting a touch, she lifted her gaze to meet his. "Not particularly."

"Because I don't." He kissed the tip of her nose.

She might never know what made her move, but she did. Lifted her face so that his lips slid off her nose and touched her lips. Time stopped. She didn't even breathe, fearful that she'd made a foolish mistake and was searching for something to say or do to explain, or even an excuse.

Before anything came to mind, his lips moved against hers. She let out a soft gasp at the pressure, the pleasure, and the satisfaction. Without thought, her lips moved, kissing him in return. Nothing had ever felt so divinely perfect. Or excited her so completely.

Until Jake's lips parted and his tongue slid across her lips.

She parted her lips, and the sensations that overtook her as his tongue gently entered her mouth had her balling a handful of his shirt with one hand.

Time stopped again as she lost herself in being kissed, thoroughly, completely kissed. It was more than she'd imagined. More electrifying and consuming, and utterly divine. Her entire being felt alive, swirling with heat and desires, and excitement.

So much excitement!

Jake ended the kiss in such an abrupt manner her eyes flew open in startlement. He was already moving off the bed, muttering something, and that's when she heard the knock on the door.

With her heart still stammering, she quickly rolled to the other side of the bed and leaped to her feet, was standing there, smoothing the sides of her dress with both hands when Jake glanced her way before he placed a hand on the knob.

"Excuse the interruption, sir," Mr. Tucker said, as Jake opened the door. "Mr. Drummond is hoping you might spare a few moments. There is something he would like to discuss with you."

"Certainly," Jake said.

It might have simply been in Caroline's mind, or perhaps she was still trying to catch her breath, and couldn't hear past the thudding in her ears, but she thought she heard a hint of frustration in Jake's voice, and saw regret in his eyes when he turned to her.

"Lock the door behind me," he said.

"I will."

He lifted his hat off the bedpost and exited the room.

She walked around the bed and locked the door. Turning about, she leaned back against it and pressed a hand over her racing heart. It was indeed full of hope.

The frustration inside Jake at being interrupted was still near a boiling point when they boarded the train the following morning. Drummond had offered him a reward for bringing Edward back to Texas. The man had explained that Faith was the oldest of his four daughters, whom he'd raised alone after his wife had died ten years ago, and he admitted that there were times when he was at a loss for how to handle his daughters. That he might have raised them more like sons. He'd also been full of questions about the family Faith had now married into.

Jake had refused the reward, and told Drummond the truth about his aunt and uncle, how they would treat Faith like their own daughter. Oddly enough, Drummond didn't ask about Edward. To Jake's way of thinking, Drummond was either confident that the talk he'd had with Edward prior to the wedding would make Edward toe the line, or he knew that Faith could handle any husband. During their discussion Drummond had stated that his daughter was strong-willed, stubborn, and not afraid of much. A true Texan born and bred.

That statement had struck Jake like water straight out of the well in January. Caroline wasn't born and bred in this country. He hadn't been, either, but he'd adapted. That was easy for a young boy seeking adventure, but not for an English lady.

Although he'd wanted to pick up right where they'd left off when he'd returned to their room, he'd restrained himself. Having had a solid taste of her sweetness, of her willingness, and her boldness, restraint was harder than ever.

She'd still been awake, wearing her nightdress, and that had tested his restraint more strenuously than ever.

He'd climbed into bed beside her, held her close as she snuggled in and fell asleep with her head on his shoulder, because he hadn't wanted her to think she'd done anything wrong.

She hadn't.

He had.

He'd crossed a line that he could never uncross.

"Where would you like to sit?" Caroline's question shattered his thoughts.

He scanned the bench seats, looking for shady characters. Seeing none and several open seats, he said, "You decide."

She chose a nearby seat and made room for him to sit beside her as she waved a hand before her face. "Your aunt was right. It's certainly warm here."

He nodded, but bit his tongue to prevent saying it was only mid-June and would get a lot warmer before it started to cool off come winter. Then it could get cold enough that cattle could end up with their eyes frozen open, blinding them. The reasons why he shouldn't have brought Caroline here just kept adding up. He'd noted it at the hotel, too. There was no electricity on the ranch, nor indoor privies.

"We lucked out," he said, finding something positive. "This train will take us to Fort Worth, and there's one heading north tomorrow morning, so we'll be in Twisted Gulch by tomorrow evening."

"I'm looking forward to that."

"Tired of traveling?"

She shook her head. "Just excited to see the place I've heard so much about."

"I may have made it sound better than it is."

"I don't believe so. You made it sound like it's a place that you love."

He did love it, but he would never fault her for not even liking it. Digging in the saddlebag he'd set on the floor between his feet, he pulled out two books. "I picked these up for you this morning." He'd gone to buy their train tickets and send a telegraph to the ranch so that someone would know to bring a wagon to town tomorrow.

"Thank you," she said. "That was very thoughtful."

"One's a catalog, for you to order whatever you might need and can't find in Twisted Gulch. The other one is novel."

"I see that. *The Belle of Texas*," she said, reading the title. "Sounds interesting."

"The shop owner's wife said that was a popular one," he replied.

Hours later, Jake determined he wouldn't visit that shop again while in Galveston. He'd hoped the book was about a refined woman living in Texas, because not all parts of the great state were as isolated as the ranch.

This book wasn't about that at all. The so-called belle was a woman who took over running a ranch after her father died. Wearing britches and packing two Colt revolvers, she protected her ranch with the guts and glory of a man. She was also married four times, outliving each husband, who all succumbed to unusual deaths after they'd defied the belle in one way or another.

He knew all of this because shortly upon beginning to read, Caroline had asked him several questions that made him wonder about the story. Ultimately, he'd leaned over and read the pages along with her.

"Well, now, that was imaginative," he said when the book ended, attempting to find a kind way of saying it was completely unbelievable.

"That's what novels are," Caroline said, her voice serious. "Stories made up in someone's mind. It would be foolish for anyone to believe that anything about it was real, or could come true."

Something in her tone, and the way she was looking out the window at the grand open space as she spoke, tied a knot in Jake's stomach strong enough to hold a bull in place. If this was last week, or even just yesterday, before they'd kissed, he would have put his arm around her and thought of something to say to make her smile.

He couldn't do that today. As much as he wanted to, as much as he wanted so many things, he had to stay planted in reality, like a big old oak tree, swaying in the wind but not giving in to the pressure.

They spent the night in Fort Worth, in a hotel room where the bed didn't sink in the middle, so she didn't sleep with her head on his shoulder. Instead, they slept back-to-back.

He accepted that. They'd agreed to keep their distance. Jake might have forgotten that agreement for a moment there in Galveston, but he wouldn't let himself forget it again, nor the very good reasons behind it. Because the truth was that anything else, anything more than sharing a bed back-to-back, could lead ultimately to pregnancy, and then, just like Faith and Edward, he and Caroline would be inseparably joined for life. There would be no undoing their convenient arrangement. Although Jake might rejoice in that fact, it would be wrong, because he couldn't force a life on Caroline that she didn't want.

Early the next morning, along with several other passengers, they boarded the train that would take them to Twisted Gulch.

"Slap me with a wet catfish!" a man's exclamation echoed off the roof of the train car.

Jake glanced up from where he'd just sat down next to Caroline, and despite all his own dark and gloomy thoughts, he grinned at the grizzled old man carrying a saddle and gear.

"Jake Simpson, what in Sam Hill are you doing in this here country?" the man asked.

Caleb Graham could be as old as the hills, or a few years younger; no one knew for sure. There was too much hair on his face and head to know what he looked like, but the hair was all gray. "Just traveling through," Jake replied. "You?"

"Heading to Cripple Creek. Hear tell they got some cat troubles. You got any in your neck of the woods?"

Jake couldn't say. He hadn't been home for nearly a month and a half. Mountain lions were known to go after calves in the spring. That had happened more than once on the Rocking S and Caleb had been hired a time or two to help with the nuisance. Caleb's gaze had caught and settled on Caroline, and Jake made the introduction. "Allow me to introduce my wife, Caroline."

Caleb dropped his saddle and gear in the seat in front of where they sat. "Well, if that don't beat a stick to death. Jake Spencer married. Never thought I'd live to see the day, but it sure does give me a goose feather tickle!"

"Caroline," Jake said, "this is Caleb Graham."

With a smile brightening her eyes, and with her demure, ladylike voice, she said, "Hello, Mr. Graham. It's a pleasure to make your acquaintance."

"Well, glory be!" Graham bellowed, loud enough to catch the attention of others still settling in their seats. "You done got yourself an English lady. Knowing your folks as I did, they sure would be proud of that."

"I did," Jake replied, feeling his chest swell with pride. His parents would have been proud of him for marrying Caroline. "We are on our way to the ranch from England."

"Newlyweds!" Caleb was grinning broad enough that one would have thought he was the one who'd just gotten married. "I'm a lucky man to have gotten on this tin box on wheels this morning." Plopping onto the seat where he'd dropped his gear, Caleb spun about so he was looking over the back of it. "Tell me more. How's the queen getting along?"

"Well, I didn't happen to see her," Jake replied.

Despite Caleb's obvious disappointment, it didn't slow him down in asking questions, and in less time than it took a horse to flick off a fly with its tail, Caleb became so smitten with Caroline he was doe-eyed. It was her that Caleb talked to all the way to Cripple Creek.

"I sure do wish I didn't have to skedaddle," Caleb said, "but I gotta catch me a cat or two."

Caroline had questioned, and Caleb had told her, all about the mountain lions attacking calves, and though it had made Jake's stomach quiver for her to learn of such things, she accepted all he'd said with a graceful common sense.

"Do take care of yourself, Mr. Graham," she said as Caleb collected his gear. "I'll look forward to you visiting the Rocking S."

Caleb hooked his saddle over his shoulder with one hand and gave her a nod. "You can bet your stars I'll be there, and looking forward to the coffeepot snorting out a fresh brew while we jaw."

"Are there more men like him?" Caroline asked, watching Caleb depart the train.

"Well," Jake replied, "Texas is bigger than all of the UK and Ireland combined, but we have a lot fewer people. However, just like everywhere else, no two people are the same. We have the young and old, rich and poor, smart ones and those that aren't quite so smart."

She nodded. "How much longer until we arrive in Twisted Gulch?"

He held in a sigh at the uneasy feeling filling him. "About two hours."

Chapter Thirteen

Dusk was starting to settle over the small town of Twisted Gulch. It consisted of little more than two rows of wooden buildings, one on each side of the street. Each building was painted differently and bore signs describing the business behind the doors and windows, all closed and unlit right now, other than one entitled the Broken Spoke Saloon. Piano music drifted out of the swinging doors of that establishment.

Caroline was doing her best to pull up excitement, or even hope, as she sat between Mack Henderson, the ranch's foreman, and Jake, on the seat of the wooden wagon that had been waiting for them at the train depot. Her luggage filled the back of the long wagon, along with Jake's, as well as supplies that Mr. Henderson had picked up in town while waiting for the train to arrive. Two black horses were hitched to the single-tree yoke, pulling the wagon through the small town.

Several houses were dotted here and there. What Caroline noticed most was the lack of trees. Hardly a one could be seen.

However, none of that was her reason for feeling so empty. That came from herself. From the fact that she'd forced Jake to kiss her, and though he'd acted as if he'd wanted that as much as she had, he obviously hadn't, and still didn't. Since leaving their hotel room that night to talk to Mr. Drummond, he'd barely touched her, or looked at her. When he did, it was as if it pained him to see her.

It did pain him. She pained him. He didn't want a wife, nor had he married her to be one. He'd married her to teach Nellie how to be a lady. That was Caroline's job now and that was the only thing she should be thinking about. It had been foolish to think, to hope, differently. If she'd learned anything from Aurora's rule book, it was that a lady should become a master at masking her true feelings.

Therefore, as Jake and Mr. Henderson conversed, she held a smile on her face and listened to learn all she could, because besides teaching Nellie, she would do all she could to not be a burden to Jake or anyone else.

Night had fallen by the time they arrived at the ranch, which had almost as many buildings as the town had, but here, flickering light from oil lamps filled the windows. As the wagon rolled to a stop, a door on one three-story home flew open and a young girl with long, black braids flapping against her shoulders hurried across the wide porch and down the steps.

"You're home!" she shouted.

"I am," Jake shouted in return as he climbed off the wagon and caught the girl as she threw herself into his arms.

A wave of happiness filled Caroline at the reunion between siblings; however, it was short-lived. As soon as he released Nellie, the girl took a step back as she stared at the wagon.

"It's true," Nellie said, sounding almost bewildered. "You got married?"

"I did." Jake said. "Her name is C—"

"We just got rid of one bossy woman and you brought home another one?" Nellie asked, spinning about. "I thought Faith was lying!"

"Nellie," Jake said.

She kept stomping toward the house. "I'd rather join the army and face a firing squad than have another woman telling me what to do and when to do it!"

"Nellie!" he repeated.

Caroline had scooted to the edge of the seat and touched his shoulder. "Leave her be," she said. "Please. She needs time to get used to me. Just like you did. Just like I needed time to get used to you."

He glanced at the slamming door, then sighed as he nodded. "I apologize for her behavior. She's normally not like that."

"She normally hasn't been separated from you for over six weeks," Caroline said.

"That is true," Jake replied, and grasped her waist to lift her down.

She was introduced to Slim, who was not slim nor tall, and Rocky, who could have easily been called slim, as they arrived to unload the trunks from the wagon, and to Lolitta, who led her into the house.

"I have water heating for a nice long bath after all your travels," Lolitta, a middle-aged woman with graying black hair, and deep brown eyes that shone as brightly as her smile, said. "But first, I delayed supper so you can eat."

"Thank you, that all sounds very delightful," Caroline replied, walking through a large sitting room with a massive stone fireplace.

"Don't worry none about Nellie," Lolitta said. "She'll come around. She's just been out of sorts having Jake gone and Miss Drummond here for so long."

"I completely understand and agree." Not wanting to be discovered discussing Nellie in case she was nearby—which Caroline was sure *was* the case, since she could spy a door to the room cracked open, with a shoe sticking out near the bottom—she said, "Jake has told me so much about the ranch, and everyone here. He missed everyone immensely and is very happy to be home."

"We are happy he's home," Lolitta said. "And happy to have you here, too."

"Thank you," Caroline replied, forcing her smile to remain in place even though she knew that Lolitta's statement certainly wasn't true for Jake.

She hadn't needed more proof of that, but received it when she never saw Jake again that night. After eating, she took a bath, and then settled into the bedroom where her trunks had been delivered. It was clearly Jake's bedroom, but he never came to bed, and the next morning, he was already out working when she went downstairs.

Accepting things for what they were, Caroline wasted no time in offering a helping hand to Lolitta, insisting that she was not here to be waited on, but to be useful.

Throughout the day, and those that followed, Caroline met all of the other ranch residents, and grew increasingly comfortable as she continued to work alongside Lolitta in the house, Luis in the garden, which was an utter delight, as were the many farm animals that she quickly included a visit to in her daily routines. She also visited with Mr. Henderson's wife, Jane, who was an absolute dear and lived in the cabin a short distance from the house with their two children, Melanie and Boyd. Both had Jane's blond hair and bright blue eyes, and were just as adorable as their mother. Melanie was eight, slightly younger than

Nellie, while Boyd was seven, and had informed her all about school not being in session right now.

Nellie tended to keep herself out of sight as much as Jake did. Caroline had quickly discovered that Jake was sleeping in the spare bedroom next to the one she was sleeping in, and took most of his meals in the bunkhouse with the men. When she did see him, Caroline did exactly as a lady would: kept her feelings masked, and made polite conversation.

The happy, charming man she'd known in England and on the ship was gone, and she greatly missed him, and the time they'd shared together, but knew it was her fault. She'd pushed him too far by making him kiss her.

There too, she kept her feelings hidden and found other things to concentrate on. Mainly Nellie, and how she could befriend the girl. So far, Caroline had only initiated conversation with her when the girl made her presence known rather than peeking through doorways or windows.

It was her fourth day there, when she noted Nellie rushing up the staircase to the second floor. The domestic chores had been completed, and there were a few hours before Caroline would be needed to assist Lolitta prepare the evening meal. Setting aside the feather duster she'd been using on the windowsills in Jake's office, Caroline walked to the staircase.

In all of Jake's descriptions of the ranch, he'd never really mentioned specifics about the house, and she'd thought it was because it would be small, or lacking in some way. It was just the opposite. Built solidly, decorated with lovely and stylish furnishings, and well-maintained, the three-story house was not only impressive; it was a place anyone would be proud to call home. She'd explored every inch of it, including the basement beneath and the uppermost third story, which was merely one large room that wasn't used for anything.

Nellie, wearing her usual trousers and a blue blouse, was near the far end of the hallway when Caroline reached the second-floor landing. Caroline's own bedroom was on that end, and for a moment Caroline wasn't sure whether or not she ought to make her presence known, because the girl was clearly up to something. But a creak alerted the girl, or maybe Nellie's senses just picked up on something, and she spun around.

"Hello," Caroline said, walking forward.

"Hi," Nellie said, holding both hands behind her back.

"I just came up to get something out of my bedroom," Caroline said. "Perhaps you'd care to help me?"

"I, uh, I can't," Nellie said, squirming slightly, and moving her arms, but not revealing the hands still behind her back, as she stepped sideways.

Caroline then saw why. The tiny head of a tan and brown snake was sticking out from behind Nellie's hip. "Is that your pet snake?"

Nothing but the girl's big blue eyes moved, almost as if she was looking for an escape route. Within a moment, she must have determined there wasn't one and pulled the snake out from behind her back. "No. Jake would tan my hide if I tried to keep a snake for a pet."

"Well, I would protest if he attempted to tan your hide, as you say, simply because of his own aversion." Holding out her hand, Caroline asked, "May I hold him?"

"A snake? You want to hold a snake?"

"Yes." Caroline had no doubt she would have found the snake somewhere in her bedroom later on today.

"You like snakes?"

"I like all creatures, at least those that don't bite. I'm assuming he doesn't, or you wouldn't be holding him."

"No, it's just a little hog snake. They don't bite." Nellie held out the snake.

Caroline took him and upon examining his quite adorable little face, giggled. "I truly have never seen such a cute snake. It's like he has a turned-up little nose."

"That's why he's called a hog-nose snake."

"Well, now, that does explain it. Where did you find him?"

"By the barn. Snakes eat mice."

"They do. I remember finding a small adder in our chicken coop when I was a little girl, which of course we had to relocate because they eat eggs." She handed the snake back. "Thank you for letting me hold him."

"You're welcome." A frown tugged on Nellie's dark brows. "What's an aversion?"

"It means a dislike," Caroline replied. "As in Jake has an aversion or dislike of certain creatures."

"How do you know that?"

Knowing her response would cause more questions, Caroline opened the bedroom door. "Because my uncle has leeches in his basement, and Jake was quite disturbed by that."

"Leeches? Why would anyone keep leeches in their basement?"

Caroline entered the bedroom, leaving the door open for Nellie to follow, or simply stand in the doorway if she was more comfortable. "Because my uncle and older brother are inventors, and leeches are part of one of their inventions. That's who I lived with, my aunt and uncle and older brother, because our parents died when my brother and I were young." She'd wanted to suggest that this was something they had in common and she'd achieved her goal, so she changed the subject again. "My aunt is a painter, and that's what I was coming up to get. Some watercolor paints, brushes and paper."

"You're a painter, too?"

Caroline opened her trunk and began lifting out the painting supplies from Aunt Myrtle. "I enjoy painting now and again, and would like to paint a picture of the pretty flowers and vines on the side of the porch."

"That's coral honeysuckle," Nellie said. "My mother planted it before I was born."

"It's truly beautiful. I've only ever seen white honeysuckle, and will have to mix some colors together to create the color of those flowers." She looked up to meet Nellie's gaze, who had entered the room and was standing close. "I have plenty of supplies. Would you like to paint a picture, too?"

Nellie hesitated for several moments before she shook her head.

With her hands full of supplies, Caroline stood. "Maybe another time, then."

With a nod, Nellie backed up, toward the door. "You, uh, you won't tell Jake about…"

"Your snake?"

Nellie nodded.

"Heavens, no. Not with his aversion to such creatures. I imagine he would have been quite disturbed to find one in the house."

"Uh, yeah, he would have been." Nellie said, then disappeared out the door.

Less than fifteen minutes later, she appeared again, as Caroline was sitting on the front porch, paintbrush in hand.

"I just thought I'd watch," Nellie said.

"I'll enjoy the company," Caroline replied, more than happy to have broken the ice between them.

It was raining. Raining hard. That meant that unless it absolutely had to be done, not much would happen at the ranch. Animals and people would find shelter and hunker down until the rain let up or ended. Which, in turn, meant Jake was in his office, attempting to look busy. He'd already used the evening hours of the past week to make entries in his ledgers and review the records that had been entered during his time away.

He'd done that to keep his distance from Caroline, as well as several other tasks throughout the days. It wasn't working as well as he wanted it to. A single moment didn't go by where he wasn't reminded of her. His wife. In her quiet, simple ways, she'd already endeared herself to everyone on the ranch. That didn't take much. A mere smile or introduction would have done the job, but she of course went beyond that. She'd embedded herself in the household by working side by side with Lolitta in the house and Luis in his outdoor tasks in the garden and barns.

She and Jane Henderson had become fast friends, and Mack proclaimed that Melanie and Boyd adored her, which was obvious from their reactions whenever they encountered her. Trusty old Clem, the cook for the ranch hands, adored her as much as the children, singing praises about how she'd helped him by peeling potatoes or carrots, or any number of other tasks.

Even the animals were enthralled with her. Ted and Fred, the yard dogs, ran to her side, tails wagging, the horses gathered near the corral fence for a pet, the pigs left the shade of their sty to greet her, the chickens flocked around her feet, and more than once Jake had espied her sitting on the stairs off the back porch with a hen snuggled on her lap.

Animals often recognized those who fed them, but this went beyond that.

It had only taken a couple of days for Nellie to warm up to her, too. The two were now practically inseparable and could often be heard laughing and giggling.

All of that should please Jake, and in many ways it did. Truth be told, he was proud of Caroline, and proud that others had accepted her so readily. However, it had only been a week.

Unquestionably the longest week of his life. He missed her. Seeing her from afar didn't compare to what they'd shared on the ship. The closeness and companionship they'd shared. Or the fun they'd had in London, dancing and dining together.

The knock on the door pulled him from his thoughts and he quickly picked up a pen and flipped open a ledger book before verbally inviting entrance.

"I need to go to town," Nellie said. "So does Caroline."

There it was. The isolation. Just what he'd expected. "It's raining."

"Not right now," Nellie replied, stopping in front of his desk, "but next time someone goes to town, we need to go with them."

"Why?"

"Because we need some pieces of glass."

"Glass?"

She nodded.

"What do you need glass for?"

"Our paintings."

He'd seen the two of them in various places with paper and paints. "What will you do with the glass?"

"Put our pictures behind it," she said with a flair of frustration that he hadn't figured that out. "Luis said he could make us some frames, but that we don't have any glass."

"Very well, next time someone goes to town, you can go with them."

"And Caroline?"

"Yes," he replied.

"She's not like what Faith said she would be."

He set down the pen and leaned back in his chair. "Oh?"

Nellie nodded before saying, "She's not like Faith, either. She never stopped telling us what to do, how to do it, and when to do it. Caroline doesn't just sit around doing needlepoint and drinking tea. She doesn't sit around painting all day, either. We can't do that until our chores are done, but that just makes them go faster. Do you want to see the picture I'm talking about?"

That was Nellie, jumping from topic to topic. "Yes, I would," he answered.

She spun about to leave, but then pivoted to face him just as quickly. "Are your hands clean?"

Taken aback by the question, because she'd often opposed cleanliness in a way that was common with children, he grinned and held up his hands for her to see. "Yes."

"Good. Because I already have a smudge on it from when mine weren't clean. That's why I need the picture frame and glass, so it doesn't get any dirtier. I'll be right back."

"I'll be here."

Minutes later, his heart hammered while the rest of him froze as Nellie entered the room followed by Caroline. She was wearing a white-and-yellow dress, but it wasn't her clothing that stunned him. It was her beauty. More than one ranch hand had said one look was all it took to understand why Jake had given up his bachelorhood. He'd agreed with good humor, fully aware of his wife's beauty, but right now, it felt as if he'd forgotten just how enchanting she was.

"Here it is," Nellie said, holding out a piece of paper.

Pulling his gaze off Caroline, he took the paper and examined the painting of the flowers growing on the side of the house. It was a close-up of two blooms. She'd gotten the color of the flowers exactly right. The same was true of the greenery and the porch column. He remembered when his mother had planted the honeysuckle. She'd been carrying Nellie, so he'd gone along with her to the creek, to dig up some small shoots of the plant that grew there, and transported them back to the house, then dug the hole next to the porch.

"This is a beautiful picture," he said.

"I know," Nellie said. "That's why I want it framed."

He took another look at the picture, then paused briefly to peer closer at something among the leaves. "That's a hog snake."

Nellie laughed, and looked at Caroline, who gave her a demure wink of one eye.

"I know!" Nellie said, still laughing. "Isn't he cute?"

In his opinion, no snake was cute, but the one in the picture did hold a charm of its own.

"Here's another picture I want put in a frame," Nellie said. "You could hang it here, in your office. Caroline painted one just like it to send to her aunt."

He handed back the first picture and took the second one. The paper was thick, like the first one, but this time the image was horizontal instead of vertical, and he instantly recognized the exact spot she'd sat to paint it. A distance down the driveway, where the entire homestead was in view. The painting displayed every building, every tree and bush, as well as a field of daisies behind the house. All in all, it was exactly what he saw, what he loved seeing, whenever he rode along the road, whether he'd been gone an hour, or longer.

The trouble was, he was beginning to wonder if his love for his ranch was enough. Was all he wanted. He'd once believed it was, believed it would always be, but that was before Caroline. He now wanted more.

"This is quite amazing," he said, looking at Caroline. "It appears I was not aware of all of your talents."

She blushed slightly. "I haven't painted in a while, but Aunt Myrtle gave me the supplies as a going-away gift, and wanted a picture of your ranch."

That was exactly how she always accepted a compliment, with an explanation as if she didn't quite believe she deserved the praise.

"I would be honored to have this hanging on the wall, and will indeed see that glass is purchased. Or perhaps Mr. Case will have ready-made frames in his store."

"Told you he'd like it," Nellie said to Caroline. "And that he'd want to hang it up."

"That you did," Caroline admitted, resting a hand on Nellie's shoulder. "Now, let's leave him to his work. We have a floor that needs mopping yet this morning."

Nellie reached out for the picture he was still holding. "I have to put these away first."

Jake reluctantly handed over the painting, and watched

as they left the room. A mixture of thoughts and emotions swirled restlessly inside him. The strongest were the ones that he'd been trying to squash the hardest. He'd never wanted nor hoped to be wrong. Today, he was badly wanting his assumptions that Caroline would never be happy here to be wrong, and was hoping there was a chance of more. More between the two of them.

Three weeks later, not much had changed. Jake was still being eaten alive with desire, and still denying even the slightest opportunity to be near Caroline because he was sure to lose his last bits of restraint. The memories of her snuggled against him, with her head resting in the crook of his shoulder and her hand resting on his chest, had become nightmarish, reminding him of what could be, or could have been.

He'd allowed himself to contemplate various scenarios, imagining what her reaction might be if he told her that he couldn't go on like this. That they either had to make their marriage real, or… That's where he got stuck. Or what?

While he was anguishing, Caroline appeared to be downright happy with things just the way they were.

Why had he ever thought that this would be so much simpler than it had turned out to be?

Others at the ranch were questioning things. No one had made a single comment, but he saw the look of wonder on people's faces, and knew they knew he was sleeping in the spare bedroom.

A flash of light split the darkness, quickly followed by a boom, signaling another storm was about to hit. Everyone was safely inside their respective shelters, probably sleeping already, so Jake merely rolled over in the lonely bed of the spare room and repositioned the pillow beneath his head.

The rain struck a short time later, with an intensity that had him tossing aside the covers and rising from the bed. A quick glance out the window confirmed hail was coming down outside. The wind was increasing, making the hailstones strike the glass with increased force.

Concerned about windows breaking, or other possible damages, he dressed quickly. He'd barely stepped into the hallway when Caroline exited his bedroom—or hers, as it was now.

"This storm is fierce," she said, hurrying past. "I'll wake Nellie and take her to the basement."

"You read my mind," he told her. Not even the storm and potential danger could prevent him from recognizing the nightgown and over wrapper that she'd worn each night on the ship. His body reacted, too, with a need that left a painful throbbing.

Giving his head a solid shake to dispel memories, he followed her down the hallway. "I'm sure everything will be fine," he said, trying to dispel any worries she might have.

"I'm sure, too," she said, then opened Nellie's bedroom door.

It took but a moment to rouse his sister and for Caroline to collect a pillow and quilt for Nellie, then they descended the stairs to make their way to the kitchen and the stone basement beneath that part of the house. Luis and Lolitta were already there with the door open, and a lamp lit below.

Blinding light was followed by a resounding boom, so close the entire house rattled, startling all of them.

"Hurry now," Caroline said, far calmer than anyone

could be expected to be as she guided Nellie into the stairway.

Jake didn't follow, because he'd heard the aftermath of the lightning strike. The recognizable crack of wood splintering and the crash of a tree falling. He rushed to the back door and threw it open, trying to see through the wind, rain, and hail.

The past weeks had given Caroline ample time to master hiding her emotions, and she was glad to have worked so hard at it, because she'd been able to maintain the control even when it had felt as if lightning had struck the house.

She quickly got Nellie wrapped in the quilt and settled on the floor of the basement, with a pillow beneath her head. "Just go back to sleep," she whispered. "The storm will be over before you know it."

Nellie nodded, and Caroline pressed a hand to the butterflies in her stomach in preparation of turning about and facing Jake. That's where she was still having difficulties masking her emotions. Though they'd barely interacted privately the past month, the feelings she felt for him had continued to grow.

She'd now understood why he loved this ranch so much and the people here. It was truly a great big family where everyone worked together, for the good of all. She loved being a part of it. Loved everything about being here. Including him. She fully understood that.

She also understood now that she worshipped him from afar, and always would.

There were nights when silent tears fell upon her pillow because in so many ways, she had gotten what she wanted, but now knew that what she'd truly wanted was the ultimate. To love, to share a life like this with someone, and that someone was Jake.

The crushing blow was also knowing that would never be what he wanted, and there was no reason why he should. He already had everything.

Even so, she couldn't stop missing him, stop missing the closeness they'd found on the ship, stop thinking about that one wonderful, life-changing kiss they'd had in Galveston.

Closing her eyes for a moment, she willed herself to maintain control, because Jake didn't have a shirt on. He had on pants and boots but no shirt, and the sight of his bare chest upstairs had sent her heart racing. She missed him so much. Missed touching him, talking with him, laughing with him.

Letting out the air she'd been holding, she opened her eyes and turned about. Lolitta was the only other person in the basement, standing near the stairway, staring up the steps.

Caroline crossed the room that was lined with shelves, filled with more provisions than some stores had held back in London. "Where's Jake and Luis?"

"Outside," Lolitta whispered.

"What? Why?"

"Because lightning struck a tree." Lolitta turned, and there were tears in her eyes. "It fell on the cabin."

Daniel's death in Aurora's book hit her all over again. "Stay with Nellie!" With terror whirling frantically within her, Caroline ran up the steps, and out the back door.

The storm was raging, making it impossible to see anything, except when flashes of lightning lit up the sky. During those brief times, she couldn't see the cabin, just a massive pile of branches and leaves.

Along with the wind and rain, she heard what sounded like shouts, and ran across the porch, hoping to see and hear better.

Another flash showed men near the fallen tree. That wouldn't be happening if the Henderson family was all right. She ran down the steps, hardly noticing the rain or wind, or the way her slippers were instantly soaked as she crossed the yard.

Slim was the first person she encountered, "How bad is it?" she asked.

"Part of the tree broke through the roof," he shouted. "Jake's trying to make his way through the branches to the door."

The tree seemed ten times larger on the ground than it had while standing; Caroline couldn't even see the cabin. Men were using axes and saws, and throwing aside branches that had broken in the fall, but it didn't seem to making a difference.

Another shout sounded. Both she and Slim heard it and ran around the tree, the house, to the back side, where a small window was open. Jake was there, on the inside of the cabin. "Mack and Jane are pinned in their bed beneath the tree!" he shouted. "I'm going to lift Melanie and Boyd out the window. Then get me an axe and some rope!"

"Hand them out, boss!" Slim replied.

"I'll be right back for the children!" she told Slim, and ran to relay Jake's needs to Rocky, who was using an axe not far away.

She was back just as Boyd was handed out, and took him from Slim, then waited until Melanie was lifted out. "We are going to run to the house," she told the children. "Get you out of this rain."

Carrying Boyd, and holding tightly to Melanie's hand,

Caroline hurried back to the house. Lolitta was standing at the top of the stairs. "These two are going to join Nellie," Caroline said, keeping her tone light and her voice calm. "Please get some towels and quilts. For as warm as it was today, that rain in notably chilly."

Once the children were settled next to Nellie, who had fallen back asleep, Caroline told Lolitta, "We will need the spare bedroom upstairs for Mack and Jane. I'll go prepare it."

"I can do that," Lolitta said.

"No, you stay with them," Caroline said. From the time she'd arrived, she'd insisted upon taking over the duties of cleaning the upstairs. Not just to be helpful, but to conceal the fact that her husband didn't want to share a bed with her as much as she possibly could. It made her feel like a failure. It was the proof that she was someone Jake had been forced to marry, rather than wanted to marry.

She chided herself for such selfish thoughts when Mack and Jane could be seriously injured, and hurried to complete the task. Afterward, she checked on Lolitta and the children, before she went back outside. The flashes of lightning had grown farther away, but it was still raining considerably, making it difficult to see how the men were progressing.

Once again, she ran across the yard, and upon approaching saw that a narrow passageway had been made through the tree branches and a lamp was lit in the cabin.

With her heart in her throat, she quickened her pace, all the way to the open bedroom door inside the cabin.

"We have to pull at the same time," Jake was saying. "There can't be too much pressure on any single point of that beam."

The tree had smashed through the roof, between the

rafters, and had knocked down most of the ceiling. Three ropes had been slung over a now-exposed frame beam and tied to the tree at different points, and men held the other ends of the ropes. Two at each end, except for one, where there were three, including Clem, the cook that she'd come to know so well. He was older, and a scruffy sort, but utterly endearing.

"Mack," Jake continued, "on the count of three, we're going to lift the tree. There's not enough room to go too high, so you and Jane have to roll out of the bed, onto the floor. Can you do that?"

"Yes!" Mack answered from beneath branches, leaves, and a very large chunk of the tree trunk that was also sticking up out of a big hole in the roof.

Caroline knelt down, peering beneath the tree and through branches that had been cut away. The bed was against the wall, leaving only one side open. She assumed Jane was on the other side of Mack and prayed that she was all right.

"One," Jake said, "two, three."

The men groaned and the overhead beam creaked as the huge tree trunk slowly began to rise.

"Can you roll out?" Jake asked, the strain of the hard work of lifting the tree making his voice sound like a growl.

"No! Something's holding the covers down, I can't kick them loose!"

The tree was high enough that Caroline could see the bed, and Mack—and that a chair had been knocked against the bedframe, near the foot. It had toppled, so the back of it was on the bed, angled so the seat was jammed against the floor. Rushing forward, she dropped to her knees and crawled beneath the branches. "It's a chair!"

She grabbed the chair leg and tugged until it broke loose. "I got it!" she said, pulling the chair farther away as she crawled backward.

Mack rolled and landed on the floor, and a split second later, Jane followed him. Caroline was out from beneath the tree and rising to her feet when Mack and Jane crawled out. She grasped Jane's arm, helping her to stand. It was then that she turned, caught Jake looking at her with such fury that she was chilled to the bone.

"We'll go down on the count of three," Jake shouted. "One, two, three!"

Mack had risen to his feet, too, but was only standing on one leg and holding on to the chest of drawers.

"Your leg!" Jane exclaimed, rushing to his side. "I knew you were hurt and not telling me."

"Get him in the house," Jake said to Bernie and Denver, who were closest to Mack. "The rest of you can go back to the bunkhouse, there's nothing more we can do until morning."

His voice still sounded like a growl, his words barked demands that the men quickly followed.

Caroline started to follow the others to the door, but was stopped by a hand seizing her arm. She glanced over her shoulder, and gasped at the scrapes and scratches she saw covering Jake's chest. "You're bleeding," she said. "You need to get in the house, too."

He didn't say a word and, lifting her face to meet his gaze, she swallowed at his angry expression.

"Don't you ever do something like that again," he said.

It took a moment for her to comprehend what he was referring to, but she'd barely opened her mouth to respond when he spoke again.

"That beam could have broken!" he said. "The ropes could have snapped!"

"I know," she replied. "That's why I had to get that chair out of there."

"You didn't have to do anything," he retorted. "You should have been in the house, where you belong!"

The weeks of masking her feelings, of hiding so many things, disappeared in a flash. Instead, she was right back in England, being told what to do, when to do it, and where she belonged. "Where I belong?"

"Yes."

She tried. For the briefest of moments, she tried to find an ounce of control, but it just wasn't there. Pain was, and anger. And hurt. And, they were all crashing and whirling together, like an internal storm with a force that could knock over trees. "It appears to me that where I belong is anywhere that you aren't! I've seen the way it pains you to look at me. Well, it pains me, too." Choking on a sob, she had to stop, swallow. Swallow the anguish of knowing that the place she wanted to belong was inside his heart. A place that he didn't want her to be. Would never want her to be.

"It doesn't pain me to look at you," he said. "I—" He shook his head. "I know you, and know you just wanted to help, but it was too dangerous for you to be out here."

She had her voice back, and her anger was growing. "Too dangerous for me, but not for you? The one who everyone depends on?" His hold on her arm had eased and she wrenched herself completely out of his hold. "And you *don't* know me. I didn't just want to help. I wanted—" Her throat constricted. She'd wanted to be more than help. She wanted to be wanted, but couldn't tell him any of that. Why had she given in to hope again? Why had she wanted more instead of being satisfied with the life she'd had? Because she could remember a time when she'd had more and wanted that again.

She'd been ready to settle for less, until she'd met him, then she'd wanted it all. Foolishly. That wasn't going to happen. Not ever. And now, by daring again to wish for more, she'd not only hurt herself, but Jake in the process.

"This isn't what I wanted," she whispered, and hurried to the door, counting on the rain to wash away her tears before she entered the house, because there was no stopping them.

Chapter Fourteen

The fear Jake had felt when he saw Caroline shoot beneath the tree was still making his insides tremble. So was regret for speaking so harshly to her. The way she'd said those words—*This isn't what I wanted...*—was cracking his heart in two with a pain he'd never known.

From the moment he'd met her, she'd scared him, left him tongue-tied, because even then, deep down, he'd known there was something special about her. Something that would change his life.

He stood where he was, staring at the door, in silence. The rain must have stopped. Either that, or the clamor of his thoughts was so loud he couldn't hear anything else. Part of him was shouting that this was all Edward's fault; another even louder part told him that he was the only one to blame. He was the one who'd gone to England. The one who'd stopped Caroline's marriage to Edward, and asked her to marry him instead.

Loudest of all was the voice saying that his real fault wasn't marrying her: it was falling in love. He couldn't deny it. He'd fallen in love. He was afraid to spend the rest of his life without her. He was pained when he looked at her because he ached to touch her. Ached to kiss her. Ached from head to toe, sunset to sunrise and back to sunset, because he loved her. Loved her more than he'd ever loved anything else.

Disgusted at himself, he shook his head, even though that wouldn't clear his thoughts. Nothing could. He looked at the ropes still dangling from the tree, at the damage done from nothing more than a storm. A strike of lightning. A gust of wind.

Just as he'd known, this place was too dangerous for a woman. For a lady.

A lady needed to be in the city, attending balls and the theater, shopping and hosting dinner parties.

Huffing out a breath, he reached down, grabbed a broken branch, and carried it to the doorway. After tossing it outside, he went back for another one. Then another. After the loose branches were all hauled outside, he grabbed the axe and started chopping off others, and hauling them outside, making a pile beyond the pathway the men had created in order to get to the door.

He hadn't waited for that task to be finished; he'd just barreled his way through the tree to get to the door. That was how he'd always faced life, by barreling forward. Just like he'd barreled to London, barreled into the church. Barreled into Caroline's life.

This was all his fault. He'd brought her to a place she didn't belong, a place she didn't want to be. A place too dangerous and isolated, and all the other things he'd always known.

"That can all be done tomorrow, Jake. You should go have those scratches seen to."

He set the axe down, turned to face Jane. She and Mack had lived in the cabin since before his father had died, and were as much a part of the ranch as him. The ranch he'd never once contemplated leaving, until now. It wasn't fair of him to put so much at stake just because he'd fallen in love. He'd been the one to force Edward into taking responsibility for his family over his own wants and needs. He needed to heed his own advice. "How's Mack?"

Jane walked to the dresser. "Caroline got his leg clean and bandaged, and he wants a pair of britches. Embarrassed about wearing only his underwear." Her smile grew. "Men, you're all the same. So strong and proud, yet embarrassed over the littlest things."

"His leg is going to be all right?"

"Yes." She lifted out some clothing and closed the dresser drawer. "He'll have to stay off it for a day or two, until it heals enough to not break open with every step."

"That's good." Relieved, he picked up the axe again. "I want to get a few of these branches out of the way so we can get to fixing this place up first thing in the morning."

"A few branches aren't going to make a difference," she said.

She was right, but he wasn't ready to face Caroline, so he merely stood there, waiting for the moment that Jane left and he could start swinging the axe again. Figure out what his next steps were going to be.

"I don't know the circumstances behind your marriage to Caroline," Jane said. "It's not my business to know, but I've seen the way the two of you look at each other. The way her face lights up when she talks about you. And I can't help but wonder why the two of you are so set on making yourselves miserable."

He was miserable, and hated knowing that Caroline was, too. Lowering the head of the axe to the floor, he leaned on the handle. "I shouldn't have brought her here."

Jane frowned. "Why would you say that? This is your home."

Nodding, he agreed. "It is. It's also in the middle of nowhere and as unlike London as any place could possibly be."

"I imagine that is true, but if you think that upsets Caroline, you don't know her."

He huffed out a breath, having already heard that tonight.

"She's found beauty here that I hadn't even noticed until she'd pointed it out," Jane went on, "captured it in her paintings. She loves this place as much as you do."

That couldn't be true, nor could he question why Jane would suggest it, because questioning it would be a step toward hoping she was right. And he couldn't hope. There was nothing to hope for. Caroline herself had just told him that she didn't want to be here.

Jane shook her head and let out a sigh. "It's not my place to say anything, but right now, I'm so grateful to be alive that I'm going to say it. You are being as stubborn as that old bull you love so much. If you'd just get over what you're stewing about and accept that you are as head over heels in love with her as she is with you, the misery would end for both of you. I lived in many places as my father moved us west, and I know from experience, happiness doesn't come from where you live. It's who you share your life with."

"Some places are safer than others," he pointed out.

She shook her head. "Oh, Jake. There are dangers everywhere. Accidents happen everywhere."

He was about point out differences between here and London when Caroline appeared in the doorway.

"Mack is questioning what is taking so long," she said.

"Of course he is," Jane said, smiling. "I will take these

to him, and let you convince Moby it's time to call it a night."

Caroline frowned as Jane left the room, then she asked, "Was she referring to you or your bull?"

She was still wearing her nightclothes and housecoat, and her hair was damp, hanging in waves well past her shoulders. He wanted to wrap her in his arms, hold her tight against him, and never let her go. If only he could. "In her mind, both," he answered.

"You should come inside and let me clean those scratches."

"The rain cleaned them." He released the axe handle, let it fall to the floor, so he could wipe his arms, and chest, show her that the scratches had quit bleeding. "I'm sorry for upsetting you earlier. It scared me to see you in danger." That was an understatement, but he had to start somewhere.

"I'm sorry, too," she said. "I never felt like I was in danger. Perhaps because I'm used to unexpected things happening. You were there when there was an explosion in the basement. Things like that happened often."

That was true, but still very different. "Maybe if we had one of those weather machines, we would have known a storm was coming."

"Perhaps, but then you would have leeches in your basement. And it wouldn't have told us that a tree was going to fall on the cabin. There is no invention that will ever predict the future."

If only there were. If only Jake knew what to do right now. "No, I suspect not."

They stood there, staring at each other for a long, stilled moment. The sadness in her eyes was like a knife in his heart. "I'm not sure what I can do to make things better," he said.

She glanced at the tree. "I'm sure the roof can be rebuilt and—"

"I'm not talking about the cabin," he interrupted. "I'm talking about us." Flustered, he ran a hand through his hair. "I could sell out. We could move to England and—"

"Did you get hit in the head by a branch?" she asked.

He felt his forehead, wondering if she'd seen a scratch there or blood, or something. "No."

"Then why would you suggest such a thing?"

"Because you aren't happy here. You don't want to be here."

She placed a hand over her mouth and closed her eyes.

The room was so silent he could hear his heart echoing in his ears. "I won't force you to stay," he said when the silence got to him.

"I'm sorry that I forced myself on you," she whispered. "I shouldn't have, I know that now." As her lids rose and her gaze met his, he could see tears welling in her eyes. "I don't want you to be unhappy, and if me leaving will put an end to that, I'll go."

His heart felt like it was being squeezed by a fist. He still didn't know what to do, other than to tell her the truth. "That won't make me happy. What makes me happy is standing before me." He stepped closer, wanted to touch her, but kept his hands at his sides. "I thought I had everything I wanted, but I didn't. Not until I met you. The friendship we formed in London. The closeness we had on the ship. Sleeping next to you. Introducing you as my wife. All of those things made me very happy."

Uncertainty filled her eyes as she shook her head. "They did?"

"Yes," he answered, with emotion turning his throat raw. "It also scared me to death because I knew it wasn't what you wanted, but I couldn't *stop* wanting it. Couldn't stop falling in love with you. I don't want to live without you, so you just tell me where you do want to live, what you do want. And I will take you there, spend the rest of my life—"

"No," Caroline said, holding her hands up for him to stop talking. She was half-afraid to believe she was hearing correctly, yet couldn't quell the joy filling her heart. "I don't want to live anywhere else, except here. Right here. Because I'm the one who fell in love with you. But I thought when I made you kiss me, that—"

"You didn't make me kiss you," he interrupted. "I'd wanted that for a very long time. Still do."

"But you didn't want to get married," she said, still afraid to believe. "I forced that on you, too."

"Do you honestly think anyone could force me to do something that I don't want to do?" he asked.

"No," she admitted, but it was the grin on his face that made her believe. Truly believe.

"You're right," he said. "I wanted to marry you. I wanted to kiss you. I want to share my life with you." He touched her arms, ran his hands up to her shoulders. "Now, did I hear you say that you are in love with me?"

She nodded. "Yes. Very much so."

The next moment, she was in his arms, and being kissed in a way that would have made Aurora jealous. There was nothing holding them back, except for the need to breathe, and when that happened, they each tried to explain their own stubbornness, but there wasn't time for that, either, because the need to kiss again was stronger.

Caroline had no idea how long they remained in the cabin, kissing and hugging, and professing their love, before Jake suggested they go to the house.

"I tried not to fall in love with you," she said as they walked hand in hand across the wet grass. "But you made it impossible, right from the start. I kept telling myself not to hope, but it was impossible. I kept on hoping that you'd change your mind about being married."

He stopped walking, cupped her face with both hands, and kissed her so thoroughly, her knees grew weak.

"I changed my mind all right," he said, while scooping her into his arms and carrying her the rest of the way to the house.

The kitchen was quiet, everyone having gone back to bed. Jake blew out the lamp and they quickly made their way up the stairs to their bedroom—which was what it would be from now on. She had no doubt on that, or on Jake's love. He was a man true to his word. She'd known that from the beginning.

Once in their bedroom, she removed her housecoat, tossed it aside, and looped her arms around his neck, feeling a tremendous sense of victory. Victory at finding love. At finding a place in Jake's heart that mirrored his place in hers. Victory in believing in hope again. Victory in having it all.

"I've missed sleeping with you," she whispered against his lips.

His hands cupped her bottom as he pulled her tight against him. "Sleeping is not all that is going to happen tonight."

The kiss that followed was only the beginning. Thoughts about Aurora and Daniel did flash across Caroline's mind more than once, but only briefly, because the real thing was better than a fanciful novel. The way Jake undressed her, looked at her, kissed and caressed her built an intensity inside her so strong that it reverberated through her entire body, washing away any inhibitions she might otherwise have experienced.

Even while lying naked on the bed, with nothing but the cool night air caressing her body, she was heated and aware of a desperate yearning deep inside. Shamelessly, she watched as he shed his clothing, examining every inch of his exquisite body, much like he'd done to hers. From the top of his dark hair, down his handsome face, muscular chest, flat stomach, impressive manhood, thick thighs, and muscular legs and feet, her eyes moved, feasting on every inch, and she welcomed him with open arms when he climbed onto the bed.

The rest of the world ceased to exist as they came together, and hours could have easily been minutes as they relished becoming husband and wife.

Somehow he knew exactly what she craved and when. When he brought her to the peak of ecstasy with breathtaking kisses and caresses, she knew that it wasn't the end, but only the beginning.

Which proved to be true. Jake entered her, and if there was any pain, she was too lost in pleasure to feel it. He was gentle, giving her body time to adjust, to receive him, before he began to move, gliding in a little deeper with each stroke forward. Their bodies quickly formed a rhythm, a dance as old as time that had her jutting her hips forward to meet each of his downward thrusts. It was all-consuming, taking her on an inner journey that was indescribable, pushing her to a height of a wondrous desperation so intense, she was certain that not even Aurora had experienced anything close. Especially when all that wondrous desperation burst into a pleasure that stole her ability to breathe.

Jake held her, kissed her, as his body went rigid all over and another, final thrust brought a second bout of euphoria washing over her.

It took time for her world to stop spinning, for her to take in more than quick gulps of air, and for her to admit that she'd never felt so wonderful in her life.

"Is that so," Jake replied, their bodies still intimately joined.

"Yes," she answered, not realizing she'd spoken her admission aloud. Letting out a satisfied sigh, she kissed his lips. "That book wasn't all that thorough after all."

Jake eased his weight off her and stretched out beside her before tugging her close to his side. "What book?"

She snuggled her head onto his shoulder and roamed a hand over his muscular chest. "One I read on the ship."

He kissed the top of her head. "The one about rules?"

She pressed an answering kiss to his shoulder blade. She was no longer ashamed of what she'd read. "Yes. It was about a lady who had an affair with her gardener. It was quite descriptive."

"The one where Daniel died?"

She lifted her head. Met his gaze and smiled at his quizzical look. "That part was sad, but the rest of it was very informative."

"How so?"

Running a hand lower, down across his stomach, she explained, "Certain scenes were quite vivid, quite...explicit. Left very little to the imagination."

"Oh?"

She nodded. "Would you like me to tell you about one?"

"Yes."

"Well, Daniel was lying on his back, naked, like you are right now, and Aurora, also naked, sat on his stomach, and—" She smiled. "Maybe I should show you instead."

His grin was filled with delight. "I think you should."

Caroline laughed as she flipped a leg over his stomach, and proceeded to act out the scene from the book. That naturally led to discussion and demonstration of a few other scenes. It was hours later before they both fell into an exhausted sleep.

When Jake awoke the next morning, he didn't quietly slide out of bed and tiptoe away. Instead, he stayed put, relishing the feeling of having both arms wrapped around Caroline as she slept. He also thanked his lucky stars that he'd finally come to his senses and admitted his love to her. If he'd done that on the ship, he could have avoided weeks of misery, and read that explicit book with her, rather than the dime novel on the train.

He would just have to make up for wasted time; that was all there was to it. And when Caroline stirred, looked up at him with sleepy, love-filled eyes, he decided there was no time like the present to do just that.

Therefore, it was later than normal when he made his way downstairs, feeling like a brand-new man.

That feeling remained throughout the day, and night, and the next day, and continued right on into the next week. He'd have had to be blind not to notice that others saw the change in him, and in his and Caroline's relationship, and he'd have had to be a fool to not accept their approval.

It was Caroline's approval that meant the most to him. He'd never felt so alive, so happy, and so grateful. Their wedding photos now sat on the mantel above the fireplace, and his heart overflowed when he saw them, knowing that marrying her had been the best decision he'd ever made.

Within a couple of days, the cabin had been rebuilt, and the fallen tree had added to their wood supply. All that still needed to be done was replacing the window glass in the bedroom window. It had to be ordered and would arrive by train.

Said arrival just so happened to be scheduled for today. Frustrated with not being able to do much while still recovering from his injury, Mack had insisted on going to town to pick it up, claiming he could drive a wagon as well as ever. Jane had gone along with him that morning.

Jake spent the morning cutting out a dozen steers to be delivered to the army post several miles north of his property in a few days. When he rode back into the yard, Caroline was on the front porch. The rejoicing he felt in coming home to her was like no other.

He dismounted and knocked the dust off his hat by slapping it against his thigh before plopping it back on his head and climbing the stairs.

She was smiling and tilting her face upward for him to kiss when they met at the top of the steps. He kissed her lips not once but twice, before asking, "Mack make it back yet?"

"No." She wrapped a hand around his arm as they pivoted to walk across the porch. "Perhaps they decided to eat in town. Your lunch is ready. Complete with a blueberry pie. The children and I picked the berries this morning."

They stopped near the door and he kissed her again. "I love you."

She giggled. "I would have picked blueberries a month ago if I'd known that's all it would have taken."

"The berries weren't ready to be picked a month ago."

He winked at her. "I told you, all you would have had to do was let me read a chapter of that book on the ship and we'd have put a few more lumps in that sagging mattress."

She shook her head, but then whispered, "Perhaps I'll tell you about another scene tonight."

"You said there weren't any more."

Shrugging, she reached for the door. "Did I?"

He grasped her waist and picked her up, held her so her body was pressed tight against his. "Damn, woman, but you are a vixen like no other." Then he kissed her, not caring who might see them on the porch.

As it turned out, her arms were still looped around his neck, and her feet dangling near his ankles when the rattle of a wagon rolling up the road had him pulling his lips from hers and pivoting.

Confusion seized his mind as he noted four people in the wagon. Two on the seat and two in the back. Mack was driving, but it was the man sitting beside him that caused a shiver to ripple over Jake's shoulders.

He lowered Caroline to her feet, and noted the expression on her face. One that said she'd recognized Edward as quickly as he had.

"You don't think…" She let her thoughts fade off.

"I have no idea," he replied, at a total loss why his cousin would be here. Faith was in the back of the wagon with Jane.

He and Caroline walked down the steps, and met the wagon as it rolled to a stop near the house.

"Picked up some guests while we were in town," Mack said.

"I see that," Jake replied, giving a nod to Edward before he moved to the back of the wagon to help Jane down.

Edward had climbed down and helped Faith out of

the wagon, and in her boisterous way, Faith was the one to explain the visit. "I told Eddie that we can't leave for England without coming to say goodbye to you all. Why, if not for you, we wouldn't be married right now, and that would be a crying shame."

Jake couldn't help but notice the smile on Edward's face as he stared at his wife, nodding in agreement.

"We were on our way to the livery to rent a rig when I spotted Mack and Jane," Faith continued, loud enough for folks in Oklahoma to hear, as she and Edward walked around the wagon. "We arrived last night, but being so late, we stayed in the hotel. We would have wired you, but we wanted to surprise you."

"It's a pleasant surprise," Caroline said. "And you're just in time for lunch."

"Thank you, kindly," Faith replied. "It'll do us good to wash the dust out of our mouths."

While Mack drove the team away and Jane just as quickly hurried for the cabin, Jake rested a hand on Caroline's back. They shared a smile. Faith took some getting used to, but it appeared as if Edward had done just that. The smile on his face hadn't faltered once.

Caroline stepped forward to lead Faith up the steps, and Edward stepped beside him. Looking at his cousin, Jake asked, "All's well?"

"More than well," Edward replied. "I never knew marriage could make a man so happy."

Jake nodded in full agreement, but he was also stunned to hear those words said by Edward.

"I'm aware that she's going to come as a surprise to some people," Edward said, "but I love her. Everything about her. She tells it like it is, whether a person wants to hear it or not, and I find that refreshing." Edward slapped

Jake's shoulder. "And I owe everything to you. I'll never forget what you did for me, Jake."

"Nor I you," Jake said, nodding toward the house where the women were entering the door. "This has turned out very well for both of us."

"I heard as much," Edward said. "I'm happy for both you and Caroline."

"I'm happy for all of us," Jake said, as he and Edward climbed the steps to the house.

Jake's happiness hit a slight bump when they stepped inside the house and noted Nellie, who hadn't been shy about her dislike of Faith during her last stay at the house, was being held in a bear hug by Faith.

As soon as the hug ended, Faith said, "Nellie and I became fast friends while I was here, but she can be a bit of a rascal. I can tell you how to nip that in the bud."

Caroline stepped forward and placed both hands on Nelle's shoulders. "That's certainly kind of you—thank you for the offer. I've discovered that Nellie rarely commits a faux pas that needs to be nipped, but I'm sure your knowledge will serve you well when your own child arrives."

Jake tried to keep a straight face, but gave in because he couldn't hide the smile on his face at how his wife had made it clear she didn't need help with his little sister. He stepped forward, wrapped an arm around Caroline, and winked at Nellie, who was smiling from ear to ear.

Faith was the only one frowning. After a moment, she asked, "That's how a lady talks, isn't it? I guess I'm gonna have to learn how to do that."

"Edward's mother, Lady Hilda, will teach you all you need to know," Caroline said.

Jake couldn't stop himself from adding, "Or you can

find yourself a book about it. There might be one in the library on the passenger ship."

Caroline jabbed him in the ribs.

He laughed.

So did everyone else, because after all, after everything, they were just one big happy family.

Epilogue

Caroline paused in the doorway of Jake's office, smiling at the sight of her husband, his eyes closed, stretched out on the sofa with their son, Oliver, sleeping on his chest. She knew exactly how soothing and comfortable it was to sleep just like that.

Without opening his eyes, Jake held out a hand, apparently knowing she was there by instinct alone. She entered the room, closed the door, and made her way to the sofa, where she knelt down to whisper, "I was wondering where the two of you were."

"Hiding," Jake whispered in reply.

Smothering a giggle, she gently smoothed the black hair on Oliver's head. He'd not only inherited his father's dark hair and blue eyes; he'd inherited his handsomeness and personality. Everyone loved Oliver as much as they did Jake, including her family. Which was why both Simpson men were hiding in Jake's office. Uncle James, Aunt Myrtle, and Frederick had arrived this afternoon, for their third visit to the ranch since Oliver had been born a year ago. Almost a year. His birthday was in two days, and more company was yet to come.

"They've retired for the evening," she whispered.

"The evening? It's dang near midnight."

"I know, but they stay up late at night and sleep late in the morning," she said. "The exact opposite of you."

He opened his eyes and gave her a sly grin. "I retire early to spend time alone with my wife, and I rise early for the same reason."

"I know, and I quite enjoy both." She kissed his lips. "I'll take him up to his crib."

"Is it safe?" Jake asked. "I tried three times, but the stairs were still being swept by the rotating stair cleaner."

"The stairs have all been cleaned, and quite well, I might add. I can see why Uncle James sold that invention." She was impressed with the round brush that fit perfectly on each stair and rotated, pushing the dirt into an attached dust bin. "He wanted the stairs cleaned before the party, and feared once more people arrive, he wouldn't have the opportunity."

"That could be true." Jake kissed the top of Oliver's head. "Our house will be quite full the next few days."

"That it will." The duke and duchess would be arriving tomorrow, along with Edward, Faith, and their daughter, Hope. Luckily, they'd had plenty of advance notice, so the house was ready to accompany so many, especially now that the third floor had been remodeled into bedrooms and a playroom for Oliver and future children.

Jake lifted his head and kissed her before he rose into a sitting position, holding Oliver tight to his chest the entire time. "By the way, we weren't hiding. We were trying out the self-contained ink pen that James brought to us. That is until someone fell asleep on me. I'm quite impressed by the pens, though. Not a single drop of ink leaked out on either of us."

"I'm glad for that," she said. Ink didn't come out of

clothes easily. "The company who bought the patent is quite impressed, too."

"I knew my investment in your family would pay off." He planted another kiss on her lips before he rose to his feet, still holding Oliver close. "It has since day one. Now let's go up to bed."

She looped her arm around his back as they walked across the room. "You know your aunt and uncle are going to ask Nellie to return to England with them, for a visit."

"I know."

"I told her that it's up to her."

He nodded. "You also told her that we could all take a trip there if she would prefer that."

She opened the door for them to exit the office. "I did."

"So did I," he said.

"I love you," she said.

"I know that, too, and I have a surprise for you in our bedroom."

"You do?" she asked.

"Yes, a special little book that Captain Goldman retrieved from his library and sent along with your uncle to give me."

She stopped dead in her tracks. "You did not!"

He kept walking toward the staircase. "I did."

Catching up with him, she slapped his arm. "Jake! What if they read it?"

"The captain wrapped it in brown paper."

"But they could have opened it."

"Trust me, no one wants to read about rules for ladies."

That was true. Or Caroline hoped it was.

Yes, she hoped. She wasn't afraid of doing that anymore.

Hope had given her the perfect life.

"I'll put Oliver to bed and meet you in our bedroom," Jake whispered in the upstairs hallway. "You unwrap the book."

She giggled, and hurried to their bedroom. The book wasn't the only surprise awaiting someone. Tonight, Jake would learn that Oliver would have a brother or sister seven or so months from now.

Oh, yes, her perfect life just kept getting more perfect.

* * * * *

If you enjoyed this story,
then make sure to read
Lauri Robinson's
The Redford Dukedom miniseries

Captivated by His Convenient Duchess
Winning His Manhattan Heiress

And why not pick up one of her other brilliant stories?

An Unlikely Match for the Governess
A Dance with Her Forbidden Officer
A Courtship to Fool Manhattan

Harlequin® Reader Service

Enjoyed your book?

Try the perfect subscription for Romance readers and get more great books like this delivered right to your door.

See why over 10+ million readers have tried Harlequin Reader Service.

Start with a Free Welcome Collection with free books and a gift—valued over $20.

Choose any series in print or ebook. See website for details and order today:

TryReaderService.com/subscriptions

RSBPA2409